The Curtain Lady

by

Andrea Shepherd

AOS Publishing, 2023

Copyright © 2023
Andrea Shepherd

ISBN: 978-1-990496-11-0

Cover Design: Jessica James

Visit AOS Publishing's website:
www.aospublishing.com

To Dawn, my best friend,
without whom I would not have survived adolescence.

Chapter 1
Winter 1980

Friday, Feb. 1, 1980

Dear Diary,

This is my first journal entry. I don't really know what to write about, but supposedly it doesn't matter because Mr. K. won't be reading this anyway. At least that's what he said.

This journal is Mr. K.'s new brilliant idea. He told us we will have to write in them for the rest of the year, just to get us in the habit of writing. We have to show him a new entry every class, but we don't hand it in, so he won't read it.

I guess I will write a bit about me. My name is Poppy, well, Penelope, but everyone calls me Poppy. I'm eleven years old and I'm in Grade Six. My best friend is Chantal and we have been best friends since Grade Four. Chantal thinks this is the dumbest assignment ever, but even though I agreed with her I actually kind of like it and I like Mr. K. even though she doesn't. I think it's because he smells like pipe tobacco, which reminds me of my dad. Uh oh, now I feel sad. I don't mind this diary homework because I like making up stories and just writing in general and my teachers always tell me I'm good at it. It's better than math at least.

Suddenly I know what to write about. I want to tell you about the Curtain Lady. But it's a long story and Mom just called me for dinner. I'll tell you all about the Curtain Lady next time!

• • •

Monday, Feb. 4, 1980
Dear Diary,
That thing happened to me again last night, when I wake up, but I can't move for a long time. I finally screamed to get out of it and Mom came running as usual and asked me what my nightmare was about as usual. I said I couldn't remember, which was the truth, but it wasn't so much the nightmare that scared me as the I-couldn't-move part. I hate it.

I have to tell you about Gabriel and how he makes me feel kind of funny and a bit sick to my stomach when I see him. I wish he went to a different school so I wouldn't have to keep seeing him and having these feelings.

We used to be good friends when we were little because our moms are friends. Last summer I went to his grandparents' chalet for a whole month. It was fun and we swam a lot and biked and made up ghost stories (I'm good at ghost stories and told him my famous China Doll story, but for some reason not my true Curtain Lady one) and we even tried to smoke a cigarette once that he stole from his mom but it was gross! But also he cried and stopped talking to me sometimes because he got depressed about his parents' divorce and then I would be all alone to eat with his grandparents who are strict and I don't think his grandfather really likes me. Also he (Gabriel not his grandfather) had a crush on Sophie two cottages away, which made me jealous and I don't know why. I don't like him in THAT way AT ALL and anyway she's two years older than us so even if she's prettier than me (not that he said that but I know he thinks it) she didn't have a crush on him back.

Then after the crush he had on her, not me, and me not having any crush on him AT ALL, when we were coming back home on the two-hour bus ride (all by ourselves!) he held my hand and I had all these feelings I kind of liked but now I don't like them at all when I think about them. Like I had happy butterflies in my stomach, but when I remember them now it feels more like I want to throw up. Also my face got, like, really warm and I felt like I was glowing, but now I feel like I was probably just hot and sweaty with red cheeks like after gym class.

Anyway, he still wants to be my good friend like when we were little but I don't really want to (what if he tries to hold hands again?) and Chantal thinks he's square and weird and I mostly avoid him at school, but sometimes he still comes over with his mom. When he comes over it's kind of OK and a bit like before and he never does try to hold my hand again and sometimes I worry we won't be friends anymore and then I feel relieved but also sad.

Enough about Gabriel. My stomach feels weird and my hand hurts from too much writing.

I know I said I would tell you about the Curtain Lady but she will have to wait.

● ● ●

Tuesday, Feb. 5, 1980
Dear Diary,
So much has happened at school that I want to write about like how we got a new teacher for *Histoire,* which is my worst subject and she is super strict and gives too much homework and also I hate gym and me and Chantal have started hanging around with Tee and Cee from the English side. Me and Chantal are the only kids from the French side in Mr. K.'s English class, because I'm "anglophone" and Chantal is half "anglophone" so she speaks English perfectly. What a dumb word, why can't we just say English?

But I promised you the Curtain Lady story so here it is:

It's actually a ghost story so don't get too scared! And I am not making this up, I swear. (I'm not sure why I have to say that, because technically I am writing to myself so I know it's true, right?)

The Curtain Lady used to live in my curtains. I don't know when she started visiting me, because I was too little to remember, but I know it lasted a few years and most of the visits were pretty much the same.

I had these red curtains and she would come out from behind them. She had no face and no voice and she was just this light gray shape of a lady and she always came toward me slowly, but for some reason I never ran away. For some reason I guess I couldn't. I would just see her floating toward me across the room and I would just lie there terrified knowing what was coming while watching her kind of float over to me.

And then she was next to me. And she would start to tickle me. She was mean and she had no mercy on me even though I was just a little kid. It might not sound so bad to you to just be tickled, but I just HATE being tickled. It's the worst. It's like torture. And I would just lie there until she was done.

I know what you're thinking. She was just a dream. But I know she wasn't, even if I was little and some of my memories don't make sense. Like sometimes I was sure my dad had come to rescue me. I would scream and he would come running and make her go away. But he never remembered that, so I guess those parts were actually just dreams or else she was gone by the time he got there. Of course my parents both said it was all just dreams.

That makes me remember about how my dad would tell me stories at night (he usually fell asleep before me and would suddenly start mumbling nonsense instead of finishing the story and then start to snore) or how he smelled like a sweet, spicy, smoky pipe (just like Mr. K. as I already told you).

I feel sad again thinking and writing about my dad and his bedtime stories and his pipe smell.

Anyway, here are the reasons I know the Curtain Lady was a ghost and not just a dream:

1. Because sometimes I did dream about her. But when I dreamed about her she was nice; I would tell her I hated being tickled and she would listen and understand and stop. But in the mornings after those nights I knew I had been dreaming, not like the mornings after she had visited me for real. Then there was no talking and no listening. Just that shape with no face and her creeping fingers.

2. Because we moved out of that house when I was 8. My same red curtains are still hanging in my room in our new apartment, and on the first night here I lied in my new bed in my new room, like just knowing the curtains would move and out she would come. But she didn't. Not that night and not ever again. So she must have stayed in the old house.

Until now I still cannot sleep without the covers on, even though the covers never protected me. I always covered my whole body before I fell asleep but every time she came I was somehow always uncovered.

And that is the true story of the Curtain Lady.

● ● ●

Saturday, Feb. 9, 1980
Dear Diary,
Chantal is sleeping over tonight. She already fell asleep, though. I just wanted to write that I'm so happy she's my friend and she is the best friend ever.

I sure hope Quebec doesn't separate from Canada. There's going to be a vote in the Spring and it's all Mom can talk about and she keeps saying no way will we stay here if Quebec becomes its own country. But where would we go and live? I've never lived anywhere else and what would I do without Chantal?

• • •

Tuesday, Feb. 12, 1980
Dear Diary,
I'm so excited! Me and Chantal and Tee and Cee made a pact to watch *The Exorcist* on TV tonight. It's about a girl who becomes possessed by the devil and supposedly it's super-scary! I've never watched a horror movie before and this one is supposed to be the best.

Mom told me I shouldn't watch but she can't stop me because she's working late as usual. No way am I not going to watch it when Chantal and Tee and Cee are all watching! It's almost time!

• • •

Thursday, Feb. 14, 1980
Dear Diary,
It's Valentine's Day today. "J" took my hand and pulled me into the back stairs at school and said, "Happy Valentine's Day, Poppy" and KISSED ME ON THE CHEEK. (I won't write his name because I bring this Diary to school and I would DIE if anyone read it and found out I find him SO CUTE but you know who he is.)

I don't even remember what I said to him after because I got a bit lost in that warm and nice feeling in my stomach and my face again and felt like I was floating. Then after school I found out he had pulled, like, half the girls in our grade into the stairs and kissed them, too, including Cee. So I don't feel so special anymore and the floating feeling went away. But I still haven't washed my face yet, not that I would tell anyone that, not even Chantal and for sure not Tee and Cee. By the way Tee's real name is Tabitha and Cee's real name is Carolyn. I don't remember when they became Tee and Cee, but it's cute, right? Chantal and me can't do that because we would be Cee and Pee, and there's already a Cee and of course I don't want to be called Pee! Besides, I like my name.

But more about that another time. What I really want to write about is that I did watch *The Exorcist*. Except for the parts when I closed my eyes and when I left the room to turn on all the lights in the apartment.

It's about a girl named Regan who becomes possessed by a demon and it's super-scary! (Kind of too scary, actually.) Then yesterday me and Chantal find out that Tee and Cee never even watched because their moms wouldn't let them! Meanwhile I've had nightmares both nights since the movie. Not about green puke or heads spinning around, though. I don't really even remember the dreams except that when I woke up I couldn't move for a long time and I could see this huge dark shape in front of me that wouldn't go away no matter how many times I blinked. Finally I remembered to scream and I kept screaming until Mom came running in and rubbed my back until I fell asleep again. I didn't really want to go back to sleep because I didn't want to get stuck and see that thing again, but I couldn't keep Mom up all night especially because I think she knows I watched the movie even though I denied it. But if I don't admit it she can't say I told you so, even though she did.

Chapter 2
Winter 1982

Friday, Jan. 1, 1982
Dear Diary,
Happy New Year!

This is a brand-new diary Chantal gave me for Christmas. She got it in Chinatown and it has birds on the front and I love it! I'm going to always use the same pen and write super neatly to keep it as nice as possible.

I realized that in exactly one month I will have been writing to you for two whole years! I hardly ever miss a single day anymore and with this new diary I will try to miss even less. Even back when I started in Mr. K.'s class I was writing at least a couple of times a week. Did I ever mention that Mr. K.'s plan to make us all journal writers did not work at all? Most of the kids hated writing and he just couldn't get people to do it so he gave up the project after two months. Chantal was really happy. But I kept writing anyway, 'til now. I bet I'm the only one who still writes in my "journal," though I call it, or you, my diary. It's kind of funny that Chantal gave me a diary when she hated that project so much, but I guess she knows that I love writing to you. It helps me organize my thoughts and it's fun to read my old entries and see how immature I was two years ago when I was only eleven!

Speaking of mature, Chantal called me today and guess what? She got her . . . period! I'm a bit jealous but I didn't tell her that, I just acted excited and happy for her but also sorry for her because she said her cramps are SO bad. She still might come over later but her mom made her chicken soup and told her to lie in bed with a hot water bottle on her stomach. I hope I get mine soon so I don't feel too left behind. We were the last two of our gang not to have ours and now I am last of all. Also some girls are already wearing bras, but I'm still flat. Chantal's pretty flat, too, but maybe hers will grow now that she got her "monthly visitor." (That's what her mom calls it. Some girls at school say "on the rag." So weird and gross.)

I don't know what I will do today if she doesn't come over. I'm kind of bored. Maybe I'll start reading one of the books I got for Christmas. Mom always gets me lots of books and this Christmas was no exception. She got me three more Judy Blume books, *Flowers in the Attic* by V.C. Andrews (I already read *My Sweet Audrina* and it was SO GOOD) and a horror book called *'Salem's Lot*.

I absolutely LOVE horror. Last week me, Chantal and Tee wore makeup and tried to get into *Friday the 13th Part 2* for eighteen-and-over.

We didn't get in but Tee has a VCR at her house (lucky!) so for her birthday we're going to have a sleepover and convince her mom to let us watch *Part 1*. I saw *Jaws* on TV a few weeks ago. It's a different kind of scary. I've never been to the ocean and now I'm not sure I ever want to!

Speaking of scary things, I've been waking up screaming more and more lately. I don't usually remember my dreams, well, nightmares, but they make me scream loud enough to wake Mom up and then not want to go back to sleep after in case they continue, which sometimes happens. It never happens when Mom stays with me and rubs my back until I fall back asleep, though. It's nice when she does that, even if it makes me feel a bit like a little kid.

• • •

Sunday, Jan. 3, 1982

Dear Diary,

Sorry I didn't write yesterday, but I've been reading *'Salem's Lot* all weekend and I just finished it. I have never read such a long book in three days before! It's by a writer named Stephen King. It's about vampires and it was amazing and so scary. I cannot even look at my window at night now. I had just one nightmare last night. I woke up screaming as usual, but I don't remember what I dreamed. I hope I don't have another one tonight. Remember after I watched *The Exorcist* and I had those bad dreams for almost two months? Mom was so mad.

Pumpkin won't sleep with me and I bet it's because of my screaming problem. Mom doesn't even like the cat being on her bed because of all the orange fur he leaves behind and yet he's always sneaking in when she's asleep. He'll snuggle with me on the sofa and he'll curl up on my bed when I'm not in it, but he never sleeps with me at night.

I am totally lending *'Salem's Lot* to Chantal. She said her cramps finally got better. So at least she'll be at school tomorrow for our first day after Christmas vacation.

I think I want to be a writer when I grow up.

• • •

Monday, Jan. 4, 1982

Dear Diary,

I'm so tired I hope I don't fall asleep while I'm writing this.

I did have nightmares last night and they were the horrible kind that makes me afraid to go back to sleep, but for some reason I made up a totally different dream to tell my friends at school. I told them I dreamed about the vampire from *'Salem's Lot* coming to my window and then things started flying around my room and I just kept making more stuff up to freak them out and impress them as much as possible. But my real nightmare was harder to explain and much more frightening. Actually I don't really remember most of the dream as usual but I sort of woke up and I was lying on my back and this big dark shape was just standing in the middle of the room watching me. Well, I couldn't see any eyes but it was standing there so I guess it was looking at me. I kept thinking it was just my clothes piled on my desk chair that looked like a creature in the dark, but I couldn't move to even blink, much less turn on the light, if I even could have gotten the courage to reach over and turn it on. But anyway I couldn't move at all. Or talk. I could breathe, though. But except for that I felt kind of like I was drowning, being pulled under by the weight of my own self, while that shape watched me and I was stuck and kept, like, feeling I needed to fight my way back to the surface. Finally I managed to scream and Mom came running and I finished waking up. The weird thing was, we turned on my light and there were no clothes on my desk chair and it was neatly pushed in under the desk for once. I guess I was still dreaming when I saw what I saw. But I really felt awake.

Anyway, Mom was too tired to stay and rub my back so when she left I kept my lamp on and read my book until I fell back asleep. *Deenie* by Judy Blume. It's about a girl who has scoliosis. I'm sure glad I don't have scoliosis, but I also wish I was gorgeous like her. I think I'll take a break from horror for a while.

• • •

Tuesday, Jan. 5, 1982
Dear Diary,

I have two things to tell you.

First, I woke up screaming AGAIN. I don't remember my dream at all this time. I heard there's a thing called Night Terrors and I wonder if that's what I have. I'll have to go to the library and see if there are any books on that. The lady next door who already never smiles has been looking at me very disapprovingly lately. Mom says she just doesn't like teenagers and also that she looks at her disapprovingly too but I'm thinking she hears me screaming at night and wonders what is wrong with us.

Second, I got it! Yes, IT! In the morning I was so tired I didn't know how I would ever get up and go to school, but when I went to the bathroom and saw those red drops in my PJs I sure woke up! There were just a few drops and not many more on my maxi pad when I got home after school and also no cramps like Chantal, but it's official! I'm a woman! (When I told Mom she was very practical and business-like about it, not emotional and mushy like some moms, which made it less embarrassing, even though I was still pretty embarrassed to have to say it.) Tomorrow I am totally sitting out of gym class now that I have an excuse. Thank God our gym teacher is a woman. How would I ever tell that to a man? I would be SO embarrassed.

It's amazing the way everything happens to me and Chantal in almost the same way or at the same time. First, we are both the same sign, Libra. She is exactly one week younger than me. Also we both live in duplexes in N.D.G. I'm an only child and she is not, but in a way she is like an only child because her brother is seven years younger than her, so she was an only child until she was seven. Also, our dads are (or were) both teachers. And now we got our periods just four days apart.

Do you think my boobs will start to grow now and I can finally get a bra?

● ● ●

Thursday, Jan. 7, 1982

Dear Diary,

Chantal and Tee and I are going roller-skating tomorrow night at the Paladium. Tee and Cee aren't friends anymore since November. They had a fight after Cee started hanging around with the preppy gang from the English side (well, Tee and Cee are on the English side, so I don't see the problem). Chantal and I aren't in a fight with Cee but since we're kind of our own gang with Tee we don't really hang around with Cee anymore even though we're officially still friends.

Anyway, I'm so excited about tomorrow. We went just before Christmas and it was so much fun. I was actually hoping for my own roller skates, but they cost like forty dollars plus I think Mom had already bought my presents by the time I asked, so I'll have to keep renting them for now. I'm not so good at roller-skating, but I'm not too bad either. I would like to learn to skate backwards like some of the cool boys who just speed around, changing directions so easily, whipping out their comb to fix their hair at the same time. Actually, some of the girls brush their hair while they're skating, too. They keep their brush in the back pocket of their Sergio Valentes and pull it out to flip their hair the way I wish I could flip mine. My red, curly hair just does not flip. Chantal's does. She always complains that her dirty-blond hair is too straight, but then her bangs always do just what they're supposed to, hanging down neatly over her forehead or feathering back from her middle part.

I was going to wear my new white jeans, but now that I have my you-know-what I won't take any chances, even though I think it might be finished already, there wasn't really any more after that first day but Mom and Chantal both said that sometimes it stops and starts again, so I'm going to just wear my tightest and favourite Jordache jeans and my white blouse and blue eyeliner and my new orange lipstick. Tee says orange looks good on me because of my red hair and green eyes. Chantal and Tee are wearing their white blouses too.

• • •

Friday, Jan. 8, 1982

Dear Diary,

We did go to the Paladium tonight and it was amazing. Chantal and Tee are sleeping over so they are next to me as I write this. I wish we could go roller skating every night! Just going around and around with the lights and the music and being with my friends and looking at boys. It makes me feel so . . . free. I do wish I had my own roller skates so I could decorate them. They played this new song called "Illusion" that is so good! I hope they play it on the radio so I can hear it again. Maybe I can even tape it. And a girl in the bathroom complimented me on my orange lipstick. *"Y'est beau ton rouge à lèvres,"* she said, with a very French-Canadian accent. So I said, *"Merci,"* of course, in my best French-Canadian accent, which probably still sounded super "anglophone."

And also . . . I have a date! Well, WE have a date. We met three boys, Mathieu, Pierre, and Richard (all French) and they asked us to go to the movies tomorrow. Mathieu is the one who likes me. Richard likes Chantal and Pierre likes Tee. I've never been on a date before so I'm nervous and excited! We're going to see *Superman 2*, but the guys don't speak much English so we're seeing it in French. I guess I'll understand it, but it will be weird. Chantal, as you know, is half French-Canadian so her French is perfect. Tee says her French is better than mine because she used to go to a French summer camp, but I'm the one who gets the best marks on our verb tests, even better than Chantal.

My ANNOYING friends are getting impatient for me to finish writing so I will sign off now. I'm going to hide you under my pillow so they don't try to read you. I'm sleeping on the top bunk and they're on the bottom. Sometimes I feel like a little kid still having bunk beds, but it's practical for sleepovers.

I hope I don't have one of my screaming nightmares while they're here.

● ● ●

Saturday, Jan. 9, 1982
Dear Diary,
My first date:

The movie was good even if it's weird to hear the actors with voices that aren't theirs and their English mouths not moving in time with the French words. Also I was pretty distracted by all the hand holding. At first I really liked it, so much that I was afraid Mathieu would hear my heart beating right through my clothes and over the movie. I got these warm, tingly feelings all up my arm and my underarms started sweating and I got butterflies in my stomach. Good ones, different from when we have a band concert at school or I have to talk out loud in class. But after a while I wanted to eat my popcorn but I felt kind of frozen not knowing if I should take my hand away or not and then I kind of stopped enjoying it and just stayed there forever feeling awkward and holding his hand and not eating my popcorn.

After the movie we all went to Mathieu's house. He lives near Pie-IX metro (pronounced pee-neuf, in case you were wondering), so pretty far. I didn't talk much because even though I'm on the French side at school and I was born in Montreal I'm embarrassed about my English accent and sometimes the boys talked so fast with their *"joual"* and their Quebec accent that I lost track of what they were talking about. But I did understand and sure liked it when Mathieu would look at me and say, *"T'es belle"* or, *"J'aime tes yeux."*

When we got to his house his parents weren't home. Just his older brother, but he stayed in his room. We all sat in the living room listening to the radio and then at one point Mathieu went to his brother's room and asked him for a cigarette! Him and Richard and Pierre smoked the cigarette inhaling and everything and they offered us a puff but we did not take one! I can't believe they already smoke. I mean they're older than us but they're only fourteen (I think Pierre is fifteen).

After that Mathieu brought me to his room. I was pretty nervous but when he stood up and put out his hand and said, *"Viens,"* what could I do but go with him? When we got to his room he closed the door and turned on his clock radio and you won't believe it, but "Illusion" came on! I told him, *"J'aime cette chanson,"* and he said, *"Moi aussi,"* and then he just kissed me. On the mouth. Then, without giving me time to wonder what I should do next, he did it again, but this time he stayed there and put his tongue in my mouth and I have to admit I was a little surprised but then I just wanted more. It sounds corny, I know, but with my favourite song playing and him kissing me and tasting like that cigarette that should have been gross but wasn't at all, it was magical. I can't even describe the feelings I had, like I wanted to hold on to him so tight to just feel more and more of the warm feelings I was feeling. We ended up sitting on his bed, still French-kissing, and it felt like it went on forever, though not long enough. Then he broke the spell by putting his hand on my boob. I actually kind of wanted him to, but it felt really fast and I suddenly got really embarrassed about being so flat and not wearing a bra yet so I pushed his hand down and said, *"Fais pas ça."*

I was afraid he would get mad and I felt childish and my face got really hot, but he actually apologized. *"J'm'excuse,"* he said. Then he looked at me and said, *"T'es belle."* My cheeks that were just starting to cool down warmed up again. Then I made what was probably my first joke ever in French. I said, *"Je suis* vraiment *belle!"* which means I'm *really* pretty. Of course he looked at me weird, like who could be so conceited (plus I'm not actually that pretty), and I explained that my last name is Bell, so that's why I am *"vraiment"* Bell. Well, my joke was a big hit! He laughed his head off and gave me this big hug that was so . . . warm. Like he treasured me or something. It's hard to explain.

Anyway, I suddenly realized it was already dark outside. It's January, so it was only five o'clock, but that's what time the stores close and our moms all thought we were going shopping after the movie so we had to leave.

When we were on the metro I found out that Chantal and Richard and Tee and Pierre made out too, on the sofa. They asked me if Mathieu is a good kisser and I said yes, but I don't actually know because I never French-kissed anyone before. Unless you count Evan that time we played spin the bottle which was awkward and embarrassing and I didn't know what I was doing, which he even said afterwards, making me ten times more embarrassed. So I won't count that time.

I think Mathieu is really nice. Also cute! His eyes are nice too, actually. They're kind of a mix of colours, blue and green and even some yellow. His teeth are crooked, though, and a bit yellow. He's going to phone me tomorrow. I'm getting those warm, good feelings again just writing that.

● ● ●

Sunday, Jan. 10, 1982
Dear Diary,
Mathieu did call me today. It was a bit hard to talk to him, because I felt so shy talking to a boy on the phone plus in French and he talks too fast so I had to keep saying, *"Quoi?"* or, *"Pardon?"* He even tried out his English on me, but it's really bad. He hardly knows any words and his accent is ridiculous. But I didn't laugh

at him because I'm always so worried people will laugh at my French accent and I didn't want to be a hypocrite. (I just learned that word the other day from Tee who said it about her mom.) Anyway, we're going to meet at the Paladium on Friday. I can't wait!

• • •

Monday, Jan. 11, 1982
Dear Diary,
Mrs. Plume gave us a cool assignment today. She wants us to write about how we got our names. Like how our parents chose them and what they mean and if we have a nickname. I kind of knew about my name already but I asked Mom again so I could have all the details. I like the story so I figured I would tell you, first, then copy it for my assignment.

As you know, my name is Penelope but almost everyone calls me Poppy, except Mom when she's mad at me and Madame Labrosse, my art teacher who insists on calling me Pénélope, pronounced the French way (which I actually don't mind but it's annoying that she won't just call me Poppy like everyone else).

My parents had picked out a boy's name before I was born, but couldn't come up with a name they agreed on for a girl. My dad kept saying that this was the guarantee I would be a girl, and I guess he was right. Anyway, I was born and I was a girl and when my mom asked my dad, "So what *are* we going to call her?" he shrugged and said, "I don't know. Penelope?" because it was the first name that came to his mind, and he thought it was a funny name but it was also a name from a great work of literature: *The Odyssey,* which we actually are going to read in English class this year.

Mom laughed and said "No, seriously!" Then, as she studied the funny tuft of red hair on the top of my head, she said, "Isn't

Poppy a nickname for Penelope?" And it was settled: My name, nickname, and me were all born on the same day.

I do wish my dad was still alive. But at least I will always have my name that he gave me.

● ● ●

Tuesday, Jan. 12, 1982
Dear Diary,
Just four more days till the Paladium and Mathieu!

● ● ●

Thursday, Jan. 14, 1982
Dear Diary,
Mathieu called me today. He wanted to make sure I'm still going tomorrow night. He said he misses me. I think he *really* likes me.

Chantal is going with me and Richard is going too, but not Tee. Her mom said no. Her parents are so much stricter than mine and Chantal's.

This time I am going to wear my white jeans.

● ● ●

Friday, Jan. 15, 1982
Dear Diary,
Friday is finally here! Chantal is on her way over to get ready to go meet the boys at the Paladium! I washed my jeans in hot water and dried them in the dryer to make them so tight I had to lie down on the bed and hook a coat hanger through the zipper to do

them up, and I even like my hair today, even if it doesn't flip. I can't wait to see Mathieu.

I got a perfect grade on my English assignment about my name. Not only that but Mrs. Plume said I have talent for writing.

This is such a good day!

Oh, and I haven't had a nightmare all week!

•   •   •

Saturday, Jan. 16, 1982

Dear Diary,

I have a boyfriend! Actually, *"un chum."* That's how you say boyfriend in French. And girlfriend (that's me!) is *"blonde,"* even if you're not blond, which I am not.

I was kind of nervous on the metro on the way to Berri to go to the Paladium. I didn't know if Mathieu would already be there or if it would be hard to find him or how I should act when I did see him. But when I walked in he was right there, like he had been waiting for me. He smiled with his crooked teeth and multi-coloured eyes and said, *"Salut"* and kissed me right away. A fast kiss, but right on the mouth and I was surprised but also happy. He waited for me while I rented my roller skates and put them on and he held my hand almost all the time while we were skating. He's such a good skater and sometimes he would go backwards and pull me along with him, which was really fun. I would have felt bad being with him all the time and not Chantal but she seemed to be having just as much fun with Richard. So at one point someone came to say hi to Mathieu and he said, *"Tu connais ma blonde, Poppy?"* The way he says my name is funny. It sounds like "Puppy" but with a really strong y. But what I noticed most about the sentence was *"blonde."* I just kind of floated around the rink after that. When we left and he kissed me goodnight, a long, amazing kiss before we went to our different metro platforms, I wished I could go with him and be alone in his room with him again.

I'm waiting for him to call me now.

• • •

Sunday, Jan. 17, 1982
Dear Diary,
It's twelve o'clock and he still hasn't called.

On top of that I'm so tired and I have homework to do. Boring *Histoire* homework.

I'm so tired because it was hard to fall asleep last night and then I had a dream. Well, a nightmare. Or both or something in between. First I was dreaming about Mathieu. I think he was someone else but then became Mathieu, you know how that happens in dreams. Well, we ended up kissing (of course!) and he touched my boob again and I let him this time, only in the dream I had real ones, like the models in *Seventeen* or even like Tee, who's fourteen but she's been wearing a bra for, like, two years already. Anyway, he was touching them and he liked them and I liked it (I'm kind of embarrassed even to be writing this and I will die if anyone ever reads it), but then I started to wake up and I was in my bed and I knew it was a dream, but it was like it was still happening and suddenly I didn't like it anymore but I couldn't stop it. I couldn't SEE him and somehow it's like it wasn't him anymore, it was an IT. Just someone or something touching, holding, pushing on my chest, back to my real-life flat chest. It didn't hurt but it was kind of tight and I felt like I couldn't breathe even though I was actually still breathing, and I couldn't talk either or move. I knew I had to scream, it's the only way to come back, but I felt like I was drowning and didn't have the strength to get to the surface, but no way was I going to stay down there with that dark thing around my chest, so I tried and tried to scream until I actually did and I woke up. I somehow remembered right away that Mom had a super early shift this morning so I stopped myself from screaming more and she didn't wake up. Good for her but not so good for me, because I had to turn on my lights and read some Judy Blume because no way was I going right back to sleep after that.

I slept a little after it started to get light, but then at ten I called Chantal and told her about it. She never has nightmares and says she hardly ever dreams at all. I can't imagine, but lucky her.

Oh, also RICHARD called HER yesterday, but he didn't say anything about Mathieu.

● ● ●

3:00 p.m.
Dear Diary,
He called!

He told me that yesterday he didn't call me because he had to go work with his dad in his garage and he forgot to take my phone number with him. Then when he got back his brother was on the phone for, like, two hours and after he was scared it was too late to call me. He said he doesn't want my mom to not like him before she even meets him. I told him I can't believe he didn't even memorize my phone number, but he swears he memorized it last night before he fell asleep so that can never happen again.

After that we just kind of stayed on the phone not saying much. At one point he told me, *"T'es VRAIMENT belle,"* and then laughed his head off like it was the best joke in the world, which I found weird and a bit dumb because I'm the one that told him that joke. Other than that, with his terrible English and me embarrassed about my French our conversation was a bit boring, actually. I guess phones are not our thing. Which is not so great with him living so far and not going to my school. Well at least we have the Paladium. And kissing.

• • •

Friday, Jan. 22, 1982
Dear Diary,
I'm sorry I haven't written all week.

Mathieu has phoned me every day after school. Mom answered a couple of times (her French is so good) and when she asked who was calling he actually TOLD HER THAT HE IS MY BOYFRIEND! I wanted to die and kill him all at the same time. She was OK about it, just emphasized the word *CHUM* when she told me to take the phone, with a surprised/amused smile on her face. She didn't even ask me that much about him later, just where I met him and how long ago. I think she doesn't believe it's a serious thing, but it totally IS.

Anyway, we (me and Mathieu, that is) still don't do much talking on the phone. We mostly just sit there and he gives me compliments once in a while. It's kind of boring. Today, as usual, he made his (my) *"T'es VRAIMENT belle"* joke again. Good thing we were on the phone so he didn't see me roll my eyes. Which I felt a bit bad about, actually, because he's so nice to me and likes me so much. At one point he said, *"Je t'aime"* and I said, *"Moi aussi,"* but it just means I like you, right, not I love you?

Tee is coming to the Paladium tonight. But she's not with Pierre anymore. I feel less excited than usual about it.

• • •

Sunday, Jan. 24, 1982

Dear Diary,

I think I want to break up with Mathieu.

The Paladium was OK. He was as happy as usual to see me and all night he kept telling me I'm *"vraiment belle"* and he likes my eyes and he likes me (I think he means like not love!) and he kept saying my phone number to me over and over again and laughing a bit dumbly like he's so proud of himself for memorizing it. Like, how many phone numbers do I know by heart? Probably fifty or more! It was a bit nice but also annoying.

Anyway, I was sleeping over at Chantal's house after and then we went to see the boys play hockey the next day. It was outside in the park, not a real game just friends playing, and it was very cold so not so fun. Then we went to Mathieu's house again and no one else was home not even his brother and we went back in his room and made out again. It felt really good again and I didn't want to stop, except I had to keep my eyes closed because when I would look at him I still liked his eyes but the crookedness and yellowness of his teeth was bugging me. Still, I let him rub my boobs over my shirt, which he seemed to like a lot, but I preferred the kissing. It made me feel very, very warm in my stomach and . . . other things I can't write about.

Anyway I feel very confused and when I think of Mathieu I just see his crooked teeth and remember his dumb laugh every time he says my phone number or *vraiment belle* and how on Friday I kept wishing I could be more with Chantal and Tee and less skating around holding hands all the time with my boyfriend.

● ● ●

Wednesday, Jan. 27, 1982
Dear Diary,
I started reading *The Diary of Anne Frank* this week for school. It is so good. But so sad because I already know she dies after the

book ends. She wrote it during the Holocaust when she was hiding from the Nazis but they found her and put her in a concentration camp. How can people be so evil? Usually I don't like books we read for school very much, but I like this one. I already read more than we had to for school. Maybe because I have a diary, too. She names her diary, though. Kitty. Should I name you something else, Diary? I will think about it. Anne Frank wrote way better than me. At least if she had to die so young she left her diary behind for the world to remember her by.

If we have a nuclear war and we all die in a mushroom cloud or of radiation poisoning, maybe someday people will find you and publish you, too. If I hide you away in a bomb shelter so you don't burn and if my writing's good enough to publish! I will have to try to find more interesting and important things to write about than Mathieu and nightmares.

Did I ever tell you I want to be a writer?

●　●　●

Saturday, Jan. 30, 1982
Dear Diary,
I did it. I broke up. It was horrible. Now I kind of wish I had just done it on the phone. But Chantal said it's mean to break up on the phone, especially when he likes you as much as Mathieu liked me.

Anyway, he was as happy as always when he saw me and I tried to be happy too. I actually wanted to chicken out from breaking up, but after one song holding hands and not being with my friends I just couldn't spend the whole night like that. So we sat down on a bench and I told him I didn't want to be his *"blonde"* anymore. I tried to say we could still be friends but he just hit his hand on the bench really hard and then skated away really angry and fast so everyone was looking at him. I figured it would ruin my night and even my friends' night because how could I have fun and be happy with them while he was there seeing me and feeling sad and mad at me. Every time I passed near him he gave me a very dramatic look and skated away in the other direction. Then at one point he shoved a napkin in my hand and he left before I could say anything. I opened the napkin and it was just a picture of a broken heart that looked like a kid had drawn it. It made me feel bad but I also found it kind of immature so I felt relieved that he wasn't my boyfriend anymore.

We stayed and had quite a lot of fun, which I feel a bit guilty about but not that much. Chantal and Tee are both sleeping over. They're on the bottom bunk and I'm on top as usual.

• • •

2:00 a.m.
Dear Diary,
I just woke up and remembered something from a long time ago that I had to tell you about.

First, I woke up with my covers off and my leg hanging off the bed. I imagined one of my friends waking up and tickling my foot, which reminded me of the Curtain Lady. Also I felt a bit creeped out with my leg dangling down, so I brought it back up and covered my feet up right away because I NEVER sleep with my feet uncovered. And then I remembered why.

One time when I was little, I must have been really young, like four or five, I read an alphabet book, you know, the ones with a big letter and a picture of a thing that starts with that letter, like A is for Apple, B is for Bear etc. Well, for the letter Q the picture was a quilt and there was a boy sleeping under the quilt with one foot hanging off the bed. So I decided to sleep like him that night, with one foot hanging down. Then, in the night, I woke up and there was this little man, like an evil elf or something, with an axe in his hands and he told me that if I ever slept like that again he would chop off my foot. He even asked if I understood, but I think I didn't answer because I think I was frozen like with the Curtain Lady visits. It only happened that one time, though, so I don't know if it was a dream or if he was, like, her assistant or something. Why would I dream such a horrible thing when I was only four? I can't believe I had forgotten all about it until now.

I just realized I said I should write about more interesting things than Mathieu and nightmares and that's all I have written about since writing that!

I am going to try to go back to sleep now.

Chapter 3
Fall 1983

Thursday, Sept. 29, 1983

Dear Diary,

I can't believe I'm fifteen!

I'm not going to have a party this year. Our apartment's not big enough to have a real party, so who would I invite and who would I leave out? For sure I'll have a big party next year, though, for my Sweet Sixteen.

On Saturday Mom is taking me and Chantal to Gibbys, a fancy restaurant in Old Montreal, then we're meeting up with Tee and Cee (since they're friends again we actually don't hang around with them that much anymore, but I'm happy I invited them) and this new girl we've become friends with named Sandrine to go to the movies.

Today at school everyone got together to give me the bumps. I pretended to hate it but it was so fun. Everyone gathers around and takes your arms and legs and throws you up in the air over and over again, the same number of times as your age, plus one for good luck. Sometimes someone kicks you in the butt while you're being thrown up and down, but usually they only do that to boys and no one did it to me.

Tonight Chantal and Sandrine are coming over and we're going to have pizza and we'll have cake when Mom gets home from work. She got a new job as a private nurse for a rich old lady who lives in upper Westmount and she's happy because she doesn't have to work nights or weekends anymore like she did when she was at the old folks' home.

So let me tell you about Sandrine. First, she's so pretty. I'm a bit jealous, but only a bit because I know I shouldn't be jealous of my friends. She has dark hair she almost always ties in a tight ponytail and she looks really beautiful that way. I don't like how my face looks with my hair tied back so I always tease mine at the front. I try to get it to look like that new singer Madonna, but it has a mind of its own and doesn't always work so well. Sandrine's makeup is always so perfect and she has really clear skin. I almost always have zits, especially on my forehead and my back, which really bugged me this summer when we would go to the swimming pool. I think she has what the magazines call olive skin. She says her dad is part Italian. Her mom is French-Canadian, so Sandrine speaks French and English perfectly, just like Chantal. (I wish I did! Then I wouldn't have to be embarrassed about my accent all the time.) Her parents are divorced and she lives mostly with her mom, but sometimes with her dad.

Sandrine only started at our school two weeks ago, almost two weeks after school had already started. She came into class late and didn't even seem embarrassed to walk in in front of everyone. I hate being late because everyone looks at you when you come in. Anyway, the desk next to mine was empty so she sat there and she just looked at me and said, "Hi" with a really nice smile. After class I introduced her to Chantal, and Sandrine asked if she could sit with us at lunch. We hardly ever eat at school and today we were going to go eat at McGill campus across the street so we invited her to come with us and she just became our friend since then.

Sandrine knows a lot about boys! She's already had, like, three boyfriends or something (I've still only had one, as you know) and I'm starting to wonder if she's not even a virgin because she acted super relieved when she got her period at school the other day and Chantal said that means she thought she was pregnant! I can't believe that could be true even though she's almost a year older than me so she'll be sixteen in a couple of months. Anyway, she's fun and nice and I feel like life will be exciting with her around.

I don't want to lose my virginity 'til I'm at least seventeen.

• • •

Friday, Sept. 30, 1983

Dear Diary,

Do you believe in spirits? I do, but I don't. I love horror books and movies and ghost stories, but at the same time I'm not religious and I think all that God stuff is made up and the Bible is just a book of stories. So if I don't believe in that, how could I believe in ghosts? But then there's the Curtain Lady. Sometimes I think it must have just been dreams, but so many times and for so long and when I was so young? And if she wasn't a ghost why would she disappear when we moved from our house to our apartment when I still had the same curtains?

I am thinking about all of this because of last night. Chantal and Sandrine came over after school. First, Sandrine gave us makeovers. She's so good at doing hair and makeup! Then I opened their presents. Chantal gave me earrings. I love them! They're green and they dangle almost all the way to my shoulders. Sandrine gave me a game called a Ouija board. Well, it's not really a game, it's supposed to be a way to contact spirits.

Of course we were all super excited to try it. Sandrine explained the rules to us including the three most important ones:

1. Never play alone. (You can get possessed, like in *The Exorcist*.)

2. Never take your hands off the pointer during play. (The spirit can escape into our world if you do.)

3. Always say, "Goodbye" to stop a conversation with a spirit. (Or it might not leave.)

Basically, the Ouija board is a board with the letters of the alphabet on it and numbers zero to nine and "Yes," "No," "Hello," and "Goodbye." You have this pointer, called a planchette, and you ask questions and if a spirit hears you it answers you by moving the planchette around the board to spell out answers.

Well, at first nothing happened, but we just kept asking, "Is anyone there?" and finally the pointer moved to "Yes." It was extremely creepy and I really had the urge to take my hands away, but luckily I remembered not to. Sandrine asked who it was and it didn't give us a name, just went to "Hello" after we asked a few more times. We didn't really know what to ask, and started being a bit silly and asking about if different boys liked us and stuff like that. Sometimes it said yes or no or just spelled nonsense. By this point we were giggling quite a lot. One more time we asked what its name was and I was a bit creeped out when it spelled out "D-A-D." Chantal actually got tears in her eyes, but after, like, a second, I remembered I had told Sandrine about my dad being dead and so I'm pretty sure that was her moving it to try to prove it works. After we finished (yes, we said, "Goodbye") I asked her and she denied it, but I'm pretty sure. Anyway, she said it works better if you light candles and think of your questions in advance, so we're going to try again sometime soon.

I'm sure it won't work, though. It's just a dumb game.

• • •

Sunday, Oct. 2, 1983

Dear Diary,

You are not going to believe this, but I went to a BAR!

First Mom and Chantal and I went for dinner as we had planned. It was fancy and expensive and we all had steak and it was good. I've been thinking about becoming a vegetarian because I like animals so much so I feel kind of bad for eating them, but then I eat a steak like that and it's hard to imagine never eating meat again. Mom drank wine and we had Diet Cokes as always. We sat in the smoking section because Mom has started smoking AGAIN. Aside from that it was actually a really good dinner. I would have invited Sandrine but Mom was already paying for Chantal and I didn't want to ask her to pay for another person. After dinner we had cake and the waiter put a sparkler on my piece and all the waiters and waitresses came and sang "Happy Birthday." I was so embarrassed! We had coffee too, even though I don't really like it that much but it's good with a lot of cream and sugar in it. Chantal was like, "Would you like some coffee with your sugar?" Ha ha, very funny. She already drinks coffee every morning with her parents and she likes it with just one cream and one sugar. She said sometimes she doesn't put any sugar. Ew.

So, after the restaurant we all took the metro together, but then we got off at Lionel-Groulx to go downtown to meet up with Sandrine, Tee, and Cee for a movie and Mom went home. She said we could stay out until one, because we were seeing a late movie that started at nine forty five.

As soon as we met Sandrine in front of the theatre she said, "I have a better idea. Have you ever been to the Annex?"

We were both like, "What's the Annex?"

And then she told us it's a bar. We thought she was crazy! I mean, some of the kids in Sec. Five go to Crescent St., but they're, like, seventeen. We're only fifteen and we don't have fake ID and didn't even plan for it and dress up like we're older or anything.

But she told us if they don't want to let you in you just pay an extra five dollars to the bouncer and he lets you in.

So Chantal and I were like, "OK, let's go!"

But when Tee and Cee showed up Tee said her parents were going to pick them up after the movie so they couldn't go somewhere else. I felt kind of bad because they went for my birthday and then we changed the plans on them at the last minute, but it was my birthday, so we should do what I want, right? Anyway, they said they didn't mind, but it felt like even though no one got mad it meant the end of our friendship. I mean, they haven't really been hanging around with us anymore anyway and to be honest I find them a bit boring these days. They hang around with the preppy kids in their Levis, Polo shirts, and penny loafers and they're not so interested in makeup or fashion or the things we like to do.

First we went to fix our makeup in the bathrooms at Les Terrasses then we walked to Bishop St., just after Crescent, to the Annex. I was so nervous and sure enough the doorman asked us for ID, but we were prepared with our five-dollar bills and . . . IT WORKED! I felt so cool handing him that money and he took it all, like, on the sly, then just nodded at us without smiling and stepped aside.

There are different rooms at the Annex and Sandrine said downstairs was the best, so we went down and there was a dance floor and loud music and, of course, a bar. We danced a bit, the three of us, then we bought beers, Labatt Bleue. I've had beer before, like last summer when Claire had that party when her parents weren't home, remember? I don't really like it, but I liked it more last night than usual. Then, later, Sandrine bought me a drink called a Tequila Sunrise. She always seems to have money. Now that drink was good! And also it made me kind of tipsy, which was fun because all of a sudden I didn't feel self-conscious anymore. I really let go on the dance floor after that. I think I like this going to bars stuff. A guy asked for my phone number, but

Chantal pulled me away before I could give it to him. We almost forgot to leave on time, though! We had to run to Guy metro station to catch the last train. At least the running got rid of my tipsiness.

I didn't sleep so well afterward, unfortunately. First I had trouble falling asleep because I kept thinking about our fun and exciting night dancing and drinking and even smoking. (Oh, did I tell you? Sandrine smokes. I tried a couple of puffs of her cigarette at the bar. It was a bit gross, but not as gross as I remembered from when I tried a long time ago.) Then when I finally did fall asleep I kept having those nightmares where I wake up paralyzed. It must have happened at least three times. I wanted to wake up my friends to change the subject of my thoughts and stop feeling so creeped out, but I didn't. Why should they suffer because of my nightmares?

• • •

Monday, Oct. 3, 1983
Dear Diary,
The only class I like at school is English. Well, band is OK, too. But even after all these years I'm not so good at the clarinet. I probably won't keep playing after high school. I wish there was dance at our school. We have all the other arts: *musique, arts plastiques,* and *théâtre.* I liked ballet jazz when Tee and I were taking that class together last year, but we didn't end up signing up again this year.

Chantal's parents are having a party on Friday for their twentieth anniversary and they invited me and Mom and Sandrine.

• • •

Tuesday, Oct. 4, 1983
Dear Diary,
I am getting a story published!

My English teacher, Mrs. Tutor, submitted a story I wrote to this anthology of writing by high school students. She's a new teacher and this is the first year our school is participating in the project, which is called *The Writing on the Wall: Stories, Essays and Poems by the Writers of Tomorrow.* So cool, right? Mrs. Tutor said she was so moved by this story I handed in about when I lost my dad that she sent it in, and they will be including it in this year's book.

I never really told you all the details about my dad dying, so I'm stapling my ORIGINAL copy of it on the next page. If I become a famous writer someday it might be worth a lot of money! Ha ha ha.

I was actually kind of embarrassed to hand it in. I thought it was corny and you'll see why.

**How I lost my father
By Poppy Bell**

When I came home from school I received the news. It didn't come as a shock. I knew it would happen sooner or later. He had been sick for almost a year and we knew the end was close.

When my mother told me about my father's death, I could see her trying to stay calm and be strong for me. I wanted to be strong for her, too, and I actually thought I wouldn't cry, but then her face kind of scrunched up and one tear rolled down her face, right down the side of her nose. Before I knew it I was bawling my eyes out. She gave me a big mom hug, which made me cry even more, and worse still because her sweater smelled like my father's spicy pipe tobacco.

Back then I only knew he had died of cancer. Now I know it was a type of leukemia that pretty much always kills you fast. That's a good and bad thing, I guess.

On the day of the funeral I got dressed in my navy blue skirt and we got a ride there with my Aunt Mary, my dad's sister who was staying at our house because she lives in Ontario and just came to Montreal for the funeral. It was only November, but it was a really cold day and it had snowed so I had to wear my boots and bring my pretty black patent leather shoes in a plastic bag. When we got to the church I was disappointed. I thought the funeral service would be at the cemetery like they always are on TV, but instead it was inside a church. I had never been to church with my mother before. Once when I had slept over at my grandparents' house (my dad's parents) they took me to church with them on Sunday. All I remember is it was really boring and then my mom got very mad at my dad about his parents taking me to church without asking. But I guess funerals have to be in church, because there we were.

Everyone was very sad including me, but I was still really excited to see my cousin Cathy who is almost the same age as me. Before the service started she wanted to go look at my father in his coffin. I asked my mother and she hesitated then said, "Yes, but you must remember how he looked when he was alive, not how he looks now."

Those words haunted me for years. I was terrified I would feel guilty forever for remembering him the wrong way, but it didn't happen. In fact, I'm ashamed to say I have trouble remembering his face at all. When I try to picture his face, I always come up with the face in the black and white photo of him I have on my desk, holding me when I was a baby.

We walked up to the front and some people I didn't know who were gathered around stepped back to let us through. I guess they knew who I was, because they all looked at me like they felt sorry for me and I got really self-conscious. Cathy and I looked at my dad lying there and it didn't feel real that he was right there but would never wake up and be with us again, smoking his pipe and telling me stories. Then Cathy said she was going to touch him! And she did. She just reached in and touched his hair. I didn't like that she had touched my dad and I hadn't, and I also wanted to prove I was as brave as she was, so I reached in and touched his hair, too. I don't know what I was expecting, but it just felt like hair. Then she went and touched his hand. She said it was cold and I did not want to feel my dad's hand dead and cold, so brave or not I did not follow Cathy's example. I secretly resented her for a long time for being the last one to touch my dad.

During the service my mother and I sat in the front row with my grandparents and my Aunt Mary and the thing I remember most is I was bored. I kept looking around and seeing everyone crying and I felt like I should be crying, too, but my tights were itchy and my feet were dangling and I didn't understand half what the minister was saying.

I didn't need to feel bad about not crying, though, because I did plenty of it later. I cried when I went to bed that night and my dad wasn't there to tell me a story (though he hadn't told me a story in a few weeks, since he had been so sick). I cried when we moved out of our nice house with a yard into an upstairs duplex apartment with a balcony. I cried the first day my mom went back to work and I had to come home from school and let myself into an empty home. I cried when I found out I had to change schools, too. (I always connected changing schools to losing my father like all those other changes, but in fact I would have had to change schools no matter what, because of a new law forcing me to go to a French school.)

Eventually I stopped crying, though. Life continued and I grew up and it has been years since I cried over losing my father. Until now. I'm crying now.

Reading my story (my almost published story!) reminds me of when I met Chantal right after all that happened. Even though those were hard times for me and Mom, and of course I wish Dad were still alive, I can't imagine life without my best friend. It's one of those things I don't think adults understand, or maybe they did once, back when they were kids or teenagers, but then they forget. Your family moves or you go to a new school and they shrug their shoulders and say things like, "You'll make new friends." But it's not that easy, and some friends are way better than others.

At least in my case, I DID make a new friend when I changed schools. The best friend ever. I used to go to English school in my old neighbourhood, Montreal West. The summer after Dad died, when I had finished Grade Three and me, Mom, and Pumpkin had just moved out of our house to an upper duplex in N.D.G. near the train tracks and Mom had gone back to work I found out that on top of everything else I had to go to a French school. (Because my parents didn't go to school in Quebec.) I thought it was the end of the world. First, of course I had a best friend back then too, who I didn't want to leave.

Her name was Amy and when I think about it now, in fact, she wasn't always that nice to me. When it was just the two of us we would have a lot of fun, but when other people were around she would often ignore me. It didn't take long for the friendship to become a thing of the past, though, once I had left school and moved to another neighbourhood.

Mom chose FACE for me for a bunch of reasons. The first was it's an art school and Mom thinks I'm artistic. I guess I am better at art than math, for example, but I'm not so great at drawing and painting or even music, especially choir. Chantal is talented at drawing. Cee is one of the best singers in the school. She's a soprano and she always gets solos. I have never had one, but I still like singing, as long as I'm with the group. Mostly I'm good at writing, which you can do at any school, really. But that brings me to the second reason Mom chose FACE. It has a French and English side, so even when you're on the French side, which I am, you can still get a proper English class with the English-side kids. I guess now I'm pretty happy Mom chose this school, because this is where I met Chantal. She had had another best friend, too, who had moved away. So we were both looking for a new friend, I guess. She was kind of quiet, in a more serious way than me; I'm just shy, but inside I'm not that quiet at all. But we had to pick a partner for something on the very first day of school and she just walked right up to me and asked me to be her partner. I was so relieved and thankful! I was not good at approaching people and I'm still not. Anyway, I guess she picked the right person, because we just hit it off and have been stuck together like glue ever since. She's like my sister, except I think real sisters probably fight much more than we do. We've hardly ever even been mad at each other. One other reason I'm glad I came to this school is because I had Mr. K. in Grade Six, which got me to start writing this diary.

• • •

Wednesday, Oct. 5, 1983
Dear Diary,
I'm a little freaked out.

Sandrine, Chantal and I walked down to Ste. Catherine St. after school today to go window-shopping. At one point we went into Jean Coutu and started looking at the makeup. Like usual, we tried out some of the tester perfumes, eye shadows, and lipsticks. Then Sandrine just took one of the lipsticks and put it in her pocket! Then an eye shadow, or maybe two, I'm not sure, and eyeliners.

I don't believe in stealing and I've never stolen anything. Until today.

Sandrine just acted like it was nothing. Obviously she has done it before. I kept my surprise to myself, because I didn't want to look square, or I don't know what, and also because I didn't want to attract attention and get her caught. Then she just looked me and Chantal straight in the eyes and said, "What are you waiting for? Take one."

I had a lipstick in my hand at that moment, and I was, like, hypnotized or something, because I didn't even hesitate. I just stuck it in my jacket pocket.

By the time I got my hand in my pocket Sandrine was already out of the store. I felt so weird, like I wasn't even in my own body. My cheeks were hot and my eyes were almost blurry. I glanced at Chantal, who didn't look happy at all, and walked toward the exit. Just as I was almost there I heard someone say, "Excuse me," and I looked and it was a security guard. A woman.

"Yes?" I said, trying to look innocent even though my face was on fire and every body part was suddenly sweating.

"Did I see you put something in your pocket?"

"No," I said, sure she could hear my heart beating and see the big flashing sign on my forehead that said GUILTY. "The only thing in my pocket is my bus pass. See?" I said, pulling my bus pass out of one pocket to show her as I simultaneously worked the stolen lipstick into the hole in my other pocket and let it drop inside the lining of my jacket.

"Can both of you please empty your pockets for me?" she said to me and Chantal in a voice that was meant to sound nice and pleasant but in fact wasn't at all.

"Do we have to?" I said, wondering where my bold voice was even coming from.

"No, you can come with me up to the office and I can call the police and your parents, if you prefer," she said, still in her fake friendly voice.

Chantal's pockets didn't turn inside out, so she let the lady guard feel in her pockets. And she came out with nothing. While she was doing that I turned my pockets inside out, making sure to hide the little hole in the right one and to put on my best sarcastic face at the same time.

"OK," said the guard. "Thank you. You can go."

I was dying to say something smart and sarcastic and full of attitude, but I couldn't think of anything, and really I just wanted to get out of there in case she decided to feel around the bottom of my jacket or something. As we walked outside I don't think we were even breathing. We barely looked at each other, but we both looked up and down the street for Sandrine.

"I guess she took off," Chantal said. "I'm going home."

After checking that the guard was nowhere to be seen, I said, "You didn't steal anything?"

"No way. Of course not," she replied, looking a little appalled. "Obviously you neither, right?"

"Right," I said, shame rising to my cheeks, because I had stolen, which felt really wrong, but also because I was lying to my best friend. Without any hesitation at all.

"I'll call you later," she said, and walked away.

Then, behind me came a "Boo!" that almost made me jump out of my skin.

It was Sandrine. "I thought you guys got caught! Where's Chantal?"

"She went home," I said. "We almost did get caught. But Chantal didn't take anything and I put the lipstick in the lining of my jacket so they didn't find anything." My feelings were so mixed up as I told her the story. I felt kind of cool and professional, explaining how I had escaped capture, but I also felt kind of sick for almost getting caught and for just stealing at all, and disloyal for telling her the truth when I had lied to Chantal. Not to mention what Mom would say, think and do if she ever found out. I don't think shoplifting is for me. Even if the lipstick does look good on me.

• • •

Thursday, Oct. 6, 1983
Dear Diary,
I don't remember the dream, just the waking up part. Or should I say the almost not waking up part.

Does this happen to everyone? This inability to wake up, to move. This struggle to get out of a dream. I hate it! And then when I finally do wake up I don't want to go back to sleep. Because I don't want it to happen again. And sometimes it does. Like tonight. It's happened twice already and I really don't think I can handle a third time. So I'm sitting here writing about it at three thirty in the morning and I'm going to be so tired at school. It's hard enough staying awake in some of my boring classes without having been awake half the night to escape my nightmares.

And the bad part is, I don't even know what the nightmare was about. But I remember that first I thought I woke up from a bad dream and I felt really relieved. But then weird stuff I don't remember started to happen again and then I started to fake wake up again, but I was trapped in that terrible in-between place where I'm awake but I can't move. I wish I had better words to describe the feeling. It's kind of like I'm underwater or in a cave or a deep well that I can't climb out of. Except, I can breathe. At least I can breathe. I just kind of lie there breathing and trying to decide whether to just stay and let it go on or to fight to come back, which sounds like the right thing to do, but it's really hard and takes a lot of effort and also kind of makes me feel panicky. In the end I always do fight; usually I try to scream, and I guess that's why I've woken up screaming so many times that the neighbours probably think I'm crazy. But I'm getting control of that part now. I don't want to wake Mom and I feel childish calling for her when I'm fifteen years old, practically an adult, so I can usually stop myself from screaming quick enough that I don't wake her up.

The problem is, if I don't wake MYSELF up enough, when I fall back asleep I sometimes slip right back into that trapped place. That's what happened tonight.

And the second time was so strange.

There I was in the in-between place, breathing but suffocating all at once, and all of a sudden I just floated off my bed. But it wasn't like a flying dream or anything (those, by the way, are the best!), as I said, I wasn't dreaming, I was awake, but my body wasn't. So I floated off the bed and over to my door and I grabbed the doorknob and the door opened, and then it just started to swing open and shut, swinging me back and forth with it. I know it doesn't make sense, because I would have gotten stuck in the door if it really happened, but I am telling you, in some way it was real. I was, again, trapped, just holding that door and swinging and somehow I felt it was like someone (or something?) else was making it happen and watching it happen. And laughing at me. Cruelly.

Eventually I managed to scream, which brought me back to my bed (and my body?) with one big, hard thump, and I only called out for a second before I caught myself, stopped myself, and then grabbed all my courage to reach over and turn on the light.

I just read over what I wrote and I know it doesn't sound so bad, but I am telling you it scared the shit out of me. Because it wasn't like a dream at all but like it was really happening.

Now I have to pee. I don't even want to put my feet on the floor, I'm so creeped out. I guess I'll just run and turn on every light along the way!

• • •

Saturday, Oct. 8, 1983

Dear Diary,

That was the most messed up night ever!

What the heck's wrong with me?

Sorry for the swearing, but there are times when you just can't help it and this is one of those times.

So Chantal's parents had their party. Sandrine and I went straight to her house after school. I was planning to take a nap, but we ended up helping to fold napkins, put out food, and make the punch. Which was very good. A little too good.

France (Chantal's mom) let us taste the punch since we helped make it. It tasted mostly like fruit punch, plus alcohol of course. Actually, it tasted a lot like that Tequila Sunrise I had at the Annex. Anyway, once the guests started to arrive (including Mom, who was all dressed up and wearing makeup and everything and looking really pretty!) and the adults were distracted we three kept sneaking more glasses of punch every chance we got. We would fill our glasses and go into Chantal's room with the door closed to drink it.

At some point Sandrine said it was too bad we didn't have the Ouija board and we all agreed. A couple of glasses of punch later we decided we should just go to my house. Since Mom was at the party, we would have the place to ourselves, which seemed more fun than standing around talking to our parents and their friends. Chantal said we should walk because, "We're all a bit drunk and need to walk it off."

"I'm not drunk!" I said. "See?" I got up, closed my eyes and touched my nose to prove it, then started walking around the room one foot in front of the other to prove I could walk in a straight line. I was actually as dizzy as hell and a bit wobbly, which made

Chantal and Sandrine start laughing hysterically, which made me laugh and fall down on Chantal's bed.

Chantal was worried her parents would be mad that she wanted to leave their party, but they didn't mind at all because they were having so much fun. The adults didn't even notice how tipsy we were and didn't see when Sandrine filled a plastic cup with more punch to take with us.

We walked all the way, which took, like, half an hour or something, but I don't think we "walked it off" since we had that extra "for the road." We laughed A LOT and quite a few people stared at us while we walked by, but we just stared back and laughed louder and harder. I love my friends!

When we got to my place and out of the fresh air I started to realize just how much my head was spinning. I lay down on the couch and told them I didn't feel like playing with the Ouija board anymore. I just wanted to go to sleep. But they weren't tired at all and they insisted. Sandrine got the board out while Chantal made coffee and they sat me up and we started to play.

Of course we were very giggly at first, calling, "Is anyone here?" in different silly voices and accents. And then the pointer suddenly almost jerked right out from under our fingers and went straight to "Yes."

"Woah," Sandrine said and pulled her hands away from the pointer.

"Put them back!" I said. "You're not supposed to let go!" My words were actually slurred, but no one even laughed.

"Come on, that was you," Chantal said to Sandrine. "Admit it."

"It wasn't," Sandrine said, pretty convincingly. Then they both looked at me. Well, it obviously wasn't me, and when I shook my head they knew I was telling the truth and we all got very, very serious.

"What should we ask?" Chantal asked.

"Are you still here?" I said. The pointer didn't move from "Yes," and I realized how stupid a question that was.

"Who do you want to talk to?" Sandrine asked.

The pointer didn't move.

"Hello?" she said.

And the pointer went to "Hello."

"Who do you want?"

And the pointer went to the letter P. Then O. Then P, and you can guess the rest. I still wasn't convinced, but my eyes kind of teared up, Chantal seemed like she had stopped breathing, and even Sandrine looked less collected than usual.

"You want to talk to me?" I said.

"Yes," said the pointer.

"Who are you?" I asked, without slurring at all.

S-T-A-Y, the board spelled out.

"Huh?" I said. "That doesn't make any sense," I said. "This is bull. Let's stop."

"Ask it one more time," Chantal said.

I sighed and said, "OK. Who are you?"

And the pointer went to C. Then it paused and went to U-R. Pause. T-A-I-N. Pause. L-A-D–

"Forget this," I said. "Goodbye!"

The pointer did not move.

"Goodbye!" I yelled, feeling pretty panicky as I stared at that pointer still not moving.

Finally, after a few more seconds that felt like hours, it went to "Goodbye."

"You're not funny," I told my friends. I was so angry I was almost shaking.

"What do you mean?" Sandrine said. "And what the hell is a Curtain Lad?"

"Curtain Lady, as you know damn well. Did you tell her about the Curtain Lady?" I said accusingly to Chantal. "Is this your idea of a joke?"

"No, I swear," Chantal said.

"This is crazy," I said. Then I said, "Oh shit," and ran to the bathroom as I realized I was about to puke my guts out. Which I did.

After I finished, washed my face, and brushed my teeth I felt a little calmer. But honestly, I couldn't decide whether I preferred that my friends had played a pretty mean joke on me or that we had just summoned the Curtain Lady of my childhood nights.

"First," Sandrine said, "I am done with the Ouija board. And second, you have to tell me about this Curtain Lady."

First, I thought, you're the one who gave me the stupid Ouija board! But I didn't say it out loud. We were all drunk and tired and freaked out, and I needed the comfort of friendship, not a fight.

We went to my room and I told them the story. As I got into it, I couldn't help but add pauses for suspense and kind of play up the creepy details. I love a good ghost story, as you know. And I must admit I felt a bit cool for having a real-life one to tell.

At one point, as I was telling them how helpless I had always felt as I saw that gray faceless shape come out from behind the curtains and move silently toward me, Chantal just about jumped out of her skin. "What the hell?" she said as the two of us jumped in response to her jump.

"What?" Sandrine exclaimed as Chantal stared at the window.

"The curtains moved," Chantal said.

"What? Come on!" I said, sounding more disbelieving than I felt.

"I swear to God, *je te jure!*" she said, seemingly on the verge of tears.

"Nothing moved and there is no one there, Chantal. We're on the second floor."

"You're not funny," Sandrine said and got up to walk over to the window.

Then we all screamed at once when there was a loud and sudden knock on the bedroom door. Sandrine jumped back into the bottom bunk with Chantal and me and we huddled together, looking in terror at the door as it flew open.

"What's going on?" demanded Mom, looking a bit frantic.

We all breathed a big sigh of relief and started to laugh a little uncontrollably. "Hi, Mom," I said. "We were just telling ghost stories," I said. "And we played with the Ouija board before, so we're a little jumpy. How was the party?"

"I had a good time," she answered, eyes positively sparkling, then said to Chantal, "Your parents seem very happy and threw a great party." Then, to me, eyebrows raised, "Open the window a little. It smells like alcohol in here." Then, "Goodnight, girls."

"No way am I going near that window," said Chantal.

"Me neither!" Sandrine and I said at the exact same time.

We laughed a little uncertainly at ourselves and our active imaginations and got ready for bed. Chantal took the top bunk and I slept on the bottom with Sandrine, who didn't want to be left alone.

I started to doze off pretty quick but then I woke up a bit later because I felt something touching my stomach. Or someONE. Sandrine? I thought, surprised and a little confused. She lifted my shirt up slowly and traced a slow line from my belly button up, up, up. I was unable to react, because I was so surprised but at the same time it felt kind of good and exciting. Meanwhile I was really afraid Chantal would wake up.

But I just kept my eyes closed and tried to let go and enjoy the sensation of my shirt lifting higher, fingers tracing higher, higher, then hands caressing lower, lower. My breathing got heavier and I was afraid Chantal would hear, but God it felt so good. My heart was racing and those hands kept touching me and suddenly I knew that it was not Sandrine. I couldn't see in the dark but something even darker was there, on top of me and all over me. It was tempting and so, so hard to resist. If I just relaxed, maybe I could just enjoy for a little longer, and besides, the fighting was so hard. But I had to fight. I had to or I might stay there (wherever "there" was) forever, or sucked in deeper (deeper where?). So I fought to move, to yell, to surface. I knew how, but it just took so much effort.

When I woke up (came back?), I let out a kind of gasp, but I managed not to scream and neither of my friends woke up. I looked over at Sandrine and she was fast asleep on her side turned away from me, even snoring a little.

I have to admit I was a little embarrassed to have wanted to give in to whatever was happening to me, not to mention how embarrassed I felt when I saw Sandrine this morning. I'm glad they left early. Seriously, what is wrong with me?

Chapter 4
Summer 1984

Saturday, June 16, 1984

Dear Diary,

Summer vacation starts TODAY!

I can't believe next year will be our last year of high school!

I know I haven't written in almost two weeks, but I had a lot of studying to do for final exams and you know me I left all of it 'til the last minute. But now it's over!

There's not much to say about exams. I'm pretty sure I passed them all, even math. Well, OK, maybe not economics, and for sure if I don't pass the exam I'm not passing the course because I had exactly a sixty, but we don't have to pass that class to pass the year so it's not a big deal if I don't.

Chantal's worried about English, as always. She thinks she can't write and that our English teachers never like her, but she speaks English a million times better than I speak French (except I'm really good at verbs and grammar). I'm not sure about Sandrine, though. She didn't even show up for two exams and the teachers were always mad at her for not finishing her homework. She doesn't seem too worried, though, and just shrugged her shoulders when I asked why she didn't show up for those exams. I wish I could just shrug it off. I've never actually failed a class before, so if I do fail economics Mom will be pretty disappointed.

She has a boyfriend, by the way. She thinks I don't know, but I do. She met him last fall at Chantal's parents' anniversary party. His name is Dave, he's an editor, and he's nice. She always calls him her "friend," and he never sleeps over or anything, but she sometimes sneaks in very late at night and plus I can just tell how much she likes him when he comes over for dinner. I don't know why she doesn't just admit that he's her boyfriend. I don't mind.

Tonight Chantal and I are going to a party Sandrine invited us to. It's kids from her old school. She says that guy she brought to our last school dance who supposedly likes me will be there. She says he's "so bad," which, in case you didn't know, is a good thing. He's a b-boy, so he breakdances and listens to hip-hop and rap music. So it's going to be that kind of party. I don't know how to breakdance and I won't know anyone except Chantal and Sandrine, and sort of Ricky, the one who supposedly likes me. I'm nervous, but excited. We're going to get ready at my place and then go together. I'm going to get Sandrine to do my hair and makeup, and I have a new jean skirt I'm going to wear.

● ● ●

Sunday, June 17, 1984
Dear Diary,
I can't decide if I liked the party or not. I guess if you asked me if I would go to another one I would say yes. But I can't say I felt comfortable or necessarily had that much actual fun.

It was at a place called The Garage, just a few blocks away from my place, so we walked there along de Maisonneuve by the train tracks. It's some kind of old warehouse, with a big garage door as an entrance. We paid five dollars each to get in and went inside and it was really dark. Sandrine, as usual, kind of led the way, looking around for people she knew. I felt like a lost puppy dog following her around in the dark.

People were kind of . . . serious. Instead of smiling when they were introduced they would just barely nod their heads. Some guys looked us up and down from head to toe, which made me understand the expression "undressing you with his eyes." When we found Ricky, he did all those things. He looked me up and down, then nodded real quick and said, "'Sup?" like he wasn't really interested in my answer.

"Not much," I said, trying to act cool, like I didn't care what anyone thought of me, but really I felt totally uncomfortable and awkward, like I was off balance the whole night. I bummed a couple of cigarettes off Sandrine so I could look and feel more relaxed. Chantal and I have been smoking once in a while the last couple of months, but only when we feel like it. I smoke a bit more often than her but I'm not addicted or anything. I've never bought my own pack. I either bum them off Sandrine, steal them from Mom, or sometimes I'll just buy one cigarette at the dépanneur for twenty-five cents. Oh, there was that one time I split a pack with Sandrine. Anyway, I can stop anytime I want.

Speaking of smoking, we went out on the back stairs at one point, where a bunch of people were smoking weed, and Sandrine took a couple of tokes like it was nothing. She's so experienced! It's like she's never trying anything for the first time. Is there anything she doesn't do? Anyway, Ricky was there, too, smoking a joint, sorry, a spliff, and he offered it to Chantal (first!), who said no, and then to me. I really wanted to try it, but Chantal had said no and I was kind of scared, more of looking like I didn't know what I was doing than the actual smoking, so I shook my head and said, "No, thank you," and immediately felt stupid and nerdy and really . . . white. Ricky's white, too, actually, but even though I heard some of his friends call him "White Boy," he just fit in with the crowd, while I stuck out like a glowing sore thumb. Maybe I'm just awkward.

"Hmm. So polite," he said, like he was making fun of me, but in a teasing way, not really mean. I don't think I've ever seen anyone stoned before, but I could tell from his half-closed eyes and slow way of talking that he was.

"Let's go in," Sandrine said, right after the guy she had taken a toke from went in. She obviously likes him. I forget his name, though. Chantal followed and just as I was about to follow, too, Ricky took me by the wrist, pulled me really close and said in a kind of deep, warm whisper right in my ear, "I want to see you again. We're going to my cousin's tomorrow. You coming?"

I just about melted on the spot, feeling like he had some power over me that would make me say yes to anything. "OK," I managed to say.

"Give me your number. And bring your friends," he said.

"OK." Man, I felt stupid. Why couldn't I talk? "I'm going to go find them now," I said, dying to break the spell he had over me (but kind of not wanting to break it, too).

Then he put his hand under my chin and tilted my face up towards his. I was sure he was going to kiss me, and I was going to let him, but then he did the most surprising thing. He kissed me *on the forehead*. He seemed like the kind of guy who would push you up against a wall in an alley, like in the movies, and then he gave me that slow, tender kiss. If I thought I was melting before, I was liquid now. Like I was in love. (Ridiculous, I know!)

He let me go then, and I found my friends and told them about his invitation (but not the kiss). Sandrine already knew about it and we all agreed to go the next day. Sandrine had this funny smile on her face and her eyelids were kind of droopy. "I'm so stoned," she said, still smiling.

We stayed for a while watching the dancing, but not dancing ourselves. Sandrine was too stoned and Chantal and I were too shy. But the dancing, though! The break-dancers were totally awesome (I never did get to see Ricky break). And besides the hip-hop and rap music there was also reggae, which I had never really heard before, but I liked it. It totally makes you want to dance and the way some of the kids could move their bodies to it was amazing. This one (very cute) guy drew a whole crowd doing this dance called "doggy style" where he held one leg up in the air and kind of bounced his butt up and down to the music really fast. It was really funny and really good; I could have watched him all night. I wonder if I could learn to do that?

I actually have to leave soon to go see Ricky. His cousin lives in Burgundy so Chantal and Sandrine and I are meeting at Georges-Vanier metro.

I'll tell you how it goes later!

• • •

7:00 p.m.
Dear Diary,
I have to go eat supper soon, but I could not wait to write about my day. You won't believe the things that happened and that I did. It's like I became a whole different person in one day.

So we got to Ricky's cousin's place and there were a bunch of people there. Ricky was there, of course; a guy with jerry curls who looked at least twenty who it turns out is the cousin whose apartment it was; Freddy, the guy that Sandrine had smoked up with at the party; a (cute) guy, who I was pretty sure was the "doggy-style" dancer from the night before and two girls who didn't look very friendly at all. One was black, one was blonde, they both had their hair slicked back into tight ponytails and they were wearing perfect makeup and tracksuits. The TV was on, there was reggae music playing (I love it!), the air smelled faintly like weed, and I felt extremely shy.

Ricky walked over to us, but then he just did his little nod and "'Sup" and went to sit down on the couch and watch whatever was on TV, I don't even know what it was. So I felt totally uncomfortable right away, not knowing where to sit or who to talk to.

Sandrine went over to Freddy and sat next to him and just started talking to him. I wish I had her confidence. Maybe if I were beautiful like her or those two girls I would feel more sure of myself. As Chantal and I stood there I felt ugly and awkward and was sure my hot cheeks were probably getting red and splotchy. I guess Chantal felt uncomfortable too, because she whispered, "Do you want to stay?" in a voice that meant she did not.

I was about to say no, but then Ricky's cousin said, "Don't be so rude, Ricky. You don't even introduce me to your friends?" He walked over to us and told us his name was Tyrone then offered his hand for each of us to shake. I instantly felt, like, a million times better.

"Do you want something to drink? A Coke?"

"Do you have Diet Coke?" Chantal asked.

He laughed, lifted his T-shirt a little to reveal a flat, muscular brown belly and said "Do I look like I need a diet?" So we took Cokes. We walked past the two unfriendly girls on the way to the kitchen and I smiled at them. They smiled back, but it didn't look very . . . sincere. Like they were imitating my smile sarcastically, in a way that said they knew a bad secret about me. I know that sounds crazy since they didn't know me and it was just one smile, but that's what it felt like.

Back in the living room, we felt awkward again, but at least we had our Cokes so we had something to do with our hands. Then Freddy pulled out a spliff and Tyrone said, "Take that shit outside."

Freddy and Sandrine got up and Sandrine looked at us and said, *"Vous venez?"*

The two girls snickered and gave each other these knowing glances. Not that I knew what they meant, but I was sure it had something to do with the fact she had spoken to us in French.

Chantal and her often speak French to each other, though not so much to me. Anyway, we were happy to have a reason to get out of that uncomfortable room and away from those judgemental looks, so we followed Sandrine and Freddy. He put his spliff in and out of his mouth a couple of times to wet it before lighting it and I suddenly got just what Sandrine saw in him. There was something very deliberate and sexy about the way he did things, and he had really nice lips.

He lit the spliff, took a toke, and passed it to Sandrine. She took her toke and offered it to me. This time, I took it.

"First time, right?" she said. I nodded, feeling childish and inexperienced, and she explained that I had to hold the smoke in for a few seconds after I inhaled. Yeah, well, it's hard to hold smoke in when you're coughing your head off, which I did. It was awful and embarrassing and really hurt my throat. And everyone laughed at me of course. I would have laughed at me, too. Then I offered the joint to Chantal and she took it.

"Take a smaller hit so you don't cough so much," said Freddy, just as the cute reggae dancer came outside. Chantal did what Freddy said, barely coughed at all, then offered the joint to the cute guy, all natural like she had done it a million times. He passed.

"What's your name?" he asked Chantal.

"Chantal. What's yours?"

"Oliver, but they call me Olive."

"Why?" I said. To me Olive sounded like a girl's name, but mostly I was just looking for a way to join the conversation, because I was feeling left out.

He shrugged his shoulders, made a look-at-me gesture with his hands like he was putting himself on display and said, "Because I'm black."

Everyone found this really funny and laughed a lot. I laughed, too, but I didn't fully get the joke so it was mostly only to follow along, and I realized that I wasn't noticing any effects from the weed at all.

Once the spliff made its way back to Freddy, there was only a little bit left and he said to Sandrine, "Shotgun?" She nodded and then they did a totally awesome thing. She brought her face really close to his and then he flipped the joint around so the lit part was *inside* his mouth and he blew the smoke through the joint and directly into her mouth, with her sucking all the smoke right in, in a little stream. Their faces and their full, beautiful lips were so close together it was like watching something really *intimate* and I was kind of envious but also fascinated. How did he not burn his tongue? How can smoking a joint look so sexy?

I just wish I could feel confident and beautiful instead of feeling like I never know what to do.

We went back inside just as Ricky got up and went into another room. Freddy took Sandrine by the hand and led her to another room while Chantal and Olive got cozy together on the sofa. There was no sign of Tyrone or the two girls.

I stood in the doorway for what felt like forever, but was probably only a couple of minutes, feeling like I was dying of loneliness and awkwardness. Then I got my courage up and went to find Ricky. I went into the room where he was and found him sitting on the bed watching something on a small TV. I said, "Why aren't you paying any attention to me?"

"Oh, you want attention?" he asked. Then he got up off the bed, came close to me, shut the door behind me and kissed me hard and full on the mouth. Then, before I even knew what was happening he had lifted my skirt, put his hand inside my underwear, and put a finger inside . . . me. It hurt and obviously caught me by surprise and I made some kind of sound and put my hand on his arm, but he just pushed his finger in farther while whispering in my ear, "Take the pain," and kissed me again. I did what he said and it was kind of horrible and amazing at the same time. I felt like he was the one who controlled me, which felt both wrong and kind of good. Even if it hurt.

I cannot explain how I felt. And I don't know how I feel now. I know I feel a bit sick writing this, like I ate something delicious but bad for me. It's so confusing the way he went from ignoring me in a way that felt kind of mean to . . . well, to being *in* me.

The rest of the afternoon is a blur. He didn't keep doing what he was doing for very long and then we went back to the living room and at some point Sandrine came back too and the three of us left. We didn't talk much about what we had done or not done. Maybe they did things they're not sure about, too. I sort of hope so because I don't want to be the only one. We did talk about the weed, though. I told them I didn't feel any different and Chantal said the same. Sandrine said that's normal the first time you smoke up.

Ricky said he'll call me, but he didn't say when.

● ● ●

Tuesday, June 19, 1984
Dear Diary,
I just woke up paralyzed again. Even though fighting is hard, so sometimes it takes me a while to get up the courage, when I fight I often wake up without having to see those creepy dark shapes watching me. But honestly, it's bad enough to be paralyzed. I mean, at least I can breathe, but it's basically like being buried alive. At least it's how I imagine being buried alive feels. Of course, if you're buried alive you know you can't get out, which is pretty fucking terrifying to think about. But when I'm trapped in the in-between place and can't move, I don't know for sure I will ever get out either.

Ricky hasn't called yet and I feel very bad. I shouldn't have let him do what he did, even though I'm kind of glad to finally have some experience.

• • •

Wednesday, June 20, 1984
Dear Diary,

Why hasn't he called? Why would he ask for my phone number and kiss me and invite me over and *finger* me (I finally told Sandrine what he did and she said that's what it's called) and then not call me?

Chantal and Sandrine both say he will call, and he's just playing hard to get and if he doesn't it's his loss. It's so great to have friends, but I know they're just saying those things because they *are* my friends.

Maybe I'm a bad kisser. Maybe he thinks I'm easy or slutty because I let him go too far. But it's not like he gave me a chance to say no.

I've even cried, like, twice today. Which I would never tell him or even Chantal or Sandrine.

When I saw Mom this morning I wished I could tell her so she could hug me and make me feel better like she did when I was little and even still does when I get the flu or something. But no way could I tell her. I would be way too embarrassed and she would probably be disappointed in me. Did I ever tell you about the time I got dressed up to go out a few weeks ago and she told me I looked like a "tart?" She said it kind of matter-of-factly, not angry or anything, and I just said "thanks" and laughed it off. But it goes to show that even your own mom can judge you.

• • •

Thursday, June 21, 1984

Dear Diary,

He called!

He invited me to his cousin's place again tomorrow, but I felt so uncomfortable last time I told him to come over here instead. He was worried Mom would mind, but she doesn't get home 'til 6 so I said he could come over in the afternoon. Chantal and Olive are coming over too. They seem to be a thing now.

I know it sounds bad because I'm with Ricky, but I'm a bit jealous. I can't stop thinking about Olive's dancing, and he's really cute, and even though I don't really know him and he doesn't say much, he has, like, an easier way about him. He makes jokes and doesn't seem to change his mood every day like Ricky.

But he chose Chantal and Ricky chose me, so I can't do anything about it now.

• • •

Saturday, June 23, 1984

Dear Diary,

Where do I start? At the beginning or the end?

I guess the beginning so I can build up the suspense 'til I tell you the big news.

As we had planned, Chantal, Ricky, and Olive came over. We sat in the living room for a while drinking soft drinks and listening to a Run-D.M.C. tape the boys had brought. Olive noticed my Ouija board on the games shelf and said, "What's that?"

I started to explain and he said, "Yeah, I know what it is. But why do you have it in your house? Are you witches or something?"

"Maybe," said Chantal with a mischievous smile. "Do you want to play?" She's quiet, but she loves to flirt and she's good at it.

"No way!" he said, making waving gestures with his hands.

"Hey," said Ricky, "Show us your room."

"OK," I said, knowing he had other ideas than just getting the tour.

"Can we bring the ghetto blaster?" Chantal asked. So I grabbed it and led the way.

"Bunk beds!" said Olive. "I wanted bunk beds so bad when I was a kid."

I felt a bit embarrassed about still having bunk beds at fifteen. They're convenient for sleepovers with my friends, and I have a lot of those, but I know it's time to upgrade to something more grown up. I have been begging Mom for a waterbed for a year, but she says we can't in a rented second-floor apartment because it's too heavy and might crash through the floor.

"Perfect. One bed for us and one for them," Ricky said, which made me feel less embarrassed but more nervous. He climbed up over the foot of the bed and I followed while Chantal and Olive sat on the bottom.

Then Olive put on another cassette he said was called R and B. The music was nice and mostly slow and kind of romantic. To put us in the mood, I guess.

Ricky started to kiss me, slower this time. Not only my mouth, but my neck and my ears. "I want you," he whispered in my ear. He seems to like whispering in my ear. Anyway, whispering was good because Chantal and Olive were right below us. "You're a virgin, right?" he said. I just nodded.

"I'm gonna be your first," he said (still whispering).

"I don't think I'm ready," I said.

"I'll get you ready," he said, and his finger was inside me again. "Just take it," he said, before I could protest. It actually felt kind of good this time, at least not as painful as the first time.

At one point he unzipped his pants and got on top of me and I think you know the rest. He went slower than with the fingering and sometimes I tried to push him away a little when it hurt too much, but then he would slow down more and whisper to me to take the pain again, which I kind of liked, so that made it better. I told him I didn't want to get pregnant, but he said he would "pull out." Which he did. I don't think I want to write any more details (I'm not a porno writer!) but I've said enough that you know I lost my virginity yesterday. I can't say I really liked it, but I didn't hate it either. It was all pretty awkward, especially with Chantal right there in the bottom bunk. Oh, and guess what? She lost hers, too. Is there anything we don't do together?

• • •

Sunday, June 24, 1984
Dear Diary,

I'm leaving to go to the Saint-Jean-Baptiste parade soon. It's not really my thing since I'm not a separatist and even though I was born here I'm not considered "Québécoise" because I'm anglophone, but Chantal and Sandrine want to go, so why not? They say that it's for everyone, not just the *"pure-laine"* Quebecers, so we're just going to go and have fun.

Before I leave I just have to tell you that I got stuck in the in-between place again. I didn't feel like fighting this time so I tried just lying there waiting to eventually wake up, but then the shadow-thing appeared again. It was different this time; well, I think it's always a bit different, but this time it looked a bit like a person with a hat on. And this time instead of just staying there watching me it moved towards me. Oh God it was terrifying. But I guess terror can make you do things, because as it came closer (well, it *seemed* to be coming closer but never actually *got* closer, though I was sure it would eventually) I managed to find my voice and woke myself up.

This has been happening more and more lately. I'm scared to fall asleep half the time.

• • •

Monday, June 25, 1984
Dear Diary,

The pools are open today, so Chantal and I are going later. I love going to the pool, but I hate the first day. I get there glowing white and leave red as a lobster every time. I should put on suntan lotion with more protection, but then it'll take so long to get a tan! I really like using the Hawaiian Tropic oil, because it makes you look darker as soon as you put it on and it smells *so good*. Like coconut. I think coconut and chlorine mixed together are what summer smells like and I LOVE SUMMER.

If the guys call we are going to invite them to meet us at the pool. But only if they call. We are *not* calling them.

Also, I don't think I like parades. Some of the people in the parade seem to be having fun, and on TV parades always look like a big, fun party, but in real life it's kind of boring to just stand there waving your flag (well, lots of people were waving flags but not me) watching all the people go by with their floats (some of which are totally lame) and their music. I think I prefer to be part of something than just to watch it. At least I was with my friends and it was a hot, sunny day, which is way better than the Santa Claus or even St. Patrick's Day parade, which are always cold on top of everything.

One thing that was really nice was when we told Sandrine we're not virgins anymore she gave this little squeal of delight and practically jumped on us to hug us. Like she was just so happy for us and even proud of us. She also asked how it was and I really didn't know what to answer. I said it was OK but that it hurt a little. She said it gets better and better every time.

• • •

Tuesday, June 26, 1984
Dear Diary,
The guys didn't call and we had a weird day at the pool.

First, I saw my old friend Amy for the first time in years. I saw her once on the metro a couple of years ago but she didn't see me. Before that I think I went to her birthday the first year after I changed schools, but I hadn't seen her or the others in so long that I felt left out and back when we were friends she had often made me feel left out anyway, so we lost contact after that. Yesterday, though, she seemed really happy to see me. I could tell we wouldn't become friends if we met each other now, just because our styles and interests are different. She goes to Villa Maria, an all-girls private school, and she's really sporty. She's on the volleyball team and at the pool she was wearing a one-piece Speedo bathing suit and no makeup. She's one of those lucky girls who looks good without makeup, unlike me. Chantal and I never go anywhere without makeup! Thank goodness for waterproof mascara! And we were both wearing our new bikinis. (I wish I looked better in a bikini. My stomach is flat, but so is my chest, always and forever the flattest of all my friends. At this point I think my boobs will never grow.) When Amy spotted me and called out my name I was sneaking a smoke by the fence. I put it out when I saw her, but she probably saw. I'm sure she doesn't smoke, or do anything bad for that matter.

Anyway it was actually good to catch up. She said she still lives in the same house and told me to call her. Maybe I will.

After she left, some guys came and sat near us on the other side of the fence. "Hey Red," said one. I figured he meant me (hopefully referring to my hair and not my sunburn), but I didn't look up. I got caught at school once last year when annoying Danny yelled out "Hey, Sexy!" in the hallway. I turned around and he pointed and laughed at me, accusing me of thinking I'm sexy. I got defensive and insisted I had turned at "Hey" and not "Sexy," but that just showed him he had gotten under my skin and made matters worse. He teased me for weeks afterward.

Back to the pool, it was time for me to learn to play things cool.

"Hey, Red." Closer, louder, but I just stayed on my towel, eyes closed, sizzling in the sun.

"Hey, you. In the pink bikini with the red hair. I know you can hear me."

I sat up, nice and slow and not too interested, turned around and said, "Me?"

"Come 'ere," said the voice that was now attached to a not-bad-looking face and solidly-built body. He looked older than us, probably about seventeen or eighteen. He was dressed in track pants and a T-shirt, over which he wore a thick rope chain. His short hair was gelled back into waves.

I told Chantal to come with me and we both got up and walked over to the fence. When we got there I noticed he had a scar on one cheek. He really was good-looking, but the scar made him look a little scary. "What's your name?" he asked, somehow making it sound more like an order than a question.

"Poppy," I said.

"And who's your friend?"

"Chantal," she said.

He looked us both over from head to toe, making me feel even more undressed than I was. Then he fixed his dangerous-looking gaze on me. His eyes were a really beautiful shade of hazel, but weirdly creepy. They seemed to peer right past me into my soul, without revealing any soul of their own. "Gimme your phone number," he said.

"Sorry," I said. "I can't. I have a boyfriend."

"What, you think you're too good for me?" he said accusingly.

"N-no, of course not." I said, "I just already have a boyfriend."

"Red here thinks she's better than me," he said to his friend.

"No, I really don't," I said. "I don't think I'm better than anyone."

Chantal jumped in, "She has a boyfriend for real. His name's Ricky."

"Did I ask you?" he said to her, really meanly.

"I'm sorry," I said, feeling a little panicked and wishing I could just vanish into thin air on the spot. "I don't know you and I don't think anything about you. I have a boyfriend and that's why I can't give you my phone number. We're going back to our towels now."

He sucked his teeth as I took a step back, really thankful there was a chain-link fence between us. "You better not be lying to me," he said with one last, hard look at me and Chantal, then he walked away.

Before following, his friend said to me, "You better watch yourself. You don't want to get on King's bad side." I couldn't tell if it was meant as friendly advice or a threat.

We went back to our towels, both shaken. We decided to stay at the pool for a while longer, sunburns or no sunburns, to make sure King was long gone before we left.

Were we in a movie? I felt (and still feel) like I was being sucked into this new world where people no longer acted the way I expected them to act. They ignore you for no reason, force you to do things you're not ready for, and accuse you of thinking things you don't think. Is this what growing up is all about? Finding out that there are no more nice people? Or at least no more nice guys?

• • •

Thursday, June 28, 1984
Dear Diary,
I woke up in the middle of the night unable to move. It wasn't
totally dark in my room because my door was partway open,
letting in light from the hall, and the shadows played tricks on me
as I lay there helpless and vulnerable. I was sure one of those
dark, scary shapes would appear any second and I had this awful
feeling that if it did it would do something terrible to me. Then I
noticed a dark spot in the corner of the ceiling that I had never
noticed before. A bug? Dirt? A splotch of paint? And suddenly it
started to spread, kind of branching out like frost on a window
pane or mould on the bathroom walls, in fast motion. It was black
like tar and worked its way across the ceiling toward me with
alarming speed. I regretted having decided to sleep on the top
bunk as the crawling mass got closer and closer, mesmerizing and
terrorizing me all at once. I don't know if it was the fear or
fascination, but I just lay there letting it come for me, entirely
forgetting to fight myself awake until the very last second, when
I managed to gasp more than scream, sitting bolt upright and
looking around frantically at my perfectly normal, white ceiling.

I stayed awake for a long time and then slept in till almost
noon . . . when Ricky called! It was about time. I can't figure out
if he's playing "hard to get," as my friends say, or if he just
doesn't really like me that much. I regret giving him my virginity
so easily. I know I didn't think I had a choice, but now I feel like
maybe I did, I just didn't know it or wasn't strong enough.
Anyway, it's too late now, and part of me does like having joined
this club of grown-up, experienced people. I just wish I *felt*
grown-up and experienced.

Ricky, Olive, and some friends are going to see this movie
called *Breakin'* tomorrow. They already saw it but they said it's

the best, so they're seeing it again and Chantal and I are going to go with them. Sandrine can't come because she said her report card was horrible and her mom's punishing her.

I feel bad for her, but I can't wait!

I got my report card, too. I passed everything except I did fail economics. I only got a sixty in *Histoire*, but all my other marks were seventies and low eighties, except for English, which, as always, was my highest mark. Not to vaunt, but I got ninety-four!

• • •

Friday, June 29, 1984
Dear Diary,
The movie was amazing. The rest of the night was really fucking strange.

The movie is about a jazz dancer named Special K who meets two break-dancers named Ozone and Turbo who end up teaching her how to street dance. The dancing and the music are amazing and Ozone is so gorgeous. I could watch that movie a million times, just like when I saw *Flashdance* last year and loved it so much I walked straight over to Sam the Record Man and bought the album. We're already planning to go see *Breakin'* again next week!

After the movie we went to Tyrone's place again. It was just him and his girlfriend there. They were both really nice to Chantal and me and I felt a lot better being there than the first time. Plus of course I was there with Ricky and he wasn't ignoring me this time, even if he's a bit cold and doesn't say much except when he wants to kiss me or more.

Anyway, they put on a movie, a Bruce Lee martial arts movie. Not my thing, even though I will admit he is an amazing fighter and it's also funny to watch how the actors' mouths don't follow the English dubbed words at all. They always make these speeches that last, like, 30 seconds in Chinese and then in English all they say is "No!" or something. But I got bored of it really fast.

So then, all of a sudden, Ricky said, "So I hear you were talking to King."

I was so surprised I didn't even know what to say. I knew I hadn't done anything wrong, but my cheeks got really hot from the accusing way he was looking at me and plus I was just so shocked. I didn't even know they knew each other and even still, how could Ricky know?

"I – how do you know King?" I said.

"Everybody knows King." Ricky said, like he's somebody important. "So why were you talking to him?"

"I wasn't. I mean I was, but only because he talked to me. I told him I have a boyfriend."

"Oh yeah? Who's your boyfriend?" he said, and I couldn't tell if he was teasing me or serious. What was I supposed to answer? If I said him, I would look like I was assuming we were a thing and I guess we weren't officially, even though, you know. But there was no other good answer.

"I – well I didn't want to give him my number so I told him I had a boyfriend," I said, which actually made it sound like I *had* lied to King, which made me a little scared even though, obviously, he wasn't there.

"And how do you think I know you were talking to him?" he said, still making it sound like it was me who approached King and not the other way around.

I shrugged my shoulders, trying to look confident and like I didn't care. But I was feeling really put on the spot and afraid of just saying the wrong thing.

"You used my name," said Ricky accusingly.

"I'm sorry," I said, throwing my hands up. I could feel a lump rising in my throat and I wanted to get out of there.

Then both Chantal and Olive came to my rescue. "*I* used your name," said Chantal. "I said you were her boyfriend when King accused her of lying.

Then Olive said to Ricky, "Why you gotta be such an asshole? You know she didn't do nothing and you know how King is."

Then Ricky actually smiled (it might have been the first time I saw him smile and it changed his whole face!) and said, "I'm just messin' with you. But watch out for King. He's messed up." He tapped his temple to show what he meant.

"King?" said Tyrone, coming into the room. "Yeah, stay away from that guy. And his brother, too. Fucked-up family. And they treat their women like shit. You gotta treat your woman well," he said, eyeing his girlfriend appreciatively and then shooting a hard look at Ricky, which made me feel kind of good. So it wasn't my imagination that Ricky was weird with me, and his own cousin was on my side.

I felt better with Ricky not accusing me anymore, but again I felt like I was in some TV show. I felt like I was in *Star Wars*, with the dark side tempting me with its sex and weed but also being dangerous with its risks and bad people. I actually laughed out loud when I thought that maybe King was actually Darth Vader.

"You crazy?" Ricky said. "What you laughing at?"

"Nothing," I said. "Don't mind me."

At that, Chantal lifted her eyebrows, pointed at me then twirled her finger around next to her ear. Everyone laughed at that and whatever tension was left disappeared.

"Smoke?" Ricky said to the room, pulling a little bag of weed out of his pocket and heading toward the kitchen. I figured it couldn't hurt to try again. We all followed him out back, including Tyrone and his girlfriend. (I can't remember her name!) Ricky rolled a big spliff while Chantal and I shared a cigarette and watched him in fascination.

Once the joint was lit and came to me, I remembered to take a smaller hit and I managed not to cough. When it came to me a second time, I did the same. (I think Olive doesn't smoke, because once again, he passed.)

We all went back inside and Tyrone put on a movie called *Up In Smoke*, about two guys named Cheech and Chong who basically smoke weed all the time. It's very stupid but funny and, I guess, the perfect thing to watch when you're stoned. So we all sat in front of the TV and suddenly out of nowhere I knew I was high. I felt relaxed in a way I had never felt relaxed before. My mind stopped trying to think of a million things and question everything and I just *was*. I realized I was staring at the TV, but not really paying any attention to what was happening; instead I was focusing on the light and the images. My focus got really intense and everything seemed to slow down a little. I looked from the movie to each of the people in the room and I felt like I was very separate from them, but able to see them . . . vividly. Then I started to feel these different sensations in myself. My face started to feel kind of strange, like it was going numb, except I could actually feel it more, not less. Then as I focused on each different part of my body, slowly travelling down from one place to another each one went numb. It was the coolest sensation I have ever experienced and I felt like I could stay there forever. It was like floating in a cushion of pure light and feeling.

At some point I realized Ricky, Olive, and Chantal were all looking at me, and Ricky was exclaiming that I must be "so high." I guess they had been trying to get my attention for a while. As I came back to the room the numbness faded and I was just relaxed like I had been at first. Ricky took me by the hand and led me to a room and we had sex again. It felt better with me all relaxed and plus it not being my first time anymore. I didn't even think about protection until after. I'm going to have to do something about that or I'll end up pregnant. He pulled out before he came, but he told me to go pee right away after, just in case. I don't know much about sex, but I do know that going to pee isn't going to stop you getting pregnant. Can't hurt, though, so I didn't argue and went to the bathroom.

After that I realized I was dying to eat something. I asked if they had any chips or anything and they laughed and told me I had the munchies. Apparently that's another thing that happens when you smoke up and I wasn't the only one who had them, so we all walked over to McDonald's for Big Macs and fries.

On the way home on the metro I asked Chantal if she had gotten high too this time. She said yes and talked about feeling relaxed and happy, but she didn't go numb like me. She thought it sounded really cool, though.

It sure was.

• • •

Saturday, June 30, 1984
Dear Diary,
I just realized Ricky never did confirm that he's my boyfriend. So I'm not sure what to call him. I guess I can say he's my boyfriend, but not in front of him.

I think I need a summer job. I can't just keep asking Mom for money every time I want to go to the movies or to buy anything. She's already getting annoyed with me and summer just started. I really don't like babysitting, but what else could I do? Mom says my cousin Cathy has a paper route, but you have to get up at, like, five in the morning to do that. No way am I doing that! One of the best things about summer is getting to sleep in every day.

• • •

Wednesday, July 4, 1984
Dear Diary,
I thought I had lost you. I almost had a heart attack.

Chantal, Sandrine, Ricky, Olive, and Freddy all came over on Monday.

First we met up at the pool, but it was already kind of late and also cloudy and not that hot so we didn't really want to go in the water and we didn't stay long. Since Mom was at work and I live in the same neighbourhood as the pool (it's still almost a half-hour walk) everyone decided we should go to my place.

We stopped at Girouard Park on the way to smoke a spliff and I was super worried we would get caught, but we didn't.

By the time we got home it was already five and Mom usually gets home by six or seven so I was nervous she would get there to find us all there and notice I was high. I checked my eyes when we arrived and they were pretty red.

We sat in the living room and put on the radio. The guys don't like listening to the radio: too much pop and not enough rap and reggae. But "In the Air Tonight" by Phil Collins came on and we all just sat back and got really quiet and lost in the song. At least I got lost. At first I just listened to the amazing music. I mean, I love that song no matter what, but after smoking up it just had an effect on me. And then the numbness came over me. I'm not sure if I started it on purpose or not, but I felt it in my hands first this time and then I got it to travel up my arms, then to my neck and my head and down my back all the way to my feet. It was faster than last time and just as cool.

"That song makes you trip, doesn't it?" said Freddy, breaking the spell before the song was even over.

We all agreed.

"You have to watch it, though. I heard that song has a special power and if you let yourself go too much, it just sucks you in and you can lose your mind and never come back."

"What? Like the *Twilight Zone*?" said Chantal. "Yeah, right. Gimme a break."

Sandrine punched Freddy playfully on the arm while Ricky and Olive just laughed.

I, on the other hand, was less amused. I knew about getting stuck in places and not knowing if you'd find your way back, so just in case I silently vowed never to listen to that song after smoking up again.

A bit later Ricky wanted to go to my room. We went, but I didn't want to start anything because I was really worried about Mom coming home. He kept kissing me and trying to get under my clothes and then I'd push him away and he'd start looking through my stuff, opening a drawer or my jewellery box, then trying to get busy with me again. At one point he opened the drawer in my bedside table where I keep you, my diary.

"What's this?" he said, opening it to a random page.

"Nothing!" I said, grabbing it from him before he had a chance to stop me. "It's private."

"Oh, private," he said, mocking me. "Lemme see." He tried to take it but I put it behind my back. "Anything about me in there?" he asked.

"Nope," I lied, "But you don't read someone's diary. It's really private and it's sacred!" I meant it, but I also would have been mortified if he read the things that were in here. Or if anyone read them, for that matter.

We struggled for a while longer, seemingly playfully but with me very serious and determined inside, and then Freddy came to ask where the bathroom was. The phone rang at the exact same moment (saved by the bell!), so I asked Ricky to show Freddy to the bathroom. I answered the phone, took a message for Mom, and hid you away in the hood of a jacket in the back of my closet before Ricky came back.

Then Mom came home while everyone was still there and I had to introduce her and I was nervous about what she would think about all those guys being at our place and maybe even what she would think about some of them being black. I hate to even write something like that because I am not racist and I know Mom isn't either, but you never know what parents are going to do or who's going to turn out to be prejudiced. But I didn't need to worry. We were all in the living room not doing anything wrong and I guess she didn't notice any red eyes or anything and Olive especially was really polite, shaking her hand and saying, "Pleased to meet you." She never said anything about them being there even after they left.

But there was one other thing that happened. I had about twelve dollars in change in a dish on my dresser and the next morning I noticed it was empty. I couldn't believe one of my friends or my boyfriend (or whatever he is) would steal from me, but I was really sure I had that money there. And then I couldn't find my diary. I remembered Ricky trying to read it and I was suspicious about the missing money and got so worried he had stolen both. My heart beat so fast, right up to my temples, when I imagined him reading all my secret thoughts about him. I thought I might throw up. Or just die then and there.

And then today I remembered I had hidden you away. How could I have forgotten? I guess there were just so many events and distractions that I forgot that one important detail. I never did find out about the money, though. Maybe I spent it and forgot.

I really hope so.

● ● ●

Thursday, July 5, 1984
Dear Diary,
What a weird dream. I don't usually remember my dreams themselves in such detail and they're always so weird and

nonsensical when you try to explain them afterwards that I don't normally write them down.

But this one needs to be told!

I was with Ricky and we were going to see *Breakin'* again, but when we got to the movie theatre it wasn't a movie theatre anymore; it was a hotel. So we paid our admission to the movie but when we got inside there was a big, fancy lobby and a grand, winding staircase.

This, of course, was not strange at all, because it was a dream and things always change randomly like that without you even noticing or questioning it.

We were a more normal and happy couple in the dream than how we are in real life, because we were holding hands as we walked to the elevator, which was one of those old-fashioned elevators with a regular door and then a grill that closes and a person in white gloves who operates the elevator for you.

We got in and stood at the back of the elevator behind the operator and I could just see the side of his face and I realized it was King! I was terrified he would see me and I turned to look at Ricky only I wasn't with Ricky anymore, I was with Chantal. She was acting really normal, though, talking to me and laughing and I kept trying to motion to her to be quiet so King wouldn't turn around and see us.

The elevator stopped on our floor and we got out and just as I thought we were home free he said, "Hey, Red!" really menacingly. I turned to look at him and when I turned back Chantal was running away and telling me to hurry up. Of course, I couldn't run fast at all. My legs were lead and I felt like I was running in molasses. After I realized running wasn't getting me anywhere I decided to hide in one of the hotel rooms instead, so I opened the first door I came to and inside was Ricky, naked. He was standing there, with a *hard-on,* saying "I want you," and "I'm gonna be your first," but Chantal and Sandrine, both naked too, were standing just behind him on either side, rubbing his shoulders and arms and looking at me in a mischievous, sinister way. The room was kind of dark and as my eyes adjusted to the dim light I noticed that there were a lot of other people in the room, including Freddy, Olive, Tyrone and even Amy. All naked, of course. Suddenly, they all looked at me and started saying, "Don't mess with King."

And then King was in front of me and *I* was naked. He started walking towards me real slow, saying, "I'm gonna teach you how to take the pain."

I couldn't move from where I stood, let alone run, so I tried to scream to the others for help, but of course no sound would come out. I stood there, able to breathe but not move or make a sound, and suddenly King became nothing but a dark shadow, just a looming shape like the ones I usually see when I'm in the in-between place. The shadow started to fade to a paler colour and change shape, and I guess I managed to scream then, because I startled myself awake. Fully awake, and fully terrified.

● ● ●

Friday, July 6, 1984
Dear Diary,
Well, today just fucking sucked.

I feel so lost, I can't even believe it and I don't know where to start.

It was supposed to be just a great day. Chantal and Sandrine and I went to La Ronde for the first time this summer. First, the Haunted House AND the new Monster roller coaster were both closed. Then we went in the Salt and Pepper shaker and all the change fell out of my shorts pocket when we went upside down. La Pitoune was fun, at least, and we got soaked, which we always pretend not to like but of course we do. We decided to go a second time, even though the wait was almost half an hour, and just as we got in our boat, clouds rolled in and it got windy, so we were really cold after the ride. We decided to go eat some beaver tails (not real ones, duh! They're these really delicious cinnamon-and-sugar-topped pastries) and drink Diet Cokes and wait to see if the sun came back out.

While we were sitting there Sandrine told us that her report card had been so bad it meant she would have to repeat her year. Her parents wanted her to go to summer school, but she would have had to do both French *and* math and she said no way was she ruining her whole summer in school. If it were me I don't know what I would do. Ruin my summer in school or have to do a whole extra year of high school? I think I would do summer school; how could I watch my friends get ready to graduate and me having to wait a whole extra year? I guess she feels a bit the same because she's going to change schools! She's going to an English school called Westmount, which she says is a really cool school. I know Freddy goes there, so maybe that's why she chose it. I asked her how she was going to be able to do that, though, because I thought she was like me and not allowed to go to English school because of Bill 101, which says that you can only go to an English school if one of your parents went to English school in Quebec. She told me the law just changed so now she's allowed, because her mom grew up in Saskatchewan. I'm going to ask Mom if that's right. (What is with this stupid law, anyway? Aren't there supposed to be equal rights for everyone? Don't we have freedom of speech in Canada? I really don't understand how Quebec gets away with it. I mean didn't racist white people in the States defend segregation by saying they were "protecting" their culture? Aren't Quebec's "protection" laws the same? I mean, I know English people are not oppressed like black people, but discrimination should be illegal no matter what, if you ask me.)

So, right after Sandrine broke the news that she was leaving FACE, Chantal looked at us really seriously and said, "I have something to tell you guys." She looked like she was going to cry so we both got really scared. (I thought, "Oh my God, she's pregnant." But it wasn't that.)

"What is it?" we both said at the same time.

"My dad got a job in Halifax, so we're moving at the end of the summer."

I felt like everything around me just crashed to the ground.

"What?" I said, instantly feeling my throat tighten and tears spring to my eyes. "You can't."

"That's what I told my parents," she said, and we both started to cry.

"Stop, you guys," said Sandrine. "You're going to make me cry, too, and all our mascara is going to run."

We all laughed at that, but half-heartedly.

"What if I ask my mom if you can live with us for a year? I'm sure she would say yes. You're like my sister!" I said.

"Really?" she asked, wiping tears away.

"For sure!" I said.

"Hey, I'm starting to feel left out!" Sandrine said. "You guys might live together now and I'm leaving for another school."

"No! Don't feel left out! But we can't let Chantal move away," I said.

All the way home on the metro we discussed how to pitch our plan to our parents and when I got home I asked Mom right away and she was actually open to the idea. She said there would be lots of details to work out but that she didn't really see why not. I was sooooo happy and relieved! I called Chantal to tell her and my world crashed for the second, no, third time today. Her parents said no, flat out.

"Il n'en est pas question," her mom said, which means, basically, no way and case closed. I won't go through all the reasons because they're parents' reasons and of course we don't agree with them.

We swore we'll have the best summer ever from now 'til she leaves and spend every moment we can together then write to each other every day until she's eighteen and can move back here, and we'll get an apartment together and be roommates and start our own magazine like we've been planning.

My conclusion for today is, yeah, it definitely sucked.

● ● ●

Saturday, July 7, 1984
Dear Diary,
I am getting really good at this going numb thing. The second I realize I'm stoned I just sit back and let the feeling come over me. I can go from head to toe or toe to head. And numb is pretty much what I want to be right now, so today I was like, "Bring it on!"

We saw *Breakin'* again this afternoon (so good) then went to Tyrone's again and Ricky got annoyed with *me* for not paying attention to *him* and for liking to smoke up too much. To be honest, I don't think he really cares if I pay attention to him, he just wanted to have sex and I was lost in enjoying my numbness and resisted (but only a little) when he insisted and broke my spell.

Oh! One thing I have to tell you about! We were listening to a new album called *Purple Rain* by Prince and the Revolution. It was *totally amazing.* When I went numb (before Ricky snapped me out of it) we were listening to the song "Purple Rain" itself. It's a long, slow song and it's romantic and beautiful and sexy . . . I *have* to buy the album!

● ● ●

Sunday, July 8, 1984
Dear Diary,
Mom is such a hypocrite!

She's been getting mad at me lately for asking for too much money, for never staying home, and not always telling her when I'll be back or calling if I'm going to be later than I said. Like, I'm almost sixteen and it's summer vacation; what does she expect? For me to just stay in my room? To not date?

Oh, she also said she knows I smoke and doesn't appreciate that I lied to her about it when she asked me before.

So I told her that if she's going to talk about lying, I don't appreciate that she has a boyfriend since last year and won't admit that he's even her boyfriend. She had the nerve to say that her personal life is not my business! I almost told her that I bet she's having sex with him (I'm pretty sure she snuck in really early in the morning a couple of times recently), but then I thought I better not bring up that subject, just in case she had any suspicions to throw back at me.

• • •

Tuesday, July 10, 1984
Dear Diary,
Yesterday I filled out an application to work at McDonald's. I hope I get it. I need to have some spending money. They pay about four dollars an hour, so even if I only work part-time, I could make, like seventy-five dollars a week! Imagine the fun I could have with that. I could go out anytime I want, buy some new clothes and makeup, stop bumming cigarettes all the time and still put some money in my savings account so eventually I can get myself a car or something. I love picturing myself driving around in a convertible and living in my own apartment. Actually I dream a lot of my own apartment these days, because Mom's super moody all the time. Chantal and Sandrine said maybe it's menopause, but I don't think so because she's only forty-five and she still buys herself maxi pads.

Today we went to the park to watch Olive play baseball. It was a practice, not a game, so there were just a few people sitting around watching, including me and Chantal.

She told me some stuff about him. He's had a rough past and yet he's so nice. He's much more friendly and easy going than Ricky, who always acts like he's too cool to just laugh or be outright *nice*. Olive lived in a group home until this spring when he turned sixteen and moved in with his older half-brother who's in his twenties. I asked Chantal why he was in the group home and she said he used to fight with his mom a lot because he wasn't good at school and she was one of those moms who just always yells and screams and never listens, and one day they were having such a big fight that he hit her.

I was shocked. I could not imagine hitting Mom, much less if I were a guy! "Hit her how? Like slapped? Punched? In the face, or what?"

"I don't know, he just said he hit her. And that's when she sent him to a group home. He feels really bad about it; he says he didn't know what he was doing, he just lost control. Anyway, they didn't talk for months but now they're talking again. But he says he won't ever move back home."

I looked at Chantal for a second and asked, "He's never hit you, has he?"

"No! Of course not. You know Olive. He's always just fun and making people laugh."

"OK, just checking," I said.

Then she confessed something to me. She said she's not sure she likes him as a boyfriend anymore. She feels bad because they've had sex and everything, but she's starting to feel like she just likes him as a friend. I think maybe she's just telling herself that because she knows she has to leave him in a few weeks, but I didn't say that.

Thinking of her leaving has made me sad again. And if I'm sad now, imagine how I'll feel when she's actually gone.

• • •

Wednesday, July 11, 1984

Dear Diary,

What the fuck is with Ricky?

I got home from the park yesterday and Mom said he had called twice. (She also just had to add that "he could use better phone manners." Well excuse me! Maybe he's uncomfortable talking to parents, and it's not my fault, anyway. I can't control how he acts on the phone.)

Anyway, I tried to call him back, like, three times, but he wasn't home. The first time there was no answer and the next two times Tyrone answered but said he didn't know where Ricky went.

So then today I waited 'til almost four, and since he didn't call, I called him again, and he was all cold on the phone. After he answered and I said it was me, he was like, "Yeah, what?"

So I said, "You called me yesterday and I've been trying to call you back."

"So where were you?"

I told him I was at the park with Chantal watching Olive and he got all weird, saying why am I following Olive around when he's Chantal's man and all kinds of stupidness. I started off over-explaining and getting defensive as usual, saying that I need to spend as much time with Chantal as possible before she moves away, and then I just stopped. I could feel he was just playing some weird kind of game, accusing me of something he knew damn well wasn't true, just like that time after I met King at the swimming pool.

"I don't know what you're trying to say," I said, "but I didn't do a single thing wrong and I'm not going to stay here being accused of shit you made up in your own head. Call me when you come to your senses. Or don't. Whatever." And I hung up.

I'm so fucking mad. But also pretty damn proud of myself.
I just hope he does come to his senses and calls me.

● ● ●

Thursday, July 12, 1984
Dear Diary,
No news from Ricky yet.

But I did have a visit from one of the shadow-things last night. It just stood there watching me, with me paralyzed and knowing it's just a matter of time before it decides to come and . . . and what? I don't know what it would do, and I don't want to know either.

● ● ●

Friday, July 13, 1984
Dear Diary,
Still no news from Ricky. Now I regret what I said. I hate to admit it, but I even cried a couple of times. I'm trying to convince my friends and myself that I don't care, but I'm going to need distraction, fun and girlfriends time. So I suggested to Chantal and Sandrine that we should go to the Annex tonight.

Sandrine said no because she's going to be with Freddy, as usual. They're always together. They had a big fight the other day, but then he bought her flowers and a teddy bear to get her back. Isn't that amazing? No one has ever bought me flowers and I'm pretty sure even Mom never bought me a teddy bear. She's not very sentimental, more practical. Sandrine has a lot of stuffed animals in her room. Tee had a lot, too. They both always keep their rooms really clean, too. Unlike me. I do have an old stuffed rabbit named Bunny (very creative, I know) that my dad got me when I was born. It's pretty faded and me and my not-so-great sewing skills mended it once so it has different colours of kind of sloppy stitching on one arm, but I'll keep it forever.

So it's just me and Chantal going out tonight. I had to ask Mom for money again, for the "movies." She didn't complain, though, because I start my training at McDonald's on Monday!

• • •

Saturday, July 14, 1984
Dear Diary,
I feel awful. Not as awful as when I woke up this morning, but feeling better is taking a long time.

We went to the Annex. I wore my blue-and-white-striped mini dress with my white pumps. I got maximum volume on my hair and with the tan I've been working on, I actually felt like I looked good. Sexy, even. Chantal wore her short red jeans with an off-the-shoulder top and, well, her hair always looks perfect. I was happy with my curls last night, but I do wish I had straight hair like her that's so much easier to style how you want. Chantal is that quiet kind of pretty that sneaks up on you. If you describe her, you're like, well, she's slim and medium height and has dirty-blond hair and brown eyes, and it's like nothing stands out, but in fact everything is kind of just right so when you really look at her she's prettier than you realized. I'm really going to miss her.

The awesome thing is we didn't even have to pay the five dollars to the bouncer. I don't know if it's because we looked old or we looked good, but we walked right in! Actually, when I was on my way to the metro a guy stared at me so hard he tripped over the curb and almost fell flat on his face! When I told Chantal we literally almost died laughing.

So at the Annex we went downstairs and got right on the dance floor. They were playing Prince's "Let's Go Crazy," so that's what we did. Oh, how I love to dance! There is nothing that helps me escape reality and just feel great more than awesome music and dancing. Of course, a couple of drinks help, too. We only had enough money for one drink, but that didn't matter, because guys bought us more. It was like the more we danced, the more drinks we got and the more drinks we got, the more we danced. I kept saying how nice the guys were and felt like we should be extra nice back for them being so generous, but Chantal seems to have things figured out in a way that's more . . . mature? Calculated? Anyway, she was like, just accepting each drink, saying "thank you," and moving on.

I was having the most amazing time. I even kissed a guy near the bathrooms; well, I guess technically he kissed me, but I sure kissed him back and it was maybe the best kiss of my life. I did not hold back and I was, for once, not the least bit insecure about my . . . skills. Chantal pulled me away from the guy, though, before too long, which annoyed me at the time but I am thankful to her now. I am sure that if it wasn't for her we would not have made it home. We actually missed the last metro, but we walked along Sherbrooke, barefoot and carrying our pumps because our feet were killing us from all the dancing, and caught the 24 bus, which stops a few blocks from my place. On the bus I started to feel really woozy and kind of sick to my stomach and when we got off I barfed in a garbage can next to the bus stop. I don't actually remember the walk home from there, but I guess we made it because here I am. What I do remember, sort of, is barfing again when I got home. First in the bathroom sink then in the toilet. I also remember Mom coming in and asking me if I just drank or if I took any drugs and me just telling her to "shhhhh," then lying down on the nice, cold tile floor.

Needless to say Mom was not thrilled with me this morning. I was not thrilled with myself either; I can't even begin to explain how disgusting I felt, and still actually feel, with my pounding, dizzy head and gurgling, lurching stomach. (Plus how slutty I acted last night kissing that guy!) I puked the first piece of toast I ate, but I think that's mostly because Chantal convinced me to drink a coffee, which, well, ew.

At some point I said to Mom, "I guess I'm in pretty big trouble, eh?" and she said something along the lines of my hangover was punishment enough in itself. So I guess I'm not grounded or anything (Mom's not really the grounding type), but now that I'm up and about and feeling better she keeps making sarcastic little remarks about me lying to her about going to the movies and she wonders just what have I been doing all the other times I've been out. (It's a good thing she actually has no idea.)

Well, she's right about the hangover being punishment enough, anyway. I don't think I'm ever going to drink again.

Besides water. Man, am I thirsty today!

● ● ●

Sunday, July 15, 1984
Dear Diary,
Ricky called.

He was like, "Come over." I didn't like the way it sounded like an order, but I was pretty relieved he called, so I didn't complain. I just went.

As soon as he opened the door he took me right to his room and, well, you can guess the rest. I have to say I do not see what all the fuss is about sex. I like the kissing and making out part way more than the actual sex. It's like that part is just for him. Plus, each time we do it we spend less time on the fun parts and just move on to the just-for-him part.

Also, I have to do something about protection. I'm not exactly going to ask my pediatrician who's been my doctor my whole life about having sex and going on the pill. I know she's not allowed to tell my mom or anything, but just talking to her about it would *feel* like talking to my mom. I'll ask Sandrine if she knows where to go.

I guess I'm supposed to tell Ricky to wear a condom. That way I won't get AIDS or anything either, but how do you ask a guy to do that? Especially now that we're already doing it without a condom. It's all so awkward and embarrassing.

Anyway, I didn't stay very long after. He didn't really seem to want me around once we were done, and even though that hurt my feelings, I didn't really want to stay either.

Tyrone had seen me arrive and I was a bit embarrassed to leave so soon, because it looked like I had come over just for *that,* which I guess I had. "Leaving already?" he said.

"I gotta work tomorrow," I said. (I really do!) "Later," I said, turning away and leaving quickly so he wouldn't see me blushing. I hate that I blush; it always gives me away.

● ● ●

Wednesday, July 18, 1984
Dear Diary,
So Chantal was the one planning to break up with Olive, but they're still together, and I'm the one who ends up with no boyfriend.

Today was my third and last day of training at McDonald's, which has not been fun at all. The uniforms are ugly, they don't let you wear lipstick or jewellery, and they expect you to stay busy all the time, even when there's nothing to do. I'm working at the cash, and if there are no customers, I'm supposed to wipe down the counter, sweep the floor, or a bunch of other stuff. Also, I feel so shy serving people. Some of them are rude and some talk fast and I don't always understand what they say the first time. I guess I have to give it a chance, as Mom says, but I really feel like quitting already.

Anyway, Ricky came in today. First, he told me I look "different" without makeup, which didn't make me feel any better about being in my ugly uniform. Then he asked for free food, which of course I could not give him, so he got all cold with me. Then he told me (not asked, told) to come over again after work.

I changed out of my uniform, of course (no way would I go out in public in that thing), and took time to really fix myself up in the bathroom before leaving. It was a beautiful day, sunny and a perfect twenty-five degrees, so I decided to walk to his place instead of taking the metro. It was about an hour after my shift finished when I got to his place and he was like, "What took you so long?" as if I had been out doing something wrong instead of rushing right over.

Then, as usual, he pulled me directly towards the bedroom. This time I resisted. I wasn't in the mood and I felt tired after standing behind the cash all day.

"Can't we do something else?" I asked.

"Like what?" he said.

I looked around and couldn't think of anything. We couldn't go out to the movies because I had no money, and probably neither did he.

I shrugged my shoulders. "Got any weed?"

"The fuck are you, an addict?" he said with an annoyed laugh.

"It was just a question," I said, feeling, once again, defensive.

"Come 'ere," he said in a friendlier tone, patting the bed next to him.

"I'm going to go smoke a cigarette," I said, heading out of the room toward the kitchen fire escape. (Tyrone gets mad when people smoke in the apartment.)

"What's with you?" he said, following me out.

"Nothing," I said.

"Don't be like that," he said and put his hand between my legs, like he was trying to turn me on. But it didn't. I didn't like it at all, like he thought he could just touch me *there* anytime he wants. Even though he has so many times before.

"Don't do that," I said, taking a step back.

"Why not?" he said, doing it again.

"I just don't like it," I said, but I didn't step back this time.

Then he leaned in close so he could do his whisper-in-my-ear thing and he said, "You always liked it before."

I turned my face away and said, "I just don't want to today," in a much weaker voice than I meant to.

"What did you come here for then?" he said, louder, making me suddenly feel really cheap.

"Is that all you want me for?" I asked more boldly, looking him in the face while dying inside for him to say something totally out of character like, "No, of course not. I like you because you're smart, pretty and fun to be with." But he just shrugged his shoulders indifferently.

"Is it?" I insisted.

"Yeah," he said, looking *me* in the face now. "I guess it is."

"OK," I said, as calmly as I could after feeling like I had been slapped across the face. I turned to walk away while I still had my composure and a little bit of pride, but tears welled up in my eyes and his cruelty stung too much. How could he be so hurtful? And why?

"You're pretty fucking mean." I said, looking back at him, not even caring that a tear had escaped and was rolling down my cheek.

He didn't even say anything to that. Just shrugged his stupid shoulders again and looked down at the floor.

"Bye, Ricky," I said, still pathetically hoping he would suddenly become a different person and beg me to stay. But of course he didn't.

As I walked through the apartment, Tyrone saw me leaving in tears and said, "Can I give you some advice?"

"Sure, whatever," I said, feeling stupid for crying and resentful of Tyrone for being a guy and a relative of Ricky's.

"You gotta have more self-respect," he said. "My cousin Ricky's a little shit, but if you don't respect yourself, who will?"

"I respect myself," I said, feeling a little defensive.

"OK, if you say so. I'm not telling you what to do or not do, but I hate to see a nice, smart girl letting herself get treated the way she don't want to be treated."

"OK," I said, feeling small. But at least he cared enough to say something, and he had called me nice and smart, which was more than Ricky had done. "Thanks. Later."

"Later."

All the way home I thought about what Tyrone said and I've decided he's wrong. I do respect myself. I mean, I stood up for myself on the phone with Ricky that time, for all the good it did me. But Tyrone's right that I should make sure to get treated the way I want. I just have to figure out how to do that. With someone else, though. I'm done with Ricky.

• • •

Thursday, July 19, 1984

Dear Diary,

I had a terrible night. I woke up paralyzed, like, three times and slept badly in between because of disturbing dreams about getting lost in a gigantic maze, about my dad dying (for the first time in years), and about my friends shunning me.

I'm still in bed and don't want to get up because I feel like such an idiot. It's not even that I miss Ricky or want to still be with him, but why did he have to be so mean? And make me feel so stupid and cheap? And unwanted. And ugly.

I mean, who would want to be with me, anyway? I'm not what you would call fresh or fine. I'm too pale and I hate my nose, my unruly hair never looks good, and I'm so flat-chested, I have zits on my back and I'm shy and awkward, I suck at my new job, I'm bad at sports, and the list goes on. I can't even sleep like a normal person! And on top of everything, now all I want to do is sit in my room crying and feeling sorry for myself. What a loser.

● ● ●

Friday, July 20, 1984
Dear Diary,
Best friends are the best. What will I ever do without one?

Chantal came over yesterday and I told her all about what Ricky said and did. I felt a little humiliated just talking about the way he treated me. I cried when I told her how he said he did only want me for one thing, and even if Chantal and me are not the kind of friends that hug all the time or hold hands or anything, she listened and didn't judge me and did give me a small hug and lots of Kleenex to dry my face with.

She, of course, said he's an asshole and that I deserve better. So what if she has to say that because she's my best friend? I know she still means it and it sure felt good to hear it. She was supposed to go watch Olive's baseball game in the evening and she even offered not to go if I wanted to just hang out at her place. I told her no, that she didn't need to jeopardize her own relationship just because mine was over, and then she invited me to go with her. I wasn't sure how I would feel being around a happy couple in my state, but in fact it was fine. I feel like Olive's my friend even if he's Chantal's boyfriend and I never feel awkward around him or them, just like we're three friends hanging out together.

I even spotted a couple of other cute guys on the team, and I felt really good when I overheard one of them say I was "fly," but then I told myself not to even think about it!

Ricky was a big mistake and he really hurt me, but it's not going to take me very long to get over him, I can feel it.

Tonight is girls' night, though. We're going to see a new horror movie that just came out called *A Nightmare on Elm Street*. Everyone says it's really, really good. Even Sandrine is coming with us for once.

Unfortunately, since I haven't been paid yet for my (horrible) job I had to ask Mom for money for the movie. She got annoyed with me again about asking for money and then when she handed it to me she asked me if I'm really going to the movies or if I'm going out to get drunk again. Like what kind of a way is that to talk to me? It's not like I'm lying to her left and right and getting drunk every night. It was one time!

I hate when she gets all accusing and resentful. Like, just let me do something or don't, but I hate the way she gives in to things then gets all bitchy about them later.

• • •

Saturday, July 21, 1984
Dear Diary,
The movie was really scary. We all went on and on about how great it was, but to be honest it was a little too . . . close to home for me. And you know how much I love horror. It's about this evil dead guy named Freddy Krueger who visits kids in their dreams and kills them. So they're all afraid to fall asleep, but eventually you have to sleep, don't you? As I know very well.

For me, it was the scariest movie I've seen since *The Exorcist* all those years ago, and you know how well I slept after watching *that*. Well, this one immediately messed with my sleep and my dreams pretty badly. Weirdly, I don't feel like it was *me* who got messed up by the movie, though, I feel like it was *them* that messed with *me* because *they* knew I was in a vulnerable place after Ricky and the movie and everything. By *them* I mean the dark, looming (and now crawling) shadow-things. I do realize I sound crazy saying that.

I am almost afraid to write this down. It was the worst . . . *visit* . . . yet and the longest, too, although really I guess I don't ever know how long I stay stuck in the in-between. But it felt like forever.

I don't remember much of the dream itself, except that I was very alone, like I had lost everyone (not a big surprise, given the summer I've had). Then I started to wake up but remained trapped where I've been trapped so many times before. This time I had no will to fight, so I just lay there taking comfort in the fact that I could at least breathe and that I would get out eventually. Well, I never feel like I *know* I'll get out, but I tell myself I will, because I always have before. This time I almost got comfortable while I waited. I just kind of settled in and lay there breathing and being patient.

And then.

Something started to *crawl up my body.* I couldn't see it (and no it wasn't Freddy Krueger), but I could feel it, starting at my feet and slowly, patiently, working its way up my legs towards my stomach. At first I just noticed it and then I tried to accept it the same way I had accepted the not moving, thinking it might lose interest and go away. Then suddenly I knew. I knew it was *evil* and that if it made it up to my throat I would never be able to scream and it would take me away and I would be lost forever. It sounds corny, I know, when I write it down like that, but that's how it felt.

It was time to scream. But of course I couldn't. I tried and tried, and still wasn't able. I can't describe how hard it is to keep struggling; it just takes everything I have, and I have never had to fight for so long. (Like I said, I don't actually know that, but it seemed like the longest time by far.) Finally I did scream (or I wouldn't be here writing this now), and for the first time in a very long time I *wanted* to wake up Mom, so I kept screaming and screaming until she came running.

She was pretty freaked out and I guess she was relieved when she realized it was "just" another one of my "bad dreams." I even asked her to go check where Pumpkin was, because the feeling of crawling was so real I thought (hoped?) it might have been him. "He's on my bed. He's been there all night. Why?"

"No reason," I said and tried to hide a sob. She could tell, though, so she hugged me really tight and rubbed my back and stayed with me until I eventually fell asleep again. I hadn't felt so close to Mom in a long time.

So I guess one good thing came out of my nightmare.

Chapter 5
Fall 1984

Tuesday, Sept. 4, 1984

Dear Diary,

So I started school all alone today and it was as depressing as I expected.

First, I was super-tired and I looked terrible because I had another visit by the shadow-thing last night. Even when I woke up enough to be able to move and blink, I couldn't stop seeing it. I don't know why it took me so long to finally reach over and turn on the light, but of course when I did, it disappeared. I didn't want to go back to sleep right away so I read for a while, but I'm reading *Children of the Corn* by Stephen King, so that didn't really help.

Chantal left eight days ago and I haven't written to you since because I've written to *her* every single day. But I figured it's time to give you an update on my sad, lonely life.

Of course I know everyone at school; we've all been together since Sec. One and lots of us since before that, since now our school goes all the way from Kindergarten to Grade Eleven, aka Sec. Five.

But I've had one best friend since Grade Four and now she's gone. I never worried so much about making other friends because I had Chantal, and I'm not good at making new friends or making myself part of a clique. I don't know how to approach people and I've never felt like I fit in to any group (I can't say we have actual cliques at our school). I sure don't fit in with the style of the preppy crowd from the English side and I'm still shy to speak French (which is dumb, I know, but I can't help it) so I stay quiet whenever I'm in a group from our side. I mean, everyone's nice, or almost everyone, and there aren't really any bullies in our school like you see on American TV shows, but I always feel like I don't quite belong. At least if Sandrine were still here I would have *someone.*

Oh, you know what? She and Freddy broke up. How's that for luck? She finally gets to go to the same school as him and they're not together anymore. They had such a rocky relationship! They were always fighting and breaking up and then he would make these grand, romantic gestures or buy her presents to get her back. Sometimes I wondered if she started fights on purpose because she liked all his attempts to get her back.

I never told you this, but remember after Ricky when I started seeing that guy Terry from Olive's baseball team this summer and he dumped me because he said I was too "hot and cold?" Well, I had actually been trying to kind of copy Sandrine's technique. She has this way of pushing a guy away just enough and then reeling him in again, like she always keeps him guessing and interested. Well, it didn't work for me. I've never been good at playing games like that and Terry ended up just thinking I was crazy.

All that to say, I'm sure Sandrine will find someone new pretty fast if she really wants to. And I bet that now that the first day of school is over she's already chosen some new friends to hang out with, too.

I'm really stressed about how lonely this year is going to be.

● ● ●

Thursday, Sept. 6, 1984

Dear Diary,

I'm going to have to try harder to make friends with people at my school. I was so looking forward to lunchtimes hanging out in the lounge with Chantal and Sandrine and all the Grade Elevens this year. And now I just feel like I don't belong there or anywhere.

So today instead of going to the lounge I left school and met up with Sandrine at her school. We went down the street to buy some food and when we got to the restaurant I recognized those two girls who were at Tyrone's place that first time I went there with Ricky this summer. You know, the ones who sat in the corner and looked at us all judgemental.

"Do you recognize them?" I asked Sandrine.

"Yeah, but I think they don't remember me. They're a year ahead like you so they're not in my classes and they've never looked at me or talked to me."

As they were walking out with their order they passed right by us and one of them looked right at me. I can't help myself, I have to smile at people when they look at me, so I smiled and then she recognized me. She gave me one of those little nods. "'Sup?" she said.

"Not much," I said.

"Aren't you that girl who was with Ricky?"

I didn't like the tone she used, which made the "with" sound nasty, like I was with him one time and then maybe someone else the next day. But what could I say? "Yeah," I said. Then, trying to make it clear we were actually an item for a while, I said, "We're not together anymore, though."

"Oh," she said, knowingly, then, turning to Sandrine and looking her up and down, "And you were with Freddy, right?"

"That's right," Sandrine said, clearly not feeling any need to explain or defend herself. I really wished more of her confident attitude would rub off on me.

"Well, later," the girl said in a slightly friendlier tone. But as they walked away, I could swear I heard her friend say something like, "What are you talking to those sluts for?"

Sandrine didn't hear it, said I probably imagined it and that she wouldn't care what they think even if they did say it.

"They're just jealous," she said. "And Freddy and I were together all summer. He loved me. We just fought too much and I couldn't take the drama anymore."

I personally think she relished the drama, but I wasn't going to say that.

Once we finished eating I realized I was never going to make it all the way back to school, three metro stops away, in time.

"I'm so dead!" I said. "I have math with Mr. Franco, *et il ne tolère pas les retards!*" I said, waving my finger in imitation of him. "And I can't stand walking into class late anyway, with everyone watching you. I hate this year already."

"So don't go," Sandrine said.

"What?" I said.

"Don't go. Let's go shopping or something instead. I know! I heard they're doing free makeovers this week in the makeup section at The Bay. Let's get a makeover!"

It sounded like a good plan to me, certainly more exciting than math and gym class. But I had never skipped school before and it felt risky because The Bay was just a couple of blocks from my school.

"But everyone else is in school. You're not going to get caught."

And I didn't. No one called home looking for me, and just in case they ask, I forged Mom's signature on a note (I've never done that before either) saying I went to the dentist.

I'm kind of stressed about tomorrow, because I'm a terrible liar and also because I feel like I'm just starting the year off all wrong.

• • •

Friday, Sept. 7, 1984
Dear Diary,
I wish I didn't have to go to school this morning.

I had another visit from the shadow-thing last night. It's been coming to me so much lately that sometimes I don't even bother to write about it. Not to mention waking up paralyzed; I barely even think about it anymore when that happens. I just breathe until I gather enough energy to fight myself awake.

But even the shadow-things. I'm so used to them looming there in the dark so often for so many years that it's almost just another part of my life. The visits all kind of blur together; I can't figure out how many times it's happened (dozens? hundreds?) or sort out what it was like from one time to the next. Sometimes it's skinny and wears a hat, sometimes it's just a black shapeless thing, sometimes it moves a little, sometimes it stays perfectly still. It's still scary every single time, but sometimes (in the daytime, not while it's actually there) I even imagine maybe it's not evil at all, that it's some kind of guardian angel watching over me.

Well that was no fucking guardian angel that visited me last night.

I was sleeping on the top bunk, which I hardly ever do these days. (It's ridiculous that I still have bunk beds. I have been begging Mom to get me a new bed for my birthday that's coming up.) You know the drill: I woke up, I couldn't move or make a sound, I lay there patiently waiting until I could bring myself to try to scream. And then it appeared. Or *something* appeared. It was, as always, a dark shape, but it crawled up onto my bed, over the foot so I could see it creeping up little by little, moving like some kind of animal. Its shape was different from other times, too. It had clearly defined arms and a head, with some kind of claw-like fingers – they're what wrapped themselves over the foot of the bed first – and pointy things on its head, like some kind of devil or demon. And even though it didn't have a face – it never has a face – I could tell it was savouring my terror, enjoying the little contest of who would get there first. Would I manage to scream and make it disappear or would it get to me and drag me down with it? Either way, it doesn't matter, because it, or something like it, will be back.

I know how crazy I sound, writing about this like it's real. But these are not normal nightmares; I know other people don't lie there paralyzed night after night and don't see these . . . visitors or shadow-things or ghosts or whatever they are. If they would just stay where they were, watching me and hardly moving, or not at all, I think I could handle it. But then they change. They crawl onto my bed or up my legs, and how am I supposed to deal with that? How am I supposed to keep going to sleep? Or keep waking up?

And now I have to go to school? I'm so sleepy and I'm kind of shitting bricks about having to lie to my teachers about yesterday, and I keep feeling like the other kids are looking at me sideways because I'm turning into this delinquent who smokes, skips school, and has a slutty reputation. I know they don't even know Ricky at my school or anything but I feel like they can all see right through me to the fucked-up person I'm turning into.

• • •

5:00 p.m.
Dear Diary,
I got a letter from Chantal!

It's the second one she's sent me, but the first one was written on the first day, so it was really short, just telling me they had arrived and she missed me already.

This letter was longer, though of course not as long as my letters, but you know me. What I'm doing is writing to her every day, kind of like she's my second diary (don't be jealous!) and at the end of each week I will mail the letters.

She said they live in a rented house that's painted blue. She started school at a high school called "The West" and it's weird for her to be all in English. She still has French class but she said it's so easy it's basically a joke. I bet she'll get 100%. The other weird thing is because they don't have Cégep in Nova Scotia, high school goes to Grade Twelve, which would be like a Secondary Six. Seems so weird to me, even though I know Quebec is actually the weird one, because it's the only place that has only five years of high school and then Cégep. So Chantal won't be graduating this year. But then she'll be able to go to university a year earlier than me. She didn't say much about the kids or if she's made friends yet, but of course she wrote the letter on Tuesday after just one day of school.

Chantal is officially the first one of us to see the ocean. They went to the beach last weekend and she said she didn't swim because the water was way too cold, but she put her feet and hands in, and when she licked her fingers it was actually salty. I've never been to Nova Scotia or outside of Canada. In fact, besides Quebec I've only been to Ontario, so I have not seen the ocean. She invited me to visit over Christmas vacation, which sounds amazing, though it will be way too cold for the beach!

I don't know if I'll get to go or not. Christmas feels like forever away and Halifax seems a million miles from here, even though it's in the same country. But thinking of visiting brings her a little closer and makes me feel just a tiny bit less lonely.

● ● ●

Sunday, Sept. 9, 1984

Dear Diary,

I went to a party with Sandrine last night.

It was a house party and I basically didn't know anyone except for Sandrine and then I was super-happy to spot Olive doing his awesome reggae dancing in the living room. Sandrine actually knew he was going to be there, but didn't tell me because she wanted it to be a surprise. I told her the other day that I missed him. I hadn't seen him since Chantal and him broke up a couple of weeks before she moved away. We said we would stay friends, but then we never called each other.

So, anyway, arriving, seeing Olive, and having a couple of drinks are pretty much all I remember except for some thankfully foggy memories of getting really sick outside the party and again at home. From what Sandrine and Olive told me I drank a lot, got pretty wasted pretty quick, then Sandrine and I went outside on the steps to smoke a spliff with some guy. I guess it was really strong weed, or maybe it was the mix with alcohol, but within a few minutes I was puking my guts out over the side of the steps.

Sandrine went back inside to get Olive, worried something would happen to me while she was gone, but nothing did. They came back and found me all alone and puking again. Olive offered to take me home in a taxi so Sandrine stayed at the party. When we got to my place he didn't have enough money to pay for the taxi so he had to ring the doorbell and wake up Mom so she could pay the rest. Meanwhile he helped me inside and I went straight for the toilet.

I remember Mom coming to hold my hair back and ask me if I only drank or if I took any drugs. Obviously I said I had not taken anything. It's bad enough she's seeing me like this *again* without knowing I smoke up, too.

Olive told me two more things: That Mom offered him money to take the taxi home but he said no thanks and walked home, and that I came onto him in the back seat! He said he swears it's true but that I was too drunk and smelled like puke so he was like no way. How embarrassing!

Mom asked me this morning if she should be "worried" about my drinking. Gimme a break! I told her I just overdid it because Chantal's gone and I'm stressed about being all alone at school. Which is the honest truth.

• • •

Monday, Sept. 10, 1984

Dear Diary,

I met up with Sandrine at Villa-Maria metro after school today. She said a lot of kids hang out there after school and she wanted to see if this new guy she likes would be there. Neither of us get off there, but I'm just one stop away at Vendôme and can walk home from there if I want to, so I was like, why not?

She showed up with a scratch down the side of her face. Apparently the friend of the girl we talked to at lunch the other day didn't like the way Sandrine was looking at her man, so they ended up fighting. The girl punched her and scratched her face and Sandrine ended up almost ripping the girl's earring right out of her ear.

First of all, I have never had a fight, have never punched someone or been punched, and I'm sure I would not know how to react if that happened to me. Second of all, get this, they are apparently all friends now!

The girl, whose name is Alma, and her friend, Lisa, gained respect for Sandrine after the fight.

I'm impressed, as always, by Sandrine, and I'm happy for her that she not only made new friends but managed to do it with girls who had judged her and chosen her (us) as their enemy. But I have to admit I feel jealous, too. Because she's so beautiful and confident, not to mention street-smart, and now tough! And able to make friends anywhere with anyone, from tough girls from Burgundy to a redheaded misfit.

The guy she likes was there at Villa, but she didn't even talk to him. Just waited for the perfect moment then made sure to walk by him at just the right time and just the right speed. Of course he stopped everything for a few seconds to just watch her walk by. For sure he'll be her man by this time next week, because in addition to all the other stuff I just said about her, she also knows how to get any guy she sets her sights on.

Speaking of sights, as we were leaving, my gaze got intercepted by a familiar and unwelcome one. We were walking by a group of guys, I thought I recognized one of them and as his face came into clearer view I realized it was that guy King from the swimming pool at the beginning of the summer. I went to look away, but not fast enough. He spotted me looking, recognized me for sure and stared right back, holding my eyes in the tractor beam of his gaze. I know it was just a look, but it was totally threatening and scared the shit out of me.

● ● ●

Tuesday, Sept. 11, 1984
Dear Diary,

I woke up from a dream I can't remember, but it must have been about King. I felt trapped again in the tractor beam of his menacing gaze, but then I realized he wasn't there, and I was just stuck in the in-between place where I can't move. At first I felt panicked, but what's the point in panicking when you're paralyzed? It makes it way worse, actually, like when you can't run fast in a dream. Why keep trying to run when it's impossible and frustrating? Why not just walk? I'll try to remember that next time I have one of those dreams. Anyway, I calmed my thoughts and focused on the comforting realization that I could still breathe, but then I saw that a – no, *the* – big, dark shape was standing in the middle of my room, watching me. I kept telling myself it wasn't real and my eyes were just playing their night-time tricks on me, but it wouldn't go away. I even told myself I was just seeing things because of my encounter with King yesterday, but nothing would make the shadow-thing go away. It just stood there, looming, like it was relishing in my mounting terror and waiting for its moment. So I let the panic in. If only I could find the words to describe how hard it is to fight, how deep I have to dig, and how much effort it takes. But in the end it works every time, at least so far. (What if one day it doesn't?) I eventually manage to scream, then I can move, and the shadow-things disappear. Until the next time.

● ● ●

Wednesday, Sept. 12, 1984
Dear Diary,
In today's letter to Chantal, I told her about how even though Danny got good-looking over the summer he's still kind of a jerk, though in a less immature way.

It's weird. He's always been that annoying boy who taunts and teases you and gets under your skin no matter how much you try not to let him.

He reminds me of this boy I knew when I was around ten years old. He was the son of a co-worker of Mom's and sometimes they would take turns babysitting us for an evening. He was a year older than me and he would tease me non-stop. As soon as Mom would get back home and he would leave I would burst into tears of frustration over the things he had said, most of which I don't even remember. (For sure he teased me about my red hair, but mostly he just knew how to find any sensitive spot and start poking it over and over again.) Mom would just sigh and tell me to ignore him, that my reactions only made it worse, and to remember that boys usually tease you because they like you. Yeah, right, I thought. Anyway, our moms had a falling-out at some point and the shared babysitting ended, to my relief.

I guess Danny has the same kind of personality as Robbie did. Over the years he has pulled my hair, hidden my school supplies, made fun of my accent, teased me about having hair under my arms (when I was all of twelve), and then there was the "Hey, sexy!" incident last year. Am I forgetting anything? Probably.

Then I walk into the lounge today and I see him on the sofa and realize he's gotten cute. Not necessarily my type, but he's got dark hair, blue eyes, and a slightly crooked nose that makes his face interesting. He used to be skinny with too-big feet, but now I would describe him as tall and athletic.

"*Salut,* Poppy," he said.

"*Salut,*" I said back.

"*Tu penses pas que tu portes trop de maquillage?*" he said, "*Tu te prends pour qui? Madonna?*"

And the moment was ruined. Literally the first thing he says to me all year is, "Who do you think you are with all that makeup on, Madonna?" I regretted even thinking something nice about him.

I wished I could think up a clever retort that would make everyone laugh, but I was too caught off-guard and shy to get into it with him in front of a room full of people, so I just muttered "Asshole," under my breath and walked out.

I could have sworn I heard him say, "Slut," back, but I wasn't sure.

I went out for a walk around the block and to smoke a cigarette, and when I got back this Vietnamese girl named Trinh was sitting on the ledge by the sidewalk reading a book.

"Hi Trinh," I said, dropping my cigarette butt and stepping on it.

"Hi Poppy," she said, smiling. She was really quiet, but when she did talk, she always smiled. "You smoke?" she asked, still smiling and looking a little surprised.

"Yeah," I said. "I say I can stop anytime I want, but I don't actually think I can anymore."

Why did I just come out and say that to her? I hadn't admitted to anyone that I was addicted, not even myself.

"The bell's going to ring soon," I said. "Are you coming?" I said, and we walked into school together.

• • •

Thursday, Sept. 13, 1984
Dear Diary,
I hate the word "slut."

You hear it in movies, people say it about pretty much any girl they don't like, and, as I've mentioned, a couple of people have said it about me, and maybe some others think it.

Sandrine says people always call white girls sluts if they hang around with or date black guys. I actually kind of know that's true, but I don't understand why. Sandrine says it's jealousy. Black girls and white guys don't want the "other side" taking their girls or guys away. I guess it's comforting to think they're all just jealous. But why are we on "different sides" to begin with? And how come girls get called sluts anyway? Why are the guys never sluts or some male equivalent? They participated in the same "slutty" activities, after all. In fact, they're the ones who do most of the initiating!

I am making a vow right now never to call another girl a slut.

• • •

Friday, Sept. 14, 1984
Dear Diary,
Trinh and I have started hanging around together at lunch. She's a really good student whom everyone is nice to but who doesn't have a lot of actual friends. Kind of like me, except for the really good student part. Well, I'm a good student in English class. On the outside we're an unlikely pair, I guess, me with my makeup, teased hair, and love of cute guys and her with her plain clothes, glasses, and textbooks. But we're both fundamentally shy and have trouble fitting in.

When the weather's nice we go to eat on the grass at McGill campus. On Thursday we had a free period right after lunch so I suggested we go to a movie at a movie theatre that's in a shopping centre that's attached to McGill metro station, right near school. I don't know why people don't do that more. Even I only did it once before, last year with Chantal. Anyway, Trinh and I were the only people in the theatre and we had a great time going up to the front to pretend we were announcing the movie before it started and making all the noise we wanted. I know it was more little-kid fun than the kind of stuff I usually do now, but it was great. We saw a science-fiction movie called *2010*. The special effects were incredible! Ever since, she can't stop talking about the fact we did that. I think it's one of the most exciting and rebellious things she's ever done. She seems to have very strict and conservative parents. She always goes straight home after school and never goes to school dances or anything like that. I would bet a million dollars she's never been to the Annex.

We both play clarinet in band, but she's way better than me. Neither of us were picked to go on the trip to Wales with the choir. Mom said she couldn't have afforded it anyway.

I guess one of the reasons Trinh likes me is she thinks I'm experienced and sophisticated, which is funny because that's exactly what I thought about Sandrine for so long. I won't be corrupting Trinh by teaching her to shoplift or encouraging her to lose her virginity, though.

• • •

Saturday, Sept. 15, 1984
Dear Diary,
Chantal always says she can't write, but she totally can!
Here is the letter I got from her today:

Monday, Sept. 9th
Chère Poppy,

I miss you. It's hard to make friends in a new place and at a new school, even though everyone's pretty nice so far. I met two girls named Arlene and Heather who I've been eating lunch with. I guess I could call them friends, but it's hard to know yet if it'll last. Even if it does, they will never replace you! I think people find me exotic because I'm "French." Imagine! Me, exotic!

Little things are different that make it hard for me, like they write long division differently in English math and I always forget to use periods instead of commas when we use the decimal system. It makes me think of how lost you were back in elementary school when you switched to French school. I never really thought of how it must have been hard for you until now. History is different too; it's less focused on Quebec, of course. And French is too easy, as I told you. Also, it's not FACE, where everyone's creative and likes art, and you're right downtown and can go hang out anywhere! We didn't know how lucky we were. And you still are.

Here they're really into sports. Mom says I should join a team, but what would I play? As you know, sports are not my thing.

Philippe loves his new school. He makes friends easily and is very proud that now he has a new name: Phil. We all have to call him that at home, now, too.

I love our house, though! It's so cool to live in a house that's not a duplex, where you don't have neighbours above or below you to worry about. We have a small yard and two bathrooms! So no more fighting in the morning.

I don't know about bars or parties yet. I don't think it's so easy to go to bars here; the drinking age is nineteen, not eighteen and, well, it's just a small city, so I have a feeling there's no Annex to go dancing at. I will let you know!

I can't wait for another of your long letters telling me all about what's happening with you and Sandrine and everyone at school.

How is your nightmare situation, by the way?

Write back soon!

Bisous!

Your best friend always,

Chantal

It would be exciting to go live somewhere else, but at the same time I think of how lost I am now just being without my best friends in a school and a city I already know and I can't imagine how it would be to be in a new place where I didn't know anyone. Then again, a fresh start doesn't sound so bad.

• • •

Tuesday, Sept. 18, 1984
Dear Diary,

I've been spending a lot of time writing my letters to Chantal and haven't been keeping up with my diary writing. Sorry! I promise to do better!

• • •

Wednesday, Sept. 19, 1984
Dear Diary,
I'm sitting here watching Pumpkin sleeping contentedly in a square of sunshine coming in through the living room window. Sometimes I'm so envious of him and his simple little life and I imagine what it would be like to be a cat. I think I would like it, just living in the moment all the time and never worrying about the future or what others think of you, lazily moving from one warm, comfy spot to another. You're adorable and soft so you invite people to love and pamper you, but you're always ready to get up and walk away when you've had enough. Cats are the perfect combination of cute, elegant, and independent. And I bet they never get visited by shadow-things. Or do they? Maybe that's who they chase (or run away from) in the night when they get startled and dart around as if they've seen a ghost.

• • •

Thursday, Sept. 20, 1984
Dear Diary,
People have started calling Trinh and me the Odd Couple, you know, like that old TV show about two very opposite roommates? So dumb. I'm pretty sure Danny initiated it, but I don't really care. I'll have to tell Chantal. I think she'll get a kick out of it, because people had names for us too. If one of us wasn't around

they would ask where our other half is. Or sometimes they would ask me, "Where's your shadow?" I'm not so big on shadow references, but they didn't know that.

Trinh is a very easy person to hang around with, always smiling and she's just . . . uncomplicated. She's really direct with me without being judgemental and she doesn't seem concerned with what other people think, which must be so nice. Well, except her parents. She is definitely worried about what they think.

Chantal won't mind that I found someone new to hang around with, right? She would want me to find new friends and be happy. And after all, *she's* the one who left *me.*

● ● ●

Sunday, Sept. 23, 1984
Dear Diary,
One thing I haven't told Chantal in my letters is that I've been hanging out more and more with Olive. I don't know why I haven't told her. I mean, we're just friends and there is zero attraction between us. We're practically like brother and sister. Plus they broke up before she left so it's not like they're waiting for each other or anything, so I'm sure she wouldn't care. I should tell her soon, because the longer I don't tell her the more fishy it will look when I do.

I like hanging out at his place. It's not the cleanest and I saw a cockroach in the bathroom the other day, which totally freaked me out, but he has a VCR and since he lives with his half-brother, there are no parents. I can smoke in the apartment and sometimes we'll even have a beer while we veg on the sofa. I always have to remind him to rent something good to watch, though, because otherwise they always just have pornos or martial arts movies.

Last night I had a shadow-thing visit. Nothing unusual, just the usual looming dark shape. I think it had been almost two weeks since I had a visit, since that time the demon-shaped one creeped over the foot of my bed. That's not so long, really. I've had months-long stretches where it left me alone for a while in the past, but it's been coming to see me a lot since the summer started. This visit felt like it was just reminding me they're still around.

• • •

Monday, Sept. 24, 1984
Dear Diary,
I will be sixteen in exactly one week.

I won't be having a big Sweet Sixteen birthday party after all. Mom said I could, but who would I invite? I can't do one of those parties where you invite everyone from school, because then I would have to invite Danny, wouldn't I? And I'm not close to anyone besides Trinh, if you can call us close, and I'm not sure she would come to a big, late-night party. Mom seems sad that I don't want to do anything special, so I told her I would invite a few friends over for dinner and also Dave, her boyfriend. She looked like the cat that swallowed the canary when I said that. So who should I invite? Sandrine, of course. Trinh. Maybe Tee? We don't hang around anymore, but we used to. Amy? We've talked on the phone a couple of times since we met at the pool in the summer and keep saying we're going to get together. Olive? I can't think of any other guys I would really invite. Sounds like a weird mix of people, but I guess that's my guest list.

• • •

Tuesday, Sept. 25, 1984
Dear Diary,

Mrs. Tutor reminded us it's time for submissions to this year's *Writing on the Wall* anthology. After class she pulled me aside to tell me personally that she hopes I'll submit a story. (She actually got in a bit of trouble for submitting students' work last year without asking them first. I wonder who complained? So this year we have to come forward with our own submissions.)

Mrs. Tutor also gave me the concerned-teacher-speech. She noticed I've missed school lately (the time I skipped the afternoon and there were two mornings when I was late so I skipped first period) and I lost marks on an English assignment last week that I handed in late. She said it's not a great start to the school year and that it's unlike me. (How does she know what's like or unlike me?) Then she said she realizes I must miss Chantal like crazy, and it's a hard age, and if I ever need to talk, her door is open. For a second I felt really touched and understood, but the moment also felt a bit too much like an *ABC Afterschool Special*. I think I'll handle my life on my own.

Anyway, I wrote this poem when I got home as my submission to the anthology.

Write
By Poppy Bell

Write and write
To make the hurt go away
For if it's on paper
In my heart it won't stay

Write and write
So I can forget
How you took my innocence
Without pause or regret

Write and write

So I can forgive
That you left me alone
And found a new place to live

Write and write
So I can erase
The things that you say
Though not to my face

Write and write
To make me aware
Of why your dark presence
Is always there

● ● ●

Wednesday, Sept. 26, 1984
Dear Diary,
I just had the living shit scared out of me.

Sandrine asked me to meet her after school to go to Villa together so she could see that guy she likes. He asked her to meet him (he goes to Marymount) but she doesn't want to go alone. So we met at Vendôme and went together.

I actually saw Amy on her way back from school in her cute private school uniform. I'm so glad I don't have to wear a uniform, but I know guys think girls are sexy in their rolled-up pleated skirts and knee socks. Anyway, it was the perfect opportunity to ask her if she wanted to come to my birthday dinner on Saturday and right away she said yes, she will come. While we were talking, Sandrine excused herself, I guess to talk to her guy. Soon after, Amy left to catch her bus, and as I turned around to see where Sandrine had gone, I came face to face with King.

"Hey, Red," he said. "Still think you're too good for me, talking to your little private school friends?"

I gathered up all my courage, looked him straight in his soulless eyes, and said, "Leave me alone."

Then I turned to leave, Sandrine or no Sandrine, but he grabbed me by the wrist, pulled me just a little closer and said, "One of these days I'm gonna find you all alone and I'm gonna take out the knife I have in my pocket and carve up that pretty little face of yours. And don't think you're gonna go runnin' to anyone, because I know where you live and I'll come find you when you least expect it and do the same to your mom and the rest of your little family."

Then he let go of my wrist and I walked away in a daze, pretty sure everyone could see how much I was shaking from a mile away. But, in fact, no one had seen a thing. He was just one more guy doing his best to chat up a girl in the notorious after-school chaos of that metro station with busses and metro cars full of loud, rowdy teenagers from a half-dozen high schools all converging within a one-hour period. Amid the mayhem, we were all alone.

Normally I would have walked or taken the 24 bus down to Sherbrooke to get home, but I didn't want him to see which direction I was going, so I hopped on the 103 bus, which goes along Monkland, and just got off a couple of stops later and walked home from there once I knew the coast was clear. He can't actually know where I live, right? If he knew anything about me he would know that my family ends at me and Mom; there is no "rest of your little family."

What kind of person randomly threatens girls like that? And randomly decides to hate someone just because she won't give him her phone number the first time they meet? Did he become that way because he had a bad life or terrible parents, or was he just born evil?

Imagine if someone like him kept a diary. Of course he probably wouldn't because he's likely too busy just going around terrifying innocent people and ruining their days. Not to mention he's probably too stupid. But if he did, what would he write? "Dear Diary, Today I woke up and thought, 'I should find a redhead to torment. So I chose the first one I saw at Confederation pool and picked the first reason she gave me to act scary and threatening. And did I ever! Afterwards I waited outside for half an hour and she didn't come out. Probably stayed 'til closing to avoid me. I am *so* scary and evil. Next time I see her I will petrify her even worse. What shall I do? I know! I'll threaten to carve her face up. Her *pretty little* face. Haha! Until then I'll just keep kicking puppies, stealing candy from children, and tripping little old ladies.'"

I feel better now. Not less scared, but still better. Writing is the best. I'm going to stay away from Villa for a while, I think. And make sure to keep our front door locked.

Sandrine called a while ago to find out where I had gone. Sure took her long enough. I told her the King story and she said I was exaggerating and he was probably only joking. Is she kidding me?

● ● ●

Thursday, Sept. 27, 1984
Dear Diary,
Last night I stared it down and I think it almost worked.

As always, I woke up and couldn't move, and it appeared, the usual big, dark shape. But this time, instead of panicking to claw and scream my way back, I just kept staring at it. And I could swear it started to move *away*. It didn't fly out the window or disappear or anything, but it's a start, right?

Thinking about it now, I wonder if I was trying to stand up to it because I hadn't stood up to King and wished I had. As if the shadow-things weren't threatening enough, now I have a real monster to deal with.

• • •

Friday, Sept. 28, 1984
Dear Diary,
So, everyone's coming to my dinner party tomorrow. It may not be a big Sweet Sixteen bash, but I feel pretty grown-up saying I'm having a "dinner party."

Trinh asked if she could bake my birthday cake. Mom hates baking, so she was, like, for sure! She's making her famous lasagna, which almost never happens since it's usually just the two of us. Well, sometimes three, now.

I'm a bit nervous about how everyone will get along. That's the problem when you're not part of one group. All your friends are from different groups and they might not mix well at all.

I wish Chantal could come. I wrote to her about what King said. She is going to freak out when she gets that letter!

• • •

Saturday, Sept. 29, 1984
Dear Diary,
I turn sixteen today, but I had my celebrations last night. And what a night it was.

First, I'll tell you about my real visitors, then I'll tell you about my shadow-visitor.

I guess I had been thinking negative thoughts about Sandrine ever since her reaction to what I told her about King, because I had got it in my head that she would be mean or snobby to Trinh. I mean, they're just so opposite. Sandrine is wild and street-smart, but not school-smart at all. And Trinh is naive and, well, kind of a nerd if I'm honest. But of course Sandrine was nice to her; why wouldn't she be? If I'm friends with Sandrine it's because she's fun and friendly, right? And Trinh is nice to everyone. When she arrived she was really formal, calling Mom Mrs. Bell, which always sounds so funny to me because most of my friends just call each other's parents by their first names. Chantal always called my mom Janet, even when we were in Grade Four. Trinh also called Dave Mr. Bell and was embarrassed when I explained that he was just my mom's "friend," and that my dad was dead. Olive also insists on calling Mom Mrs. Bell. He was obviously a little uncomfortable as the only guy, plus he's not that good around parents. He was very polite and everything, but he didn't talk much. Now that I think about it, he's not that much of a talker anyway. He's so boring on the phone! Just sits there and doesn't say anything half the time and I'm like, why did you call me again? Then he can be so funny in person when it's just us. Anyway, Mom was really excited to see Amy again and asked about her parents and our old neighbours and it was really nice to have Tee there, too.

The lasagna was delicious and Mom and Dave poured wine for everyone. Trinh had never tasted wine before, took one sip and could barely swallow it. You could tell she didn't want to be rude so she would have drunk the whole glass if we hadn't all laughed and told her she didn't have to. To be honest, I'm not a big fan of wine either, so there was not much danger that I would drink it too fast and get sick to my stomach again. Oh, and you should have seen the cake Trinh brought! It was like something straight out of a bakery window! It was a huge chocolate layer cake with white icing and red poppies made out of sugar and "Happy Sixteenth Birthday, Poppy" written on it. I once tried to write on a cake with icing and it looked like something a five-year-old would write. Everyone was so impressed with Trinh's cake, which she baked and decorated all herself, I think she almost passed out from the attention and compliments.

I got some good gifts, too. Sandrine got me the *Purple Rain* album!!! As soon as I opened it I went and put it on as loud as Mom would let me. Trinh's gift was the amazing cake and a card. Tee gave me a silver bangle and a bunch of black gummy bracelets to add to my growing collection. Amy gave me a framed picture of us playing on her backyard swings when we were seven. I put it next to the picture of me and Dad on my desk. I actually didn't expect Olive to give me anything; he doesn't seem like the gift-giving type and he never really has money, but he gave me a reggae tape he made and also a card. The card was a really sappy one, not like him (or me) at all, and he just wrote Happy Birthday Poppy From Olive in writing so messy I could hardly read it. Even Dave gave me a present just from him, the *Collected Works of Edgar Allan Poe*. He said he noticed I like Stephen King, but that Poe was the original "master of the macabre" so he thought I should expand my horror horizons. Mom's gift is coming soon, she told me mysteriously. Chantal called earlier to wish me happy birthday and to ask if I had received her gift, but nope, not yet.

I kind of loved my dinner party. Nobody fit together so everybody did. It was the kind of mix of characters you could write a story about. Maybe I will someday. And the best part is for once I didn't feel like I didn't belong.

Once the table was cleared and Mom and Dave went to do the dishes, the rest of us went to the living room and turned up Prince. "Darling Nikki" came on and I remembered how Chantal and I used to dance to it in my room, all raunchy. I looked around and thought, "No way." Sandrine would get it, but Trinh would be shocked, Amy and Tee maybe too, and I could never dance like that in front of Olive.

Then Olive spotted the Ouija board. "Still got that thing?" he said.

"We should play!" I said.

No one but me seemed very into the idea, but everyone agreed reluctantly because it was my birthday, after all. We headed for my room to have more privacy, but then the doorbell rang and it was Trinh's mom there to pick her up. After we said our goodbyes, Tee also said she had to leave, and then Amy went home, too. Then it was just me, Sandrine, and Olive. I pulled the board out of the box, but Olive said no way was he taking part in that "witchcraft shit." He suggested we go to his place to watch a movie, Sandrine called her new guy to invite him, and we headed over there, stopping on the way at the video store so we could be spared the porn and endless Bruce Lee fighting.

We rented *Trading Places*, which is hilarious. I love Eddie Murphy! Things were a bit awkward, though, because Sandrine and Victor were all over each other. After the movie Olive was nice enough to walk me all the way home, which is almost half an hour away. He's such a good friend.

Then two things happened when I got home that I have to tell you about. First, as soon as I walked in the door Mom came tiptoeing out of her room to tell me that Dave and her had drunk too much wine so he was going to stay the night. Her hair was all messy and I could tell she was really worried about how I would react, but I have been sure they're doing it (ew, gross) for ages now, so I'm really not bothered. Second, when I walked into my room I froze in my tracks because the Ouija board was sitting on my bed all set up with the pointer sitting on the word "Hello."

I thought and thought, but I know I did not take that pointer out of the box before I left, much less place it on the word Hello. I even went and knocked on Mom's door to ask if either of them had, by any chance, touched my Ouija board and of course they said they had not. (Also, Dave turned purple with embarrassment when I opened the door.)

I went back to my room and had the urge to knock the board on the floor, or maybe take it outside and just burn it, but instead I picked it up carefully and placed it on my desk without disturbing it. Why I did that I do not know, but it had a result.

I woke up in the night, having another one of my paralysis episodes, and there sitting on my desk chair like a regular person was the thin shadow-man-in-a-hat, and he was bent over the Ouija board. I wondered if I could even see the pointer moving around under his black, shadowy hand. I can't even begin to describe the mix of fascination and fear I felt, lying there helplessly watching . . . him? It? And then I started to rise up off the bed. I still couldn't and didn't move my body or make a sound; I just levitated. It was at once an incredible feeling and a horrible feeling, like I was experiencing the most wonderful sensation, but that it meant giving up something really precious or important if I wanted to keep it going. Then something in me kicked in, I panicked, gasped, and woke up, lying in bed quite normally, fully under the covers. Once I got my composure, I turned on the light, gathered my courage, and got up to look at the Ouija board on my desk. It was just as I had left it, except the pointer was on "Goodbye."

● ● ●

Monday, Oct. 1, 1984
Dear Diary,
Let the celebrations continue! When I woke up this morning I smelled something cooking. I kept my eyes closed for a while and just let the smell of bacon, pancakes, and coffee fill my nostrils and wake up my taste buds. Mmmmm. (I may not like the taste of coffee, but I love the smell of it brewing.) I could hear kitchen noises, too: water running, pots clanging, dishes clinking. We're not big breakfast eaters in our house, so the busy sounds and

delicious aromas made the day feel special – I guess it's birthweekend, not just birthday!

School was good. I got lots of happy birthdays and I got the bumps, of course, which made me feel less sad, lonely, and friendless than I have lately. Maybe this won't be such a bad year after all . . .

When I got home from school I got a great surprise! Mom wasn't home yet, so I wasn't expecting anything at all, but when I opened my bedroom door I had a new bed! I do not know how she/they did this so fast, but in place of my bunk beds there was a double bed with purple sheets and a green and purple flowered comforter. (I still wish I could have a waterbed, but I do love my new double bed that makes me feel way less like a kid. And purple! My absolute favourite colour these days.)

Smack in the middle of the bed was a package in brown mailing paper and when I opened it, it was my birthday gift from Chantal: a writing set including stationery so I can write to her, a notebook to use as a diary (of course) and a fountain pen.

This has been such a good birthday weekend.

• • •

Tuesday, Oct. 2, 1984
Dear Diary,
I think Sandrine is mad at me. She asked me to go to Villa with her after school today, but I said no, because I'm afraid of running into King again. Anyway, she just doesn't want to arrive alone, but once she meets up with Victor she ignores me anyway. I mean, it took her two hours to call and find out what happened to me last week when I escaped from King.

I'm feeling unsure about my friendship with Sandrine. When I'm with her I like her and I still find her exciting, charming, and fun, but we don't have that deep trust or connection that I have with Chantal, where you know she'll always have your back and be your friend no matter what. Plus, when Sandrine gets a new boyfriend she totally abandons her friends. I guess we all do that a little bit when we meet a new guy, but I think she does it even more than the rest of us.

Since we don't go to the same school anymore either I feel like we're starting to make other friends and grow apart. Maybe I'm overthinking.

• • •

Wednesday, Oct. 3, 1984
Dear Diary,
Gross!

Today after school I went shopping and then I decided to go to Bonaventure metro since it's on the orange line and I wouldn't have to change trains at Lionel-Groulx. I went in from this entrance on de la Gauchetière near Peel that hardly anyone uses and so when I was on the escalator I was alone.

Then I noticed a person, also alone, going up on the other escalator. I could feel him looking at me really intensely, so I looked at him without really thinking about it, and he said something like "Hey, *bébé*," and he had his zipper open and was, you know, *jerking off* while looking at me.

I immediately averted my eyes and somehow managed to keep my cool until I had passed him, trying to act like I hadn't seen anything, and then I *ran* to the metro, where I felt safe surrounded by all the people. He didn't follow me or anything and I've heard flashers usually aren't dangerous; they just want a reaction.

So disgusting! I mean, it's not like it's anywhere near the first time something like that has happened to me; Chantal and I have been flashed more times than we can count. But when you're alone it's still a little scary, and, again, gross! Why do I feel like there are creeps everywhere I turn?

• • •

Friday, Oct. 5, 1984
Dear Diary,
Tonight over dinner Mom said that she and Dave are thinking of moving in together. I was totally floored! But I think I'm also totally fine with it.

Meanwhile, she goes from pretending there's nothing happening between them to asking if he can move in? Anyway, as I said, I'm so fine with it I even surprised myself. The only inconveniences I can really think of are having to share the bathroom with another person and not being able to walk around in my underwear so often.

But, honestly, Dave's nice. He just acts like a friend and never tries to tell me what to do or anything and he makes Mom happy. Maybe that will even make her less moody with me.

She says it's not a done deal yet, whatever that's supposed to mean, but he might stay over sometimes while he's getting ready to make the big move.

• • •

Saturday, Oct. 6, 1984
Dear Diary,
So, apparently sleeping over "sometimes" meant sleeping over "tonight."

This morning I woke up to find Dave at the dining room table reading the newspaper! I had actually come out of my room in my underwear and a T-shirt and turned around quickly to go put on some PJ bottoms.

"Good morning," he said, clearing his throat nervously. He was reading the *Gazette* and asked me if I wanted the funnies. I don't think I've heard anyone call them the funnies since my dad. It was weird. I just got this memory rushing back of me sitting on my dad's lap and asking him to read me the funnies. I don't even know if that's something that happened one time or something we did every morning.

I actually said that to Dave, that he had just brought back this old memory of my dad and he tried to apologize and say that he hoped it was OK that he was there and that if I wasn't comfortable with the idea of him moving in he wanted me to say so and he would understand and that he wasn't trying or assuming he would become my dad or anything and I was like, "It's OK. It will be nice to have a dad around again."

As soon as I said it I felt kind of embarrassed, because it came out different than what I meant to say, because he's not my dad and at my age I don't expect him to ever be, but then he came over and gave me a quick awkward hug that was just the sweetest thing. Ew, now I'm getting all mushy and sentimental.

• • •

Tuesday, Oct. 9, 1984
Dear Diary,
I'm sick. It seems to be the flu and it's *horrible.* Yesterday I couldn't even read or watch TV, let alone write; I had a high fever so I just lay in bed in a shivering fog, sleeping on and off, being roused now and then by Mom bringing me Aspirins or chamomile tea. At least I wasn't throwing up, which is the absolute worst.

And there could be no better mom in the world to have when you're sick than mine. First of all, she's a nurse, so she knows just what to do. She's usually a pretty practical and unsentimental kind of person, but whenever I'm sick she adds some extra TLC to her professional nursing skills and I feel so well taken care of that it almost makes me not mind being sick. Almost.

With my mind all twisted from having a temperature, I had some really fucked-up shadow-thing visits (yes, plural) last night. I keep telling myself that it was just the sickness and fever messing with my head, but that does little to allay my memory of the fear or chase away the dark shapes still swirling through my thoughts.

I think I got visited three times. I can't sort out whether that was three totally separate episodes or three creatures in one visit, but I know there was a first visit by the looming, watching shape, a second one by the thin man in a hat, and then a third visit that is very vague and murky but I remember being touched or caressed in some way. Maybe it was the crawling demon again, I don't really remember. Basically it feels like I spent my whole night with the shadow-things and even though I've been sleeping for a lot of the last thirty-six hours I feel like I didn't sleep at all last night.

● ● ●

Wednesday, Oct. 10, 1984
Dear Diary,
My head is clearer today, though I still get a fever every time the Aspirin wears off.

Mom already said I can stay home from school again tomorrow.

Thank God, because I'm not feeling rested at all with all the shadow-things visiting me at night. Why can't they leave me alone and just let me sleep?

Like I said in my poem (which, by the way, was accepted for the anthology), with most things I always feel better after writing about them. It's like when I get them down on the page it helps to get them out of my head. Like when I wrote those things about King last week I felt so much better afterward. Somehow I keep hoping that's what's going to happen with the shadow things: I'll write about them during the day and they'll stop haunting my nights. But it doesn't seem to be working so far, does it?

• • •

Thursday, Oct. 11, 1984
Dear Diary,
One thing about Dave moving in is it means there is a *man* in the house. I didn't say man *of* the house, because I'm pretty sure Mom wears the actual pants in their relationship, but it means not only can I not walk around half-naked, and do I keep pushing the thought that they're probably having sex out of my mind, but I have to check that the toilet seat is down, which I learned the hard way this morning when I got a cold surprise. It's funny now, but at that moment I was pretty pissed (no pun intended). I wanted to say something to Dave, just to remind him, but he's so nice and he would have felt so guilty so I don't think I'm going to mention it. Maybe I'll ask Mom to remind him, but I already heard her get mad at him about it once and don't want to cause a fight. So I guess I will just have to remember to look before I sit from now on.

• • •

Friday, Oct. 12, 1984

Dear Diary,

I think I'm done with weed. And I haven't even been smoking up that much lately.

Remember when I was with Ricky and we were smoking up so much that he even accused me of being addicted at one point? Well, mostly I guess it was new and also just *there.* I never really felt like I wanted or needed to smoke up when I was by myself or anything, plus I don't know where you go buy it in the first place and I also suck at rolling joints. I tried once and it was a disaster.

All that to say, since school started I think today was only the second time I got stoned. And I swear it might be my last.

So the thing I used to like the most about getting stoned was the going numb. It was the coolest sensation, but the setting has to be right for it. I have to be really able to chill out to be able to do it. If people are laughing and joking around, or if I'm making out with a guy or something, I can't focus on going numb.

So today after school a bunch of us met at the park. There was Sandrine, Victor, Olive, a girl named Linda who I'm pretty sure likes Olive, and a guy named Stevie, who pulled out a dime bag and rolled a joint. Olive actually didn't take any, because he says it makes him paranoid, something that people say but I have never experienced. Everyone else did, though, including me. The weed was strong! I got really stoned from just a couple of tokes and I decided I would try going numb for the first time in a while. Out in the park with everyone joking around it didn't work so well, though. Too many distractions. Then we saw a cop car driving through the park towards us. Stevie took off right away and the rest of us got up to leave, too. I knew Mom was going to be out with Dave this evening, so I asked if everyone wanted to come by me since I live so close to the park, but Linda must have thought five would be a crowd and she didn't come. So Sandrine, Victor, Olive and I headed to my place.

I was more stoned than ever when we got here with a bottle of Coke and a bag of chips and sat on the sofa to look for something to watch on TV. It was time for me to try going numb again. I started with my toes, and they started to tingle right away. I hadn't lost my knack for it. Then I got the feeling to travel to my feet and my legs. I'm not actually sure numb is really the right word, because it's not numb like the way you feel when your foot falls asleep and it's kind of an unpleasant feeling. It's more like a feeling of radiance, with everything tingling and glowing and just full of the sensation of just *being*. Anyway, I got the sensation to travel all the way up my body until I was basically bathed in it, almost like I was floating inside some kind of aura. I was still aware of everything going on around me, but it's as if I was separate from it all, watching it on a TV screen or something.

And then the sensation changed. It started at my feet again, but instead of the warmth and the tingling it was a cold, crawling feeling, like a darkness enveloping me, extinguishing all that radiant light, bit by bit. I was trammelled by it, unable to move or speak. I could just watch and feel, completely helpless as the darkness came over me like a slow wave.

I sat there willing someone to shake me or slap me or something, to snap me out of the state I was in before I disappeared completely into the darkness – and then someone did. I first became aware that the others were talking about me, saying "She's gone!" and "She's trippin'!" and "Should we shake her or something?" as my brain was screaming "Yes, yes!" and then Olive put his hand on my shoulder and the darkness retreated almost instantly, like black ink being sucked down a drain in the floor.

I gasped, feeling exactly like I do when I awake from my paralyzed state at night, and Olive pulled his hand away like he had touched something gross and said, "Why are you so cold?"

At first I thought he was referring to my personality and then I realized he meant my body temperature. "Am I?" I said, trying to feel my own forehead.

"Like a dead person," he said, clearly grossed out.

Sandrine laughed, felt my forehead and told Olive he was being ridiculous. "She's actually a little hot," to which Olive replied, "Yeah?" and looked me over from head to toe, making me blush. Then he put a warm hand on my rapidly warming cheek and said, "She is pretty hot. Must have been my imagination."

The flirting and joking around were good, because they chased what was left of the darkness away, but, like I said, I won't be smoking up again any time soon.

Chapter 6
Summer 1985

Friday, June 28, 1985
Dear Diary,
I can't believe grad night is over already! I feel like Chantal just moved away and Grade Eleven just started and now not only the year but high school itself is done!

I hadn't slept well because of a creepy visit by the dark, looming shape in the night. Sometimes I wonder if they visit me more often when I'm stressed; I was definitely nervous about how my big night would go!

Well, it was not the night I expected and I have a lot to tell you, so you are going to have to be patient until I get to the end.

As you know, since I'm not seeing anyone right now, I did not bring a date to grad. On American TV shows everyone stresses about finding a date for "prom," but in Montreal it's not really like that, at least not at FACE. Most people just went with their friends. Trinh and I met up in front of the hotel so we could go in together; we didn't rent a limo or any of that stuff. Some people met at the Vieux-Port and arrived by horse-drawn *calèche*. I kind of wished I had done that, too.

Of course everyone looked beautiful or handsome, all the guys in suits or tuxes and especially the girls in their colourful long dresses. I could not get over how beautiful Trinh looked. She put on makeup, not a lot, but it showed off how pretty she actually is. Her dress was very simple and classic, navy blue with spaghetti straps, and she didn't wear her glasses, which was also funny because she kept exclaiming that she was blind. My dress was purple and strapless with a lace top and I found lavender satin pumps to wear with it. I splurged by going to the hairdresser and got my hair pinned up with tendrils hanging down for a more romantic look instead of my usual teased hairdo. I loved it! I wish I could go to the hairdresser every day.

The most amazing dress was Rosa's. It was a red dress that looked more like a designer dress out of Vogue than a prom dress, and she made the whole thing herself! Some people have serious artistic talent! She said she's going to LaSalle college next year to study fashion design.

After the dinner I went outside for a smoke (best one of the day, right?) and I was not the only one. There was a small group of my classmates out there, including Danny.

I told him I was surprised to see him smoking and he said he's just a social smoker. (I remember when I used to say that about myself, too.) Then he told me I looked nice, and he didn't tack on any hidden (or direct) insults this time. Someone else pulled out a flask of vodka and passed it around and after a couple of sips I felt like I disliked Danny less and less every minute. We all ended up going back inside together and I sat right next to Danny. I don't know what was getting into me.

Well, at some point it was time for some slow songs and guess which song came on? That's right: "Purple Rain." I watched people getting up to dance couple by couple: Jimmy, my long-time but long-ago crush, and Aanya, who had been together since the beginning of the school year; Tee with *her* longtime crush, Lucas; Cee and Pierre-Paul; even Trinh got invited to dance, shooting me a happy look as she was led by the hand to the floor. I looked around to see if anyone was going to ask me; it was kind of killing me that my favourite song was passing me by and I was starting to get that old left-out feeling, even though I was certainly far from the only one not dancing.

I thought maybe I would just escape outside for another smoke and as I shifted on my chair to get up Danny looked at me and put his hand out by way of invitation.

"Pourquoi pas?" I said, shrugging my shoulders with as much indifference as possible while internally laughing at myself for accepting a dance with my faithful tormentor.

We got on the dance floor and I found myself caught up almost instantly in the magic of the moment. The elation of saying goodbye to high school, the little bit of alcohol, the most beautiful song ever, and the arms of a tall, handsome guy, even if he was Danny. "Purple Rain" is, like, 8 minutes long, so we had lots of time to gradually hold each other a little bit tighter and get comfortable in each other's arms. At some point he kind of rubbed my back in a weird way and I could have sworn he was trying to figure out if I was wearing a bra (I wasn't). I pulled back a little to look at him, meaning it as a warning that I could tell what he was up to, but I guess he took it as something else, because he looked at me really seriously and asked if he could kiss me. Part of me thought "Why not?" while another part screamed "Never!" and what came out was a sweet, inviting smile that got just a little closer to his face and a very soft, but firm "No." Then I wrapped my arms around his neck and lay my head on his shoulder, feeling like maybe I had learned something from Sandrine about what makes guys tick. I felt something in him let go and relax as he held me tighter one more time, too, but in a way that felt more sincere. I might be totally mistaken about what I felt, but I suddenly realized that it's actually true that guys are insecure, too. And when they tease you it's more about them than about you.

Now, don't get any ideas! Nothing else happened with Danny and I wouldn't be surprised if I never saw him again. But I did end up feeling just a little turned on, I'm embarrassed to say.

And something else did happen.

As the party wound down people started breaking off into groups and going their own ways. Trinh had to be home by eleven, so she left and we said our goodbyes, promising to stay in touch and get together over the summer, but I have a sad feeling we won't. I like her and she's one of the only reasons this school year was bearable, but we're so different and hardly ever hung around outside of school, so I doubt we'll see each other much anymore.

I guess I could have tagged along with Tee's gang or some of the kids from my classes after the dance, but I wanted to be with friends I was close to. I'm used to Chantal living far away now, but I really wished I was sharing this momentous night with her. It was after ten, so too late to call Sandrine or anyone else who lives with their parents, and anyway, we have grown apart since being in different schools. Finally I decided to call Olive. He was home playing Nintendo with his brother and was surprised to hear from me; I haven't seen him much this spring since we were both dating other people for a while plus I've been busy studying for exams and he got a job at Burger King. Before tonight I think I hadn't seen Olive in a month.

He said come over and I asked if he had any alcohol. He didn't, so I stopped at the dépanneur for beer but decided on a bottle of Baby Duck instead. I was celebrating, after all! I was a little worried I would get carded – in my grad dress it was pretty obvious I'm not eighteen yet – but they never card anyone at that dep.

When I arrived, he said, "It's Cinderella!"

"That's right," I said, "We better get celebrating quick before my coach turns into a pumpkin at midnight."

I dug around in the messy kitchen for some clean glasses – of course they didn't have actual wine glasses – while they finished their game of *Donkey Kong*. Darius said "Cheers" with us (the wine was so yummy! And pink!), then he complimented me on my dress, congratulated me on graduating, said he would leave us two "kids" alone, and went to his room.

I played *Donkey Kong* with Olive for a while, but I suck at video games – except I'm not too bad at *Ms. Pac-Man* – so he just kept winning and I got bored. Plus I was uncomfortable sitting on the couch in my fancy dress, so I asked him if he had a long T-shirt I could borrow. I had to get him to unzip my dress for me and when he did I got a bit of a reaction to his touch that I really wasn't expecting, but I brushed it aside, went to change, and settled in on the couch for some TV and more Baby Duck.

And then, as you've probably guessed by now, one thing led to another. To be specific, we were laughing at something really stupid on TV and I spilled some wine down my chin. Then, out of nowhere he just leaned over and kind of sucked it off me. I was shocked for a second, then he kissed me on the mouth and I didn't hesitate for a single second more, I just kissed him back, pushing all thoughts of "What the fuck are we doing?" aside.

I did wonder once or twice how far he would try to go and how far I would let him. In the meantime, I enjoyed every moment. His kissing was different than I would have imagined, not that I had. He can be moody, going from funny to quiet and withdrawn. He's not a big talker (I've mentioned how he's so boring on the phone, right?) and has always treated me pretty much like a sister, so I wouldn't have expected him to be so . . . sensual. Like he was just enjoying it, too, instead of just using it as a gateway to sex. And everything he did was like that. When he kissed my neck and my ears, when he pulled my head back, gentle but firm, then just brushed his lips against my throat . . . (My body is starting to ache and tingle a little just writing about it.)

When he put his hand between my thighs I thought maybe I should stop him, but it was a very fleeting thought. I let him move higher and get his fingers inside my underwear (I can't believe I am writing this) and then he didn't . . . penetrate me, he just kept moving his fingers and teasing, and I swear I forgot that anything else existed; I was enjoying what he was doing so much. And he just kept going, not trying to go further or anything, though at that point I would have let him for sure, and then in an instant this rush came over me. I mean, I basically exploded with pleasure, but it was a slow release that I really wish I had the words to describe. Well I guess I do have one word: Orgasm.

I was kind of in shock then, and a little shy, too. I didn't want to look at his face and I didn't want to let go of him either, so I kind of buried myself in his chest and hugged him and then once I caught my breath and my heart stopped racing I think I just said something like, "Wow. What was that?" Though I knew exactly what it was.

He laughed a little, looking just slightly pleased with himself, then handed me my glass of Baby Duck and lit a cigarette to share.

I kept wondering if I should ask or say something about it or about us, but since he didn't say anything I didn't either, and I had to be home by one, so I called a taxi and left, with our usual brother-sister hug, no big passionate kiss or anything.

So I'm sitting here, wide awake at three feeling confused and still pretty surprised. At all of it: Him, us and . . . *it*. And even more because he didn't try anything else after.

I mean, I've only had sex with three guys, but none of them ever settled for foreplay if the opportunity was there for more. The last guy, Derek, kept asking me during sex if I came yet and I never knew what to say. Finally one time I was like, "I don't know," and he stopped, looked at me and said, "Believe me, you would know." And he was right.

I'm going to go to bed now and try not to stay up all night wondering what this means for Olive and me. Will he expect more? Do I want more? Will it kill our friendship? Do I tell Chantal? (And did he do to her what he just did to me?)

● ● ●

Saturday, June 29, 1985
Dear Diary,
I feel so free!

High school is behind me and the summer lies ahead!

I was thinking of looking for a full-time job, but I'm going to visit Chantal for ten days, so it would be hard to get a job and still be able to do that.

Jodee, the mom of Sally, you know, the girl I've been babysitting, offered to pay me to vacuum and dust her house every two weeks on top of the babysitting. I guess she hasn't seen my bedroom! But seriously, I'm going to do it. I wish I had asked for more money, but you know me. I already was trying to find a way to ask for a fifty-cent raise for babysitting, so when she offered the same two dollars an hour for cleaning it was the perfect opportunity, but of course I didn't speak up, I just said "OK." The babysitting part is so easy. Sally's ten and she just loves me and looks up to me. We mostly just watch TV or we talk and she asks me lots of questions about teenage life (there's a lot I don't tell her!). Every single time I babysit she wants me to make her spaghetti with butter and cheese for dinner (which about covers my cooking skills) and after she goes to bed I watch *Hill Street Blues* until Jodee comes home.

So that covers four nights and a couple of days a month, then there's my trip to Nova Scotia (yay!) and aside from that, I have to say, I don't know what else I'll do this summer. I guess I'll see Sandrine once in a while but we really don't hang around that much anymore. Trinh lives far away and doesn't do much socializing so I don't know how much we'll see each other. Maybe we can go to a movie sometime. I'll probably call Amy and see if she wants to go to the pool or something. And then there's Olive. I wonder if he's going to call me today and what he'll say if he does.

• • •

Sunday, June 30, 1985
Dear Diary,
Olive called. He asked if I want to go watch him play later. I said sure. I'm all nervous, wondering how he'll be and how I should act. Imagine! Nervous about seeing Olive!

I think I'll just act normal and see how it goes. I'm not going to get girlfriend-y or anything.

I still go a little weak and get this hollow, longing feeling deep inside when I think about the other night, but then today he was just the same boring-on-the-phone Olive whose friendship I don't want to mess with. I was remembering that I found him cute that first time I saw him at that party a whole year ago, but then he became off limits and off my radar once he went out with Chantal. I mean, he de-virginized my best friend! It's hard to regret something that felt that good, but I think my moment of (extreme) pleasure is going to complicate my life.

• • •

Monday, July 1, 1985
Dear Diary,
Happy Canada Day!

The countdown is on. Ten days until my big trip!

I feel like this is going to be a great summer.

I went to the park to see Olive last night and it wasn't complicated at all. It was just like it's always been between us, like nothing climactically out-of-the-ordinary happened two nights ago.

I didn't go to his place after, just hung out in the park with everyone, and got the same old hug I always get when I left.

What's weird is: Things not being weird between us is a little weird.

● ● ●

Wednesday, July 3, 1985
Dear Diary,

I was sleeping in bed next to Olive and he reached over, pulled the covers down, and touched me just like the other night, waking me up just enough. No kissing this time, just touching. Such amazing touching. Then I realized it wasn't him doing it, it was me. Another first. And still so good. And then I realized it wasn't even me, but whoever it was I really, really didn't want it to stop. I only needed a few seconds more, I was sure of it. I just needed to sink back in, back down. It was so, so good, and I couldn't move if I wanted to, but it didn't matter because I just wanted to stay and then – no!

I woke with a start and a gasp, feeling just like I do when I wake up from a shadow-person visit, except this time I hadn't wanted to come back, and I wasn't afraid at all, just a little disappointed.

Sounds like a dream, I know, but it was so real I looked over at the bed next to me, almost certain someone would be there. Of course, no one was.

Frankly, if I have to have strange and vivid dreams, I will take ones like last night over shadow-people visits anytime! (I think shadow-people is a better name than shadow-things. There is definitely something human about their shape and the way they watch me . . . and touch me.)

• • •

Thursday, July 4, 1985

Dear Diary,

I called Amy last night and asked if she wanted to go to the pool, but she told me her parents just put a pool in her backyard and invited me over.

We had fun and I am also pretty envious of that pool! I'm sure I would use it every day if I could have my own swimming pool. We listened to music, dancing around to "Everybody Wants to Rule the World" – she's more into stuff like Tears for Fears, U2, and Duran Duran than the rap, reggae, and funk I usually listen to. But I pretty much like all music. Well, except heavy metal. Ew. We drank iced tea, ate egg salad sandwiches, talked about high school (She said she'll miss it. Not me!) and what we're going to do in the fall. I'm going to Dawson in Languages and Literature. She's going to Marianopolis, another private school. She plans to become a lawyer, like her dad. Her mom's a doctor. I guess that's why they have such a nice house with a pool in the backyard. Even when we lived on the same street back when I was a little kid, our house was a lot smaller than hers. I didn't realize it back then, but now, going back, I see the difference.

She said she's going to have a pool party for her seventeenth birthday later this summer and she's going to invite me. Also, on Saturday she's going shopping for a new bathing suit, and I'm going to go with her. Maybe I can get one too, for my trip to the ocean!

When I left, I actually walked by my old house. Even from the outside it looks smaller than I remembered. Whoever lives there now made a really nice garden in the front. It's full and lush and just bursting with flowers of every colour. I stopped to admire it and then gazed up at the house wondering who lives there now.

I had this crazy urge to ring the doorbell and tell them I used to live there and ask if anyone ever saw or heard any ghosts in the house. Obviously I didn't actually do that, because they'd probably think I was crazy and slam the door in my face, but I did look up at the second-floor window that used to be mine. The curtains, some kind of floral pattern, were closed, but just as I was about to turn and walk away, I saw them move. They didn't get pushed open, and no face appeared in the window, but the curtains definitely moved. Despite the July heat I actually shivered with the chill that ran down my spine. What if the Curtain Lady does still live in that house? And what if she knew I was there?

●　●　●

Saturday, July 6, 1985
Dear Diary,
The freakiest thing just happened to me, which made me wonder if I'm losing my mind or something. I was walking home from the metro, along de Maisonneuve by the tracks, which I don't usually do at night. It's faster to get home that way, but it's dark, a little grungy, and pretty deserted, so if I don't take the bus I prefer to walk the long way, up Décarie, along Sherbrooke, and then back down my street. But I was tipsy and feeling carefree, so I took the shortcut.

Even though it's a warm Saturday night, the street was even more deserted than usual. One person sped by me on a bike, but other than that I didn't see another soul. It really is a creepy area at night, one side lined with chain-link fence and then the train tracks and the other side with rows of low-rent apartment buildings, garages, and warehouses with graffitied walls. As soon as I had crossed to the other side of Décarie I regretted my decision. Just like it does at 3 a.m. in my dark room, my mind started concocting all kinds of chilling scenarios, giving me shivers despite the hot summer weather. Every dark alley I passed, every rustle I heard further convinced me I was being watched or stalked. Whether it was by someone (or something) made of flesh and blood or shadows didn't matter; within minutes I was sure I was being pursued. Shadows lurked while footsteps closed in behind me, but every time I looked to the side or over my shoulder, there was no one there. The level of desertion of the street was surreal. It was too dark, too silent, too still. At one point I must have heard the echo of my own footfall, because I spun right around, sure I would come face-to-face with some form of dark and evil being, but again there was no one. Then I turned back around, thinking I would sprint the rest of the way home, and I stopped short as I spotted a tall, slim, dark figure with a hat standing half a block ahead of me on the overpass, looking over the guardrail. I continued to walk forward as time seemed to stand still. I was certain he had not been there five seconds before. It made no sense. Was I dreaming? And who wears black head-to-toe, including a hat, in July? As I approached, in reverie-like slow motion, my pulse pounding in my ears, he turned toward me. I couldn't see his face, just his shape, and then I knew: It was the thin man of my nightmares. He had done it. He had found a way to fully enter my world and was going to take me here and now. Just like I couldn't move when he visited me in the night, now I couldn't stop my feet from moving, each step bringing me closer to his faceless, waiting self.

As I arrived within arm's reach, he spoke: "Got a light?"

"Sorry, what?" I said, as his voice and then very human face pierced my awareness.

"A light. You got one?" he said, holding up an unlit cigarette.

"Sure," I said, letting out a big breath of relief as I dug around for my lighter while being sure to keep some distance from the pale goth face shadowed by the brim of an eccentric hat.

I lit his smoke, he nodded a smileless thanks, and turned back to watch the traffic, while I ran the whole rest of the way home.

Aside from that, I had a great time with Amy and this is turning out to be a pretty fun summer already. My childhood friend is not as conservative as I thought!

After we went bathing suit shopping today she suggested we go to Peel Pub for a beer. I had never been and as usual I was worried about getting carded, but apparently I really don't need to worry so much, because carding is actually not much of a thing, it seems.

Peel Pub is, well, a pub. There's music in the background but no dance floor. It's just tables and chairs and pitchers of beer. As you know, I'm not a big fan of beer and I thought no way were we going to finish a whole pitcher, but it actually goes down really easily, especially when you get a big plate of French fries with gravy to go with it. At one point I lit up a cigarette, sure she would wrinkle her nose or make a judgemental comment, but she asked me for one! She's another social smoker. Only when she drinks. Once we had ordered our second pitcher, Amy said, "Dare me to go talk to those guys at that table over there?" motioning towards a table of three preppy guys.

"Seriously? OK." I laughed.

"What should I ask them?"

"Um. I dunno. Ask them if you have spinach stuck in your teeth," I joked. And she did! She just walked over, sat in an empty chair at their table, smiled and, from what I could tell from her body language, asked them exactly what I told her to. They looked a little confused, but what half-drunk guys wouldn't be happy to have a pretty girl like her strike up a conversation? She stayed for a couple of minutes while I watched and laughed from a distance and when she came back she told me their names and that they are from the States, up here to take advantage of our low drinking age, and then she said it was my turn! You know how shy and bad at approaching people I am, but alcohol makes me a little bolder so I reluctantly agreed to the challenge.

"Give me an easy question," I insisted. "Nothing too embarrassing!"

She told me to go sit with this man who was alone and ask him if turquoise was my colour. (I was wearing a turquoise top.) I was like, really? Him? He was old, like probably forty, and busy reading a newspaper.

"I dare you," she said, as seriously as she could after a pitcher and a half of watery beer.

And I did it! I walked over on wobbly legs, not believing I was going to do it, right until I got to his table and asked, "Excuse me, may I sit here?"

"Uh, sure," he said, a little suspiciously. And then I said, "I would just like to know if you think turquoise is my colour."

He kind of laughed and shook his head, and said, "Yes. *Turquoise* is definitely your colour. It brings out the colour of your eyes, in fact."

"OK, thank you!" I said and almost ran back to our table.

We continued to play the game for at least half an hour, asking stupid and sometimes slightly naughty questions (we got bolder with practice) to most of the guys in the vicinity. Sometimes we asked questions about ourselves ("Can you guess what my name is?"), sometimes about them ("Have you ever gone outside in your underwear?") At one point I asked a guy if he thought my lips looked like Cyndi Lauper's lips (they don't, but someone once told me they do) and he got the wrong message and wanted me to kiss him, so we stayed away from lip questions after that. We also stayed away from girl-only tables and couples, of course. We got a couple of free glasses of beer out of it and eventually ended up joining a table of Cégep students for the rest of the evening. We didn't tell them we were just out of high school, we simply told them we went to Dawson and

Marianopolis, worried they would catch us out eventually, but they never did.

• • •

Monday, July 8, 1985
Dear Diary,
I'm on the plane!

I was a nervous wreck about finding my way through the airport and everything by myself, but it actually wasn't that hard. Mom accompanied me as far as she could, and once I went through security it was easy to find my way to my gate.

I wondered if I would get airsick, because I do get car sick and I can't read or anything in a car or a bus, but here I am writing and I feel fine. My ears are a bit blocked, though.

I can't wait to see Chantal for the first time in almost a year!

• • •

10:00 p.m.
Dear Diary,
Here I am in Nova Scotia with Chantal!

They (Chantal, her mom, and her brother) picked me up at the airport in Halifax and I almost jumped on Chantal, I was so happy to see her! On the plane I kept thinking that maybe we'd have changed so much that we'd be awkward around each other, but not at all! We were talking and laughing so much in the car that Philippe – excuse me, *Phil* – kept telling us to be quiet and her mom kept shaking her head and rolling her eyes, but with a smile on her face.

Halifax is such a cute city, and how amazing to be right beside the ocean! (Her house isn't right next to the ocean or anything, but it's close enough that you can walk to it.) I always think of the ocean being super far away, like in Hawaii or Miami or Greece, but here it is, right in Canada.

And her house is super nice! She had sent me a photo of the outside once so I knew it was cute and painted blue. After Chantal's descriptions I thought it was going to be tiny, but it's not at all. I guess it doesn't really have more rooms than her duplex in Montreal did, except for one more bathroom, but it's on two floors so it feels bigger. Her mom's photos are all over the walls, just like in her old place, but somehow I notice them more here. She's a really good photographer; she should work for a magazine or something.

I haven't decided if I'm going to tell Chantal about what happened with Olive. I'm sure she wouldn't mind, I mean it's been so long since they broke up, and how can I not tell her about my first *orgasm?* But it feels weird.

• • •

Wednesday, July 10, 1985
Dear Diary,
It's hard to find the time to write when I'm spending all this time catching up with Chantal, seeing the sights, and meeting up with her friends.

Yesterday it rained and we stayed home most of the day. When her dad, Paul, came home from work he brought us fish & chips, which they said is the "poutine of Nova Scotia," meaning the greasy, yummy, French fry-based snack of the province. I'm not big on fish normally, but it was actually really good!

Today we went to the Halifax waterfront and hung around with a couple of Chantal's school friends. I was hoping to meet Jonas, the guy she's dating, but he's away for a few days so he wasn't there. I was nervous about meeting her new friends, wondering if they would like me and if I would fit in. They're kind of preppy and even Chantal dresses much preppier now, so right away I felt like I stuck out with my jewellery, teased curls, and layered tank tops. But actually they were all nice and very curious about me and about life in Montreal. Chantal and I spoke French to each other sometimes. Normally we don't really speak much French together and you know how I'm shy about my accent, but here they don't really hear my accent or speak French half as well as I do, so it was fun to show off a little. In fact, they kept insisting that we have French accents when we speak English! Even Chantal doesn't really, only with a few words here and there, but me? To me, they're the ones with the accent, actually. They also have this idea that Montreal is, like, this huge city where all the teenagers party all the time. I don't know if it's Chantal who gave them that idea or if our city just has a reputation. I mean, the drinking age is one year lower in Montreal than here, and the bars stay open later, and it is definitely a bigger city. Anyway, it was fun to feel like the sophisticated, big-city girl.

• • •

Friday, July 12, 1985
Dear Diary,
I haven't told Chantal about Olive and me. I think at this point I won't be telling her. I mean, is there really anything to tell? It was just a one-time thing, right? Like his graduation present to me or something. Why risk making things awkward?

I actually kind of brought up the subject last night when we were in bed. I asked her why she wanted to break up (besides the fact that she was going to move away) and what he was like as a boyfriend. She said he wasn't romantic enough and she always felt like he had a weird attitude towards women under the surface even though he was always nice and decent.

"So . . . was he good in bed?" I asked, wiggling my eyebrows up and down to keep it lighthearted, like I was just teasing her rather than searching for information.

She laughed and replied, "Hard to say. He was my first. I guess it was fine. I don't think I was good in bed yet."

Somehow, I hadn't really thought about that before. Am I good in bed? Then she had a question for me: "Have you ever had an orgasm?"

It was my big chance to come clean, but I didn't have the guts. "Have you?" I asked, deflecting.

"I think so, I don't know. I'm not sure. It's been really good with the guy I've been seeing here. Jonas. He's away for a few days, but you'll meet him before you leave."

"If you had had one, you would know," I said before thinking twice.

"So you have! With who?"

"The last guy I was with. It was basically a one-night stand. Let's change the subject; this conversation's getting too personal!" I said.

So I escaped having to outright lie to Chantal at least. And I must remember to figure out how to make sure I am, or how to become, good in bed.

Tomorrow we're leaving for a two-day trip to a part of Nova Scotia called Cape Breton. None of her family has been there yet. When we come back I'll only have a few days left here and then it's back to Montreal, far away from the ocean and my best friend.

• • •

Monday, July 15, 1985
Dear Diary,

Cape Breton was so beautiful! I've never seen anything like it! We drove around the whole island, I mean *peninsula*, on the Cabot Trail. We stayed overnight along the way so we would have time to do the whole thing.

I think I am in love with the ocean. It's so vast and wild and powerful. We went to one beach where we could swim, near the beginning of the trail. The water was calm and they said it was the warmest water in Canada. We went in, but I can't say it was that warm! Then at other places where we stopped the water looked terrifying, crashing over rocks and looking like it would sweep you away in an instant. Chantal's dad, Paul, said it actually can. There's a thing called an undertow that can pull your feet right out from under you, dragging you down and out to sea. A terrifying and fascinating thought. But it was majestic; I could have watched, smelled, and listened to the sea for hours. At some places we drove so high up and so close to the edge of the cliffs that I felt dizzy and had to close my eyes. But then I would open them again because I didn't want to miss anything.

Oh and we saw a moose! We were all hoping we would, but as we got close to the end of the trail yesterday we figured we were out of luck and then one just walked out of the forest and crossed the road. It was far enough away that we had plenty of time to stop, and I even managed to get my camera out and snap a couple of pictures. I hope they turn out! Of course France took a ton of pictures, and with her professional camera, I'm sure she'll get great shots. Paul said it was a young moose, but it was still quite big and impressive, with long legs and such a graceful walk. Then we had a discussion about whether the plural of moose is moose, mooses or meece, ha ha! (Chantal, Phil and I voted for meece, much to the annoyance of Chantal's parents.)

And the people are so nice! We stopped for ice cream, fish and chips, and souvenirs and everyone was just so friendly. Some people even spoke French. They said they're Acadians, and they have a funny accent.

That was enough family time for me, though, with five of us in the car and me dying for a cigarette the whole time. I guess I could have smoked in front of her parents if I wanted to, but I was afraid of what they'd think.

• • •

Thursday, July 18, 1985
Dear Diary,
I'm on the plane on my way back home. Did I ever cry when I walked away from Chantal at the airport! I did not expect that, but I guess now that our visit is over and she's staying there and I'm going back I realize that we have different homes now. And different friends and different lives. She might come back some day, but we might never live in the same city again. It makes me miss her all over again.

On Tuesday we went to a beach nearby with some friends of hers from school. We made sure to go at low tide, walked along a rocky beach to the end and then we had to walk through some fenny water to get to a more secluded part of the beach. As my feet sank into the sludge at the bottom I was kind of grossed out by the soft, dark squishiness of it, but then I suddenly got a strange desire to just let myself sink. I stopped walking and wiggled my toes, letting the muck seep in between and start to wrap over the tops of my feet. The feeling was at once repulsive and strangely appealing and I was reminded of a childhood visit to my cousin's place in Toronto. She lived in a small house up the hill from a huge pond at the edge of High Park. You weren't allowed to swim in the pond and my cousin told me it was because the bottom of it was all quicksand. I remember being both petrified and strangely awed by the idea of quicksand: mud that would pull you under slowly but unrelentingly, like something alive, hungry, and without mercy. It haunted my thoughts for months afterward.

Then a wave came in and almost knocked me over, and I remembered about the undertow. I imagined the quicksand and the current working together to pull me down and carry me away to another world, a dark world beneath the sea inhabited by shadow-people.

"Poppy!" Chantal called, pulling me out of my daydream. "What, are you stuck? Come on!" They had made their way quickly through the muck and were already getting settled on some smooth, flat rocks where we could lie down, drink beers, and soak up some sun.

At one point I spotted Chantal holding hands with the guy she's seeing, Jonas, who's quiet and good-looking with curly hair and caramel-coloured skin. He's kind of preppy, like most of the kids around there, and very clean-cut looking. I was happy for her and kind of struck by the romance of the moment; I mean you couldn't get a more romantic setting than secluded rocks being splashed by ocean waves.

Until your friends break the spell by literally throwing cold water on it.

It was an amazing afternoon for me and it's still hard to believe that this is her *life* now. She probably has days like that all the time! I wonder if I could live in a place like that. Halifax is small and doesn't have the wild nightlife of Montreal, but the ocean! I think I could get used to it.

Also, I realize that I didn't have a single visit from the shadow-people the whole time I was on vacation. Maybe they didn't know where to find me all the way in Nova Scotia. I hope they never find me again.

● ● ●

Friday, July 19, 1985

Dear Diary,

It was a cloudy day today and I felt a little lonely. I wrote Chantal a letter then I read for most of the day.

First I read some Edgar Allan Poe. I've had this book Dave gave me for two years, and though I liked the idea of reading it, I kept putting it back in the to-read-next pile and going back to Stephen King or something else more page-turner-ish. But I have to say, I like it! Today I read *The Raven*. I guess it's Poe's best-known poem. Though I like to write poems, I'm not much of a poetry reader outside of school. Besides the dark creepiness of it, I like the fact that Poe's poetry has rhythm and rhyme. I almost always write rhyming poetry, and my teachers have often criticized me for it. They say rhyming poetry tends to sound juvenile and the rhymes are usually forced. But I like the musicality of it, as well as the challenge of sticking to a rhythm and finding the rhymes, and I'm happy to see I'm not the only one. Go Poe!

I had dinner with Mom and Dave, who is pretty much all moved in now, I guess, and then headed over to Olive's.

I decided to walk over instead of taking the bus, which turned out to be a mistake. I had walked up to Somerled and turned left to walk over to Walkley, where Olive lives. I actually was getting sick of walking so I turned around to see if by any chance the bus was coming so I could hop on, but it wasn't. At that moment a car stopped at the stop sign on the same corner. The driver stayed stopped until I passed, and although I tried not to look, I could see he was staring at me as I walked by. It's not like men don't stare at girls all the time, so I wasn't too worried. But then he caught up to me and slowed down to drive right alongside me for about half a block. I tried not to worry, but then I thought of all the times I've been flashed and the time that guy grabbed Chantal when she was fourteen and we screamed our heads off before he let go and ran away. There was a dépanneur up ahead I could run into, but it was still a few blocks away, and then the car waited for me again at the next corner. Why were there no people on the street on a beautiful summer night? I looked straight ahead as I passed the car again, and then as he crossed the intersection I quickly changed direction and ran down the cross street, which was a one-way going the wrong way so he couldn't just turn around and follow me down the street. Every time I saw headlights coming up the street I ducked behind parked cars until they passed, but none of them seemed to be the same car. I continued south and then zigzagged along the most populated streets all the way back home.

Mom was confused when I got back only thirty minutes after having left. I told her what happened and she said not to go back out alone. As if I would! My heart was beating hard and my mouth was really dry.

I called Olive to tell him I wouldn't be going to his place after all, and he said he would come over and get me! So he did. He took the bus all the way to my place just so he could accompany me back to his place. And just in case you're thinking what I know you're thinking, he didn't try a thing! We just hung out watching TV like old times.

I don't know what Chantal was talking about with his feelings about women. With me he's been a friend and now a gentleman, too. Plus one little extra gift. I'll admit he's hard to figure out, though. I think he's what's called an enigma.

● ● ●

Saturday, July 20, 1985
Dear Diary,
Last night, I dreamed of the shadow-people.

The dream is already fading from my memory, but I was basically living among them, going about my daily routine as if it was totally normal to be surrounded by faceless ghosts and spirits. Faceless, but not voiceless.

That's how I know it was a dream. Because they talked to me and normally when they visit me for real (I know what you're thinking, but what else can I call it?) they never, ever speak.

And I wasn't afraid, whereas when I see them in my room at night I am about as terrified as a person can be.

Maybe I'm done with them – or them with me – and they really won't come back.

Chapter 7
Fall 1986

Monday, Sept. 29, 1986

Dear Diary,

So, eighteen started off pretty weird.

I woke up in the night, or very early in the morning, to be more precise, and I could have sworn I was levitating off the bed. I was just lying there, not moving, and kind of mesmerized by the sensation, and then I started to get pulled toward the foot of the bed, as if I were trapped in some kind of tractor beam or something. In the moment it was the coolest sensation. Now that I'm thinking about it and trying to describe it, it sounds a little nuts, and also I can't figure out if my body itself was being pulled or whether I levitated out of my body somehow. And no, I have not taken up drugs! I haven't smoked weed in, like, two years.

Also, I want to be clear: it was not a dream. I've had flying dreams before and they are truly the best, but I know a dream when I have one. This was totally different because I was not asleep. I was on my bed – well, above my bed – and in my room. And once I landed back on my bed I didn't have the sensation of waking up, the way you do when you have one of those dreams where you think you wake up, but you're actually still dreaming, and then you wake up a second time but for real. It wasn't one of those.

Ugh. I have to go. I'm going to be late for class. Again. And on my birthday!

• • •

11:30 p.m.

I just got home from Peel Pub. My big moment of going to a bar legally for the first time was pretty damn anti-climactic since they didn't even ask for ID. I wasn't going to do anything special today since I already had my annual weird-mix-of-guests dinner party on the weekend, but once my card-playing friends found out it was my birthday they insisted on marking the occasion. So we played quarters and got pretty drunk until we decided it was time to go home if we wanted any hope of getting to school in time for morning classes tomorrow.

But guess who I ran into? Olive! It had been over a year since we had seen each other, since the summer after high school when we made out that time (and he gave me my first orgasm) then were just friends again, then we kissed that one other time and he acted like nothing had happened again and things felt too weird for me so I backed away from the friendship.

But when I saw him across that crowded room tonight I had to go say hi. Anyway, it's not like we're on bad terms or anything, we just grew apart. We promised to call each other this week and get together soon.

• • •

Tuesday, Sept. 30, 1986
Dear Diary,

I thought I would do better. Cégep is so much better than high school in so many ways, but I'm still me, I guess. I still party too late, miss morning classes, leave my schoolwork until the last minute and have a lot more fun playing cards in the cafeteria than studying. I mean, it was my birthday yesterday, so I have a good reason for having partied too late to get up for class this morning, but it's the third time I've missed that class . . . out of five classes. I should know better than to schedule anything at eight thirty.

The thing is, I actually enjoy quite a few of my classes. Some are boring and pointless, of course, but overall the teachers are more easygoing and less pedantic than many of my high school teachers. Started a sentence with "And"? No problem, if it works. I'll always remember that time in Grade Six when I handed in a poem I had worked so hard on and was so proud of. It was a silly, rhyming poem about animals who were all the wrong shape, size and colour and I used the word "ridiculiculous" to keep both the silliness and the rhythm intact and the teacher crossed it out in red and corrected it to plain old "ridiculous." I felt she just hadn't understood what I was trying to do and when I told Mom she said I should go back and explain it to my teacher, but I was way too shy to do something like that.

As I was saying, in Cégep I've taken some literature courses where I've read great books I always wanted to read (*War and Peace*!), there was that Greek mythology course I loved, and then there was that cool humanities teacher who liked to swear and let us smoke in class. The creative writing class I'm taking this semester is fantastic. Every class the teacher gives us a challenge to spark inspiration. He gives us a word, an expression, or a character we have to include in a short story. For example, today's word was "abaft," which means toward the stern of a ship, so I came up with this little adventure story about a pirate that I'm quite proud of and would never have thought of writing on my own. He also teaches a poetry-writing course that I'm going to sign up for next semester.

But it's still school. There's still studying and homework and even gym class, though I found a jazz dance class that fit my schedule this semester, which is at least more up my alley than all those years of forced team sports in high school.

I met this really funny guy today. He's in my otherwise kind-of-boring philosophy class that I'm taking at another small building a few blocks away from my usual Selby campus. I had noticed him because he's really talkative (everyone has noticed him), but today we got paired up for a little project. He was hilarious! His name's Stefano and he's like a caricature of himself. He's tall and skinny with a slightly too-big nose and hair styled just like John Travolta in *Grease*. He never stopped talking for a second, with his almost certainly exaggerated Italian-Canadian accent in a slightly nasal voice and accompanied by tons of hand gestures. He seems like one of those people who's always in a good mood. Most of the time he's making jokes, some of them really funny and some really bad, and then he just fills all the spaces in between with random thoughts and comments. Oh, and he also talks really fast!

It's a bit exhausting to be around him because he has so much energy and kind of demands your attention all the time, but at the same time it's sort of relaxing, because since he does all the talking you don't have to come up with anything much to say yourself.

After class we went to hang out in the small, quiet cafeteria, very different from the crowded, bustling, smoke-filled one at Selby. His friend Stéphanie was waiting for him and when he introduced us, before I could say "Nice to meet you" or anything he explained that they became friends because they basically have the same name. They met in a class, like us, but since they were sitting next to each other and had the same name, he had no choice but to become her friend. I think he told the same story three different ways, all quite redundant, but equally entertaining. He also does impressions. Mostly Italian TV and movie characters, like *Rocky* or *The Godfather*, but they're right on and kept me laughing non-stop. I must say, I look forward to philosophy class way more than I did at the beginning of the session.

I wonder what it must be like not to have a shy bone in your body!

● ● ●

Friday, Oct. 10, 1986
Dear Diary,
Why, exactly, do Ouija boards have to be so popular? I mean, they're sold in the *toy* section, for heaven's sake.

This girl Belinda I play cards with at school invited a bunch of people over and another girl, who had just seen *Witchboard* (kind of creepy but also cheesy), brought a Ouija board.

Another thing I wonder is how come the guys never want to play? Are they smarter than us or just a bunch of chickens?

So the guys went to watch sports on TV while the four girls, Belinda (the fun one who I find a little fake), Di (who brought the board), funny Giselle with the great legs, and me, sat down to summon ghosts. In the past the spirits have tended to centre on me, so I was tentative, to say the least.

But we started to play and I realized pretty quick that everything was going to centre on Belinda today, so I relaxed to watch the show. The questions were general, but the answers all seemed to somehow relate to *her* past, *her* family (her evil stepfather, to be precise) and *her* trauma. It was all pretty dramatic, actually, and I am definitely being more detached now than I was at the time. Even I was affected by her shaky hands and shimmering blue eyes when the pointer spelled out D-A-D-D-Y and B-E-L-I-N-D-A and B-A-D-G-I-R-L.

But theatrics aside, I do believe in spirits (there, I said it!) and I've had my share of freaky Ouija experiences, so I kept my fingers firmly on the planchette and my attention on the answers, even the ones that were clearly manipulated.

Finally one of the girls, I forget if it was Di or Giselle, told me to ask a question. I didn't really want to, but didn't want to be the one spoiling the fun either, so I went for it and asked, "Are you the man of my dreams?"

Just as Belinda exclaimed, "Ooh," the planchette whipped right to "Yes." It was so fast that we barely could keep our fingers on it and everyone was just slightly taken aback. The giggling mellowed for a moment and I thought it was an opportune time to steer the game toward "Goodbye."

Then Giselle said, "What's your name?" with a mischievous smile directed at me.

"C-U-R-T-A-I-N-L-A-D-Y"

I looked around and for sure no one there had ever heard of the ghost from my childhood. And I swear to you, cross my heart, hope to die, stick a needle in my eye, that I did not move that planchette.

"Curt Ainlady? What kind of a name is that? And isn't Curt spelled with a K?" said Belinda.

And then: "P-O-P-P-Y."

I stared at the board, fingers still planted but really trembling now, and I could feel everyone else staring at me.

And then: "C-O-M-E-H-O-M-E."

It didn't make much sense, but I didn't like it one bit so I looked kind of helplessly at Belinda, Giselle, and Di then back at the board and said, "Goodbye."

Nothing moved.

"Goodbye!" I repeated, yelling louder than I meant to.

And after a short pause that felt eternal the board gave in and said, "Goodbye."

"Such a drama queen!" Belinda exclaimed. I know she wanted to make it sound like she was only teasing, but I also know she really didn't like the way the evening's focus had veered so abruptly from her to me. "I know it was totally you who was moving the pointer around. So obvious," she said. Well, she would know, right?

I didn't say anything to defend myself to the group, but I'm telling you now, it wasn't me.

• • •

Monday, Oct. 13, 1986
Dear Diary,
Stefano is soooooo funny. He does this impression of Vinnie Barbarino, you know, from *Welcome Back Kotter*, that is just so right on! He throws his shoulders back and puffs out his chest and starts prancing around, singing "Ba-ba-ba Ba Barbarino," *exactly* like John Travolta. I swear, he could do that impression every day and I would laugh my head off every single time. He is such a freaking character! (I mean Stefano, not John Travolta, ha ha!)

He called me on Saturday to see if I wanted to go out for smoked meat. He picked me up at home in his red Chevy Chevelle. When he showed up, Mom said, "Who's the guy in the muscle car?"

I was like, "What's a muscle car?" Well, now I know. It's a red Chevy Chevelle.

So anyway, we went to Ben's downtown for dinner. I was trying to figure out if he meant it as a date, because I'm really not interested in him that way, but I'm pretty sure he didn't. I mean, we both paid for ourselves and he didn't try to kiss me or anything like that. Also, I actually think he might have a thing for Stéphanie.

As I said, he's a character and he is a bit *loud,* so in public I felt a little embarrassed with him, I'm ashamed to say. Plus, because he's so funny with his mannerisms and his impressions – he did Barbarino for me right there in the packed restaurant – I kept laughing too loud so if people were looking at us it was as much my fault as his.

Considering I barely have to do any of the talking when we're together, I felt surprisingly exhausted at the end of our non-date. Keeping up with a non-stop, high-speed, hyperactive narrative is draining, it turns out.

I keep wondering how he would fit in with my other Dawson friends, whom he hasn't met. He doesn't go to the Selby cafeteria and says he doesn't like playing cards anyway, so maybe I won't ever have to introduce them. I just don't think they'd click, so what's the point?

It makes me think back to Gabriel, my childhood friend whom I feel like I just abandoned. I always feel guilty when I think about it, how I suddenly got embarrassed by this guy I had played with for my whole childhood, because he grew up to be strange and different and also gave me my first sexual feelings, if I can call them that, that time he held my hand on the bus when we were, like, ten or something. I probably shouldn't feel guilty, right? After all, he might have abandoned me just as much as I abandoned him. I don't remember my phone ringing off the hook or anything. Then in Grade Nine he changed schools and I've never seen him again.

Seriously, who am I anyway to judge anyone for not fitting in?

● ● ●

Tuesday, Oct. 14, 1986
Dear Diary,
Have I ever told you how afraid of the dark I am?

It's three and I've been lying here, terrified, staring at the shadows and expecting them to take shape for I don't know how long, and then I thought, "Have I ever written anything about my fear of the dark?"

I guess it sort of seems obvious, because I'm afraid of my night time visitors and my nightmares and everything, but I am also just terribly afraid of the dark. Like little kid afraid. Mom actually thinks I learned to be afraid of the dark from Grover on *Sesame Street* back before I was even in Kindergarten. He was lying there listing all the reasons he was scared and I'm pretty sure the point of the episode was to teach kids why they *shouldn't* be afraid of the dark, but Mom says I started getting scared after that. I don't think that's it, though. I think it was because of the Curtain Lady.

Light and shadows play tricks on you in an almost-but-not-quite-completely dark room, as they did tonight, and sometimes I lie awake looking around expecting something to manifest itself and come for me. Or when it's pitch black, like the time we went camping and I woke up in the tent and couldn't find the flashlight. It was so dark I couldn't see my hand in front of my face. I kept imagining there was something or someone lurking just in front of me, and that if I did turn on a light it would be right there in front of my face. What it would look like and what it would do, of course I don't know, but when I'm lying there in the dark my fear takes over and I just know the shadows will come alive.

But they never have. Never when I'm awake. They only come for me when I'm asleep or halfway towards awake and they can catch me off-guard. Cowards.

● ● ●

Thursday, Oct. 16, 1986
Dear Diary,
I finally get it. I understand why people like coffee.

Everyone around me loves coffee and I have never understood it. I mean, once in a while I drink a cup with plenty of milk and sugar just not to feel left out, but I'd rather drink hot chocolate, to be honest.

So, there we were after class, Stefano, Stéphanie, and me, and they got coffees and I said no thanks and mentioned that I don't actually like coffee. Which really wound Stefano up. He went on and on about how could I not like coffee and all the benefits of it and the qualities of it and how if I only tried Italian coffee and in the end he took us both to a crowded, old-fashioned restaurant called Caffè Italia in *La Petite Italie* (I didn't even know Montreal had a place called Little Italy) to try a real Italian espresso.

I wanted a cappuccino, but he was like, no way, nothing diluted, you have to jump in with both feet and have a strong, short espresso in a tiny cup, the idea of which had always grossed me out. But I figured if I can survive a tequila shot I can survive a coffee shot and . . . it was amazing!

"*Certo,* you like it," Stefano said, pinching his thumb and fingers together and waving his hand up and down the way he often does. "Who couldn't like an espresso from Caffè Italia, eh?"

I could tell Stefano was really pleased with himself that he had introduced me to this cool new place and experience, and that I liked it.

The place *was* really cool, old-fashioned with a line of vinyl-covered stools at the counter, super-busy, even a little chaotic, with lots of older men actually speaking Italian. I hoped Stefano would order for us in Italian, but he says he doesn't really speak it that much, just understands it. I couldn't believe it, with him being so stereotypically Italian!

But anyway, he was right, all I needed was the real thing to learn to like coffee. If only I could make it at home!

• • •

Friday, Oct. 17, 1986
Dear Diary,
I don't know how to explain to you what happened tonight.

Olive invited me to join him and some friends at PJs, a sports bar on St. Jacques. You know how I hate walking into a room full of people I don't know, so I was feeling a bit nervous, but in fact I knew a couple of people from the old days and anyway, once the plates of wings and pitchers of beer start coming everyone gets comfortable. I even ended up exchanging phone numbers with one of the guys at the table, someone Olive works with.

Once the party split up Olive asked if I wanted to go back to his place and catch up, since we hadn't really had a chance to with all the other people around.

When we got there his brother was passed out on the couch in front of the TV so we had to go to Olive's room. We just chilled on his bed talking, but he's still not that good a talker and I was really tired from being up since seven, and then all the beer, so I kept dozing off. I fought it for a while but eventually gave in.

Sometime later I half woke up. I had that all-too-familiar feeling that I can't drag myself out of sleep and I'm too heavy to move. And someone was on top of me. Not just on top of me but inside me. I couldn't move because someone was lying on top of me and having sex with me while I slept. And that someone was Olive.

I was suddenly a lot more awake, though my mind and emotions were a confused mess. "Olive, no! What are you doing?" I said, managing to place a hand in front of one of his shoulders. Then he took my hand and pinned it to the bed next to me. "What the fuck, Olive? I was sleeping!" I said, confusion starting to turn to something between hurt and anger.

"Shhh," he said, and I remembered that Darius was in the apartment. Maybe that should have made me get louder, but I was still basically in shock and also not keen on anyone walking in on us. Olive was totally in the throes of it by this point and I just closed my eyes, turned my head to the side, and waited for him to finish.

Then I pushed him off me, sat up, put my underwear back on and pulled my skirt back down. My hands were shaking, my breathing was shallow, and I felt dizzy and a little sick to my stomach, probably as much from the beer as from what had just happened.

"What was – how could you – I was fucking *asleep,* Olive. I can't even stand to be touched when I'm sleeping, and I haven't seen you in, like, a *year,* and we're not – you're supposed to be my friend," I said, my throat closing up and my eyes filling with water.

Furious with myself for being so weak, I turned my face away. Then he came over to me, sat down and took me in his arms.

So what did I do? I melted into his chest and let the tears flow. I wanted to hit him, to hate him, but instead I let him comfort me.

It didn't last long, though. I pushed him away soon enough and got up to leave, saying, "I still can't believe you would do that to me."

"I'm sorry," he said, "I've just wanted you for so long and I hadn't seen you for ages, and you were lying there with your skirt up looking so – I'm sorry," he said, with a shrug. A *shrug.*

"You still live with your mom? You want me to walk you?" he said, like any normal friend would ask any normal day.

I stared at him a little incredulous for a second before saying, "No, I'll call a taxi." Didn't he get what he had just done?

"OK. I'll call you this week."

I gave him a pursed smile and a curt nod and turned to leave, then turned back and said, "No, Olive. Please don't."

I called a taxi from the living room, trying to be quiet but waking Darius a little. "Hey, Poppy," he said, rubbing his eyes. "'Sup? Long time no see."

"Hey Darius," I said, with a normal, pleasant smile pasted on my face. "Nice to see you." Then I walked out.

What I keep asking myself is: Did Olive . . . rape me? I mean, I wouldn't go to the cops or anything. Who would believe me anyway with my history and our history together? And it wasn't *that* kind of rape: He didn't hit me or threaten me; I'm sure he didn't even mean to hurt me. So is that actually what he did? And if he did, does he even know it? Would he, my friend Olive, knowingly do that to me?

My mind is very confused and my heart is a little broken.

• • •

Saturday, Oct. 18, 1986
Dear Diary,
I don't want to lose my friend. But I can't keep being his friend, can I?

Maybe I should just forgive him and forget it. I'm sure he didn't mean it. But it's not like I could pick up the phone and call him. That would be like telling him what he did was OK. And it wasn't, right?

I feel lost and alone again, like I have no friends after all and no one to talk to. I don't think I can tell Chantal because it's Olive and I never told her about what happened between us that other time and anyway, she's far away and will probably never come back at this point. She's still my best friend in my heart, but how long will she really be with all this distance between us? Do I have even one other person I would tell something like that to?

Olive and I had grown apart and just when we were about to rekindle our friendship he betrayed me. Sandrine has moved back out west and we've pretty much lost touch. My card-playing friends at Dawson are fun, but they're not confidantes, and I don't really trust Belinda. She's charming and fun, but I always think she's not quite sincere. Stefano and Stéphanie? Maybe in six months or a year if we're still friends, but it's too soon and we're not close enough yet. Amy? I could tell her, but I feel like she'd want me to report it or something and maybe she'd judge me, too. We're so different, her with her goals, good grades, and preppy friends and me with my bad grades and, let's face it, sleeping around.

Do I even have one real friend?

●　●　●

8:00 p.m.

Dear Diary,

I'm supposed to go play cards with Belinda and the gang, but I don't know if I have it in me. I just woke up from a nap (When's the last time I took a nap?) and now I'm freaked out on top of being depressed.

So, as you can probably guess I woke up unable to move again. You'd think it wouldn't scare me anymore, it's happened so, so many times, but it still does, as much as ever. Maybe more than ever. I lay there trying to wait it out calmly at first, but then I could feel someone watching me. I couldn't see anyone, and nothing was touching me or anything, but I had the distinct feeling there was a presence in the room with me. I fought myself awake, but even once I sat up I still felt there was someone (or something) there. Then suddenly, out of the corner of my eye I saw my curtains move. I whipped my head around to look, and of course there was nothing there, but I know they moved and I was not imagining it. I sat there for what felt like ever, shivers down my spine, wanting to check behind the window and even in the closet and under the bed, but I didn't have the courage. I just sat frozen, feeling terrified. And also stupid, because who is still scared of looking under the bed at eighteen? (Answer: me.)

● ● ●

9:00 p.m.
Dear Diary,
Olive just called. I did not answer. I am so glad Mom got call display.

Maybe I will go out tonight after all. I could use a dose of Belinda's wildness and if I get wasted enough perhaps I'll forget all about Olive, the shadow-people, and everything else that haunts me.

Chapter 8
Winter 1987

Thursday, Jan. 1, 1987

Dear Diary,

Well another year is off to a pretty messed up start.

First of all, the shadow-people were the first to wish me a "happy" New Year with one of their typical visits just before dawn today.

Second of all, it's like minus thirty outside today. Brrr. I am not a winter person. I'm super tired after having gone out dancing last night and I think I might just stay in bed all day today.

And third of all, I think I'm pregnant. Yeah, I know it's not the first time I've said it, but this time I think it's for real. I'm such an idiot. I mean, when will I learn?

Every time I meet a new guy it's the same. I think, "This one's different," but they never are, even when they are. What I mean by that confusing statement is each one is different from the one before because I do try to learn from my mistakes and pick guys with opposite qualities to the previous one, but somehow it all turns out the same anyway. Tons of passion and loads of hope at the beginning and then after a few weeks or months either they get bored of me, I get bored of them, or we both get bored of each other.

This time *I* got bored. Of course I picked a nice guy after everything that happened with Olive. Not that Olive's not nice. I mean, he was one of my best friends for a while there now that I think about it, and I'm pretty convinced he didn't mean to hurt me. Maybe he doesn't even *know* he hurt me. Sometimes I feel like calling him and asking him if he even realizes what he did and why I never called him back and how come we're not friends anymore. Then sometimes I want to call him just to say, "Hi," like old times. We could sit in bored silence on the phone and then I could go hang out at his place. But of course I can't do that. No way. I couldn't trust him enough to be alone with him again and I do have *some* pride in me. Anyway, enough about situations and people that should stay in the past.

I need to worry about right-now situations and people. As you know, Kareem is (was) a sweetie, so devoted and caring and calling me *all the time.* The attention was so nice at first, and the way he acted like such a gentleman, not even trying for sex the first time he stayed over. And then once he did (the second time, maybe not so much of a gentleman after all, ha ha) it was so good and made me want to be so close to him that once again I didn't insist on protection and, well, you know the rest. He didn't give me enough space, I felt smothered, and eventually I ended it.

And here I am now with no more Kareem and no period either. Obviously if I am pregnant, which I am pretty sure I am at this point, I will not be keeping it.

I guess my first step is to go get a pregnancy test done at the pharmacy. Apparently you just take a sample of your pee to the pharmacist and they test it for you. How embarrassing. What if I see someone I know in the store? Or someone who knows Mom? I'll have to go to one downtown, where it's crowded and more anonymous.

• • •

Saturday, Jan. 3, 1987

Dear Diary,

I went out dancing with Belinda again last night. We both looked really good and got lots of attention and if I hadn't been so worried about being you-know-what I would have had the best time. I just love going out and dancing and feeling young and free . . . only I wasn't feeling quite so free. Like every time I bought another drink or smoked another cigarette I felt guilty about poisoning the little life inside me. Then I reminded myself that I'm not even sure and I'm not keeping it anyway and it's not anywhere near a . . . baby . . . yet.

Ew. I feel kind of sick just writing that word. I'm so not ready for anything like this.

I still haven't done a test, by the way.

After about my third drink I almost told Belinda, but somehow she's not the person I want to tell my secrets to. I feel like even though we hang out all the time and she sometimes even says I'm her best friend, she's the type of person who might spread my secret around or use it against me some day.

And no, I haven't told Kareem either. There's no point until I know for sure. And even then. What if he got all weird about it and wanted me to keep it or something?

I don't think I can tell Mom. I mean, she wouldn't disown me or anything, but she does have a judgemental side and I can just imagine how disappointed in me she would be for doing something so dumb. I can almost picture her face and it makes me want to cry. Then I instead imagine her giving me a big, comforting, understanding hug and it makes me want to cry, too. I wonder which way it would go if I did tell her? I'll probably never know.

I'm pretty alone in this world, aren't I?

• • •

Sunday, Jan. 4, 1987
Dear Diary,
I know I'm not supposed to bring him up any more, but I am just remembering the last time I was scared I was pregnant. It was after what happened with Olive. It was, like, two weeks later and I realized my period was late. It's always hard to tell how late I am because I'm not very regular and most months I already go like thirty to thirty-five days between, but I remember counting and I was at around forty days.

So I started praying: "Oh, please, oh, please don't let me be pregnant. I swear I will go back on the pill and be more responsible if you give me one more chance!"

I felt like a total hypocrite at the time, praying to a God I don't really believe in, but I was desperate. I even got down on my knees by my bed. But while I was down there, instead of picturing whatever a god or goddess (why can't she be female?) is supposed to look like, I kept seeing the shadow-people. Dark ones, pale ones of different shapes and sizes, coming out from the floor, the window, under the bed. The memory is super-clear right now, and I guess whoever or whatever I was praying to heard me, because two days later I got my period.

I might have said this before, but there are times when I wonder if my shadow-people are actually some kind of guardian angels, looking out for me and protecting me from the worst things despite my recklessness. How else could I have such luck when I do such stupid things?

Well, my prayers were answered last time, but I didn't hold up my end of the bargain, so this time I'm pretty sure my luck has run out.

• • •

Monday, Jan. 5, 1987
Dear Diary,
I read once that lots of women have miscarriages and don't even know it, so when you have a late or very heavy period it could actually be an early miscarriage.

How wrong would it be to hope for that? I don't think I can pray to God for such a thing, whether he (or she!) exists or not, but I'm not sure I want to be summoning the shadow-people for help either. (I am suddenly thinking, "Hey, what if that's what happened last time?" Better *not* to think about it, I think.)

Oh man, one day I am going to re-read this and realize just how crazy I sound.

All this writing about praying has reminded me of something Mom told me years ago. When she was little her family was kind of religious and they did things like go to church on Sunday, say grace at meals and pray before bed. They would say that classic children's bedtime prayer that even I know, which goes like this:

Now I lay me down to sleep,
I pray the Lord my soul to keep
If I should die before I wake,
I pray the Lord my soul to take.

Well, one day she realized just what she and her siblings had been saying all those nights and she was horrified at the idea that every night before bed they were basically planning for their own death, and she stopped reciting the prayer. I guess that was one of the many things that turned her completely off religion.

I swear I will go get a pregnancy test done this week.

● ● ●

Wednesday, Jan. 7, 1987
Dear Diary,
It's three thirty and I just threw up and my hands are shaking so bad I can hardly write this.

I woke up about half an hour ago in one of my states of paralysis. At first it was no different than usual: I was trapped in the in-between, where I can't make a move or a sound. As usual, my initial panic subsided once I realized I could at least breathe and I decided to wait it out instead of struggling against the thick quicksand pulling me down, which takes almost unbearable effort.

Then I felt something pushing on my stomach. It was a startling feeling that made me want to bolt upright, see what it was and furiously brush it away like when a spider lands on you, but of course I couldn't. It didn't feel like a bug, though, more like fists pushing into me . . . and then I suddenly sensed that they weren't on the outside pushing in, but on the *inside* pushing *out.* It was one of the creepiest, most horrifying things I have ever felt, and those words don't begin to describe what it was actually like.

Well, it was time to fight my way out of that place and away from that thing. I was so freaked out by the sensation that I had a shadow-being inside me that I must have struggled harder than usual and I resurfaced pretty quick. Then a wave of nausea came over me and I ran to the bathroom and puked my guts out.

Is this a sign that I really am pregnant? What am I going to do???

• • •

Thursday, Jan. 9, 1987
Dear Diary,

I was thinking of doing the test before school today. I got a clean jar from the cupboard this morning and was on my way to the bathroom when Mom came out of her room. I hid the jar behind my back and was sure she had seen it and immediately figured out exactly what was going on. My face got really hot and probably all red, giving me away even more. But she was still half asleep and not wearing her glasses so she never noticed a thing, actually. The close call took away all my courage and resolve, though, so I didn't go to the pharmacy after all.

I'll do it tomorrow. Promise.

● ● ●

Friday, Jan. 10, 1987
Dear Diary,
I think it's time to move on from Stephen King. Don't get me wrong, he's the master, but I'm starting to feel like all his books are too similar. Not the storylines but the writing style. I need something new.

I heard about this series called *The Vampire Chronicles* by Anne Rice, so I might go buy that and I've been thinking about reading the original *Dracula*. I think vampire stories are my favourite horror genre. Followed by demonic possession stories. I guess since *'Salem's Lot* was my first Stephen King and *The Exorcist* my first horror movie it makes sense. Stories of zombies or axe murderers don't scare me the same way. I also like a good, old-fashioned ghost story.

But back to vampires. I sometimes like to imagine what it would be like to be a vampire, and when I think about death, which I unfortunately do more than I would like, I think I would like to come back as a vampire. I mean, eternal life is an appealing idea since I don't really want to die, plus vampires are often kind of sexy – I would totally want to be a sexy one! I'd have to change from blue eyeliner to black, of course. Not so crazy about the idea of sleeping in a coffin or being allergic to sunlight, but owning the night sounds pretty good, and I imagine you get used to the taste of blood . . .

Is it weird that someone like me, whose nights are plagued by nightmares and shadows, *likes* horror? Shouldn't I run away from it instead of being drawn to it? Mom can't stand it. She doesn't like anything dark or scary or violent. Chantal is like me, though. Since she's been gone it's harder for me to find people to see horror movies with. You know, I think she has read even more Stephen King books than I have.

In case you're wondering, I'm going to do the test tomorrow. Or the next day for sure. Unless I get my period before then. Please?

• • •

Sunday, Jan. 12, 1987
Dear Diary,
So I decided on *Dracula* and am most of the way through it already. I thought it might be a heavy read, being written so long ago, but it's very good and I've hardly put it down.

Now check out this passage I just read:

"I felt the same vague terror which had come to me before and the same sense of some presence . . . Beside the bed . . . stood a tall, thin man, all in black. I knew him at once from the description of the others. The waxen face: The high aquiline nose, on which the light fell in a thin white line; the parted red lips, with the sharp white teeth showing between; and the red eyes . . . I would have screamed out, only that I was paralyzed."

Doesn't it sound familiar? I mean, besides the fact that I never can see their facial features, so no aquiline noses or red eyes, this is the description of my shadow-people visits. In fact, it sounds incredibly like my thin man in a hat, minus the sharp white teeth.

Am I being visited by vampires? The idea is less appealing all of a sudden.

● ● ●

Monday, Jan. 13, 1987
Dear Diary,
Have you ever wondered if something could be real, something you don't really believe could be, but deep inside you know it actually might?

And then you suddenly get confirmation that what you didn't believe could happen is happening and the imagined becomes reality and your entire world feels like it has turned inside out and upside down?

Yeah. I got the test done. It's confirmed. I'm pregnant. Fuck.

● ● ●

Midnight
Dear Diary,
So I just got off the phone with Chantal. I told her and oh my God I feel so much better. After her initial reaction of, "Shit, Poppy," which honestly sounded a little judgemental, she became the supportive and sympathetic best friend I remembered and needed.

Mom's going to get annoyed when she sees the phone bill. I'm only supposed to phone long distance for special occasions

180

like birthdays, but I'll make up a reason I had to call and spend a whole hour on the phone.

Anyway, angry Mom or not, I feel so relieved now that I've told someone. And not just anyone, but my best friend. Even though she's far away I feel so much less alone. I sure do wish she still lived here so she could be with me while I go through this. She said they won't let me go alone anyway, that you're supposed to have someone with you, so I have to tell Kareem (no), Mom (no way) or a friend. So, the question is, Amy or Belinda?

I'm going to call the clinic at the hospital tomorrow. Chantal told me I shouldn't have waited so long to get the test done and there's a time limit so I need to make the appointment soon. I so wish she could be next to me holding my hand while I make that call.

● ● ●

Wednesday, Jan. 14, 1987
Dear Diary,
I made the call and the appointment. Then I cried myself to sleep.

It's not really about the life inside me, though of course I have some guilt about that. But it's an unwanted life, so what kind of life would it even be? I feel OK about my decision. But I don't feel so OK about how I got here. Basically, I feel stupid. And immature and irresponsible. This would have been preventable, obviously, if I had made more responsible choices. But I rarely do, do I? So I have no sympathy for myself and feel like nobody else would or should either. Which is why I don't know who to tell or to ask for help.

I guess it's the loneliness that hurts the most. And it doesn't help that it's freezing cold outside and gets dark at four thirty in the afternoon. So depressing.

• • •

Friday, Jan. 16, 1987

Dear Diary,

So I told Belinda. I went to her place and we sat on her bed, and when I got the courage to get the words out, a big sob and flood of tears tumbled out along with them.

Belinda cried, too, and hugged me and stepped up as the exact supportive friend I needed. But even while I was grateful for her sympathetic response I kept thinking it was too exaggerated somehow, like she was *acting* supportive rather than actually *being* supportive, but that's probably just me being insecure because I don't think I deserve any of it.

She also kept going on about how I must have agonized over the decision and how hard it must have been for me to choose to end the pregnancy. But no, that's not it at all. I hate having to do this and I hate that I got myself into this mess, but as I wrote before, I'm fine with my choice. I know it's the right one for me. No question. But she didn't seem to hear me when I said that.

Whatever. She's there for me and she's going to come wait for me at my appointment, which is what counts. It turns out she really is a good friend, just when I need one the most.

• • •

Thursday, Jan. 17, 1987

Dear Diary,

So it's done.

It was Tuesday, but I've been really out of it for a couple of days and kind of feel like I've been to Hell and back.

First, the doctor was super mean and judgemental. When I first went in on Monday I was relieved she was a woman, thinking she would be more understanding than a man. Like a female doctor would have to be kind of a feminist or on my side or something.

Wrong.

She asked me a bunch of questions I think they have to ask about how I got pregnant and my relationship with the guy and why I wanted to terminate, and I felt embarrassed and ashamed, unable to make my answers come out sounding like they even made any sense. At some point she asked why I hadn't come in as soon as I knew I was pregnant and I don't even remember what I was exactly going to say, but my sentence started with, "I thought–" but she cut me off right away and said, "Well, obviously you didn't *think* much at all or you wouldn't be here, would you?"

I didn't say anything in reply, just sat there like a scolded child, and I stopped trying to explain myself after that.

Because even as I was sitting there feeling small and defensive about all her judgements and thinking of comebacks that would never actually make their way out of my mouth, I was silently judging myself, too. Still, I couldn't stop thinking how unprofessional she was to make such comments to me. That's not her job, is it? She doesn't know me or anything about my life or what made me get into this situation or come to this decision.

They gave me an ultrasound, which made it feel like a real pregnancy. I mean, it is a real pregnancy of course, but – well, you know what I mean. The worst part, though, was they made me drink tons of water first so my bladder would be full. Apparently that made them see it better when they pushed as hard as they could on my stomach and ready-to-burst bladder over and over again! I kept my eyes closed the whole time and didn't look at the screen. It didn't need to be any more real than it already was.

Anyway, I got my appointment for the actual thing the very next day. Belinda skipped school to go with me. I was pretty scared and felt pretty grateful to her for being there for me. Especially since everyone else was really cold to me, even the nurse who was supposedly there to comfort me. Belinda wanted to come in with me but they said that's not allowed. I was kind of glad, but it also would have been nice to have a friendly person in the room.

I don't actually remember the . . . procedure . . . very well, because I was a little bit drugged, but not nearly enough. It actually hurt like crazy. Like my insides were being twisted in knots and then torn out. I think I cried a lot and I asked them to stop at least once, but they said, "Just a few more seconds" and kept going. Maybe it *was* just seconds, but I swear each one lasted an hour.

Most of the time since then is kind of a blurry haze of cramps, bleeding, tears, shadow-people, and random, disjointed memories.

There have been a lot of phone calls from Belinda. Also I'm pretty sure she got insulted and sulky when I didn't invite her to come over after. She came home with me in the taxi, but then I just wanted to go to bed and I guess that made me ungrateful. There have been questions from Mom, too. I told her I have food poisoning and that's why I've been in the bathroom so much, but she seems to be able to tell I'm hiding something. What I'm hiding, besides the truth, is a ton of blood-soaked maxi pads. It's actually a bit scary how much I'm bleeding. I hope it slows down soon. They said I don't have to worry unless I get a fever. So I'm reminding myself not to worry, over and over again. Also, they said I have to use maxi pads for the whole time and even for my next period. Gross. I've been using tampons since I was fifteen!

I guess I should go call Belinda (again) while I have some energy. I feel like a bad friend. I also feel like a bad ex-girlfriend for never telling Kareem. But it's too late now that it's all over.

It's all over. At least that.

• • •

Saturday, Jan. 19, 1987
Dear Diary,
What a day.

I felt a bit better today, so I went shopping downtown with Belinda. I had to act normal and get out of the house so Mom would stop worrying and questioning me, and Belinda really wanted me to go to Bikini Village with her so she could get a new bikini to wear in Florida when she goes for March break with her family.

I hate bathing suit shopping, especially in winter when my skin is so white it glows in the dark, so you can imagine how much it glows under those fluorescent changing-room lights! No way was I going to try on bikinis wearing this horrible, bloody, diaper-sized pad anyway, so I just hung around waiting to give advice to Belinda while I silently envied her womanly boobs and thin legs. (Her stomach's actually not very flat, though. I would wear a low-cut one-piece if I had her body, but she got the tiniest string bikini she could squeeze into. It's blue so it really shows off her eyes, but you might not notice that so much because of the way her other parts totally spill out of it. For sure she won't be able to swim in it at all. But I'm sure none of the guys on the beach will be complaining.)

We went to the food court after for fries and Diet Cokes and Belinda totally freaked me out when she looked past me, her blue eyes bulging dramatically, and said, "Oh my God, is that Kareem?"

I was a hundred percent sure she was just messing with me, in a not very funny way at all, and I was about to get mad at her for being so inappropriate, but when I turned around it *was* Kareem!

Maybe he wouldn't even have seen us, but she had exclaimed pretty loudly (on purpose?) so, he turned and, of course, came over to say hi.

He was a little cold, but more in an awkward way than, like, mad or mean or anything. I'm pretty sure I hurt him pretty bad when I broke up with him, so maybe he's not over me yet. I, of course, was awkward, too, for reasons you know but he doesn't.

"'Sup, Poppy?" he said. "You look good."

I know that's just something you say, but I was really shocked because I'm pretty sure I looked as awful as I felt. I was actually embarrassed to see him while looking so terrible, because you always want to look good when you see your ex. Even when you're the one who broke up. I still have some cramps, plus I felt so gross and self-conscious with my bulky pad, and I was really hot in my boots and winter coat in the mall. I hate going shopping in the winter.

"No I don't," I shot back too abruptly.

"It wasn't an insult," he said, looking confused and sounding a bit insulted himself. Then he nodded in Belinda's direction and said, "Hey."

"*Hi Kareem*," she said, widening her eyes again and putting too much emphasis on his name. "It's *so* weird that we ran into you!"

"Why?" he said. "Don't you run into people all the time? What's the big deal?"

I suddenly had this horrible feeling that she was going to find a way to let the skeleton slip out of my closet. She had the fact that she was bursting with a big secret written all over her face and I could tell she was totally enjoying it. My blood started pulsing in my ears.

"No big deal at all," I said, again sounding cold and abrupt. "You're so weird, Belinda."

I could tell she didn't like me dismissing her like that at all, but I just kept talking, dying to get away – get *her* away – from

Kareem. "I have to go, actually. I'm late and my mom's going to kill me."

"Hm. You're always late for something, aren't you Poppy?" Belinda said, a taunting tone in her voice. I could have slapped her, knowing exactly what she was referring to, but I just ignored her stupid comment as if it meant nothing.

"Say hi for me," Kareem said.

"Huh?" I said, my mind a little clouded with panic.

"To your mom. Say hi. She's – was – always nice to me."

"Yeah, she liked you," I said, regretting the use of the past tense.

"Hug?" he said.

"Of course," I said and moved into his outstretched arms uncomfortably. He held me a little extra tight for a couple of seconds and as I relaxed into his body this huge wave of sorrow washed over me. I felt like here was this nice guy who had liked me and respected me and I had done him wrong not once but twice, first by breaking up for no good reason I can remember, and then by not telling him what he probably deserved to know. I might not have thought all of those things in that moment, but I know I felt profoundly sad, and now I guess those are the reasons why.

"Aw, you guys are so cute! But we have to go, don't we, Poppy?" Belinda said. So now she was the one impatient to leave.

We said bye to Kareem and headed to the metro in silence.

"Why so quiet?" she asked cheerfully once we were on the train.

"Am I quiet?" I said. "Just thinking, I guess." Inside I wanted to yell at her, to tell her off for being insensitive in such a sensitive situation, but then I realized she hadn't actually said or done anything outright, so what did I actually have to accuse her of?

Could it all be in my head? After all, she's been there for me through all of this. Why do I keep thinking the worst of her? Shouldn't I be grateful?

• • •

Monday, Jan. 20, 1987
Dear Diary,
I feel much better and I'm going back to school today, but before I leave I want to tell you about this very strange feeling I occasionally have first thing in the morning.

Sometimes when I awake I have the lingering sense that I have been living a completely other reality, which sounds crazy, I know, but I have this vague notion that what I just experienced, as in the dream I just had, is a continuation of something I have in fact been living for a long time. But it always fades too fast for me to actually remember anything concrete.

I really wish I could remember more or explain it better, because in the moment the feeling is so real.

Last night I woke up from a dream – an actual dream, not a shadow visit – with the absolute conviction that I live two complete existences in parallel, one in my waking life and one in my dream world. Sometimes I open my eyes and quickly close them again, trying to grasp the memories of my dreaming existence, which are so close, like a word you can't quite remember but it feels like it's right there on the tip of your tongue. But the memory fades again, every time, until the next time.

• • •

Wednesday, Jan. 22, 1987
Dear Diary,
I hope I'm not too tired to enjoy myself tonight. I'm going to a party with Belinda. I don't know what kind of people throw a party on a Wednesday night, but she wants me to go with her so

I am. I'm trying to feel more positive toward her and about our friendship.

She's always bubbly and fun, after all.

She bought a striped crop top just like one I have and insists we both wear them so we can be like twins. Yeah, right. I actually like the top on me, because it shows off my (still) flat stomach while making my boobs look a little bit bigger, but next to Belinda, well, I already know I'm going to pale in comparison and feel jealous of her all night. There I go again! What's wrong with me?

I would back out if I could, actually, but Belinda would get too mad.

My cramps are gone and I'm not bleeding so much anymore, just like a light period now, but I'm still tired and more so today, because the shadow-people woke me up last night and then my fear kept me up most of the rest of the night.

It was the thin man in a hat who came to watch me this time. He seems to like showing up after I've done something bad. As if I don't have enough real people judging me, I need him, too?

I'm trying to be funny, but I think he scares me more than the other ones. Unless they're all the same one and it – he?, she? – takes on different forms on different nights? Anyway, I was so sleepy today I kept dozing off in class. I would practically just black out, actually. I was afraid I would start to snore or something and get in trouble, or embarrassed at the very least.

Anyway, I slipped into the Bistro at one point to grab a coffee and saw the most amazing thing. On the bulletin board there was a flyer advertising a lecture. It said: "Sleep Paralysis and Night Visitors: An eye-opening presentation." The event, presented by some sleep clinic, was last weekend, so I missed it. But sleep paralysis? Night visitors? You don't have to tell me more for me to understand that they are talking about what happens to me! That means my nightmares have a name. And more important still: finally, for once, I'm not alone.

Chapter 9
Fall 1988

Monday, Sept. 5, 1988

Dear Diary,

School starts tomorrow, which is exciting, but I'm actually a little disappointed that I'm not working. I've reduced my schedule to four days at Macabre, the bookstore I've been working at all summer. It's fun to finally have a job I actually like, unlike the fast-food jobs, the cleaning, and even the babysitting. I mean, what could be more perfect for me than working in a bookshop that specializes in fantasy, horror, and the occult? I have to remember to thank Dave again for getting me the job through his connections in the publishing world.

I'm only taking three courses this semester. School overwhelms me easily, and I figure it didn't kill me to stretch Cégep over a third year, so I can do my university gradually too, at least to start. I'm taking some literature courses and hoping to switch into Creative Writing by next year. I'm still disappointed that I didn't get into the program, but it's my own fault for slacking off and not getting the marks I could have in Cégep.

I just don't understand how you turn down a party or a night with friends to stay home and *study!*

I have to go. I'm meeting Alex downtown for a movie. We're seeing an action movie called *Die Hard*. What else do you see with your boyfriend but an action movie, right? Well, this one is supposed to be really good, at least.

I have a confession to make. I've been starting to think I might want to break up with him. What is wrong with me? I make no sense!

We're just about to hit the six-month mark, longer than I've been with anyone, and he is, truly, the perfect boyfriend. Besides being smart and considerate, he's good-looking (I still get lost in his transparent, hazel eyes that glow like a cat's eyes against his dark skin) and, as you know, good in bed. I mean, sometimes I feel like we could be a bit more adventurous, but how many guys make sure to give their woman an orgasm *every single time*?

OK, gotta go.

$$\bullet \ \bullet \ \bullet$$

Tuesday, Sept. 6, 1988
Dear Diary,
I can't believe it.

Chantal is back!!!

Alex wanted me to stay over at his place last night, but I told him we both needed a good night's sleep since we both have our first university classes today. When I got home there was a message on the answering machine from Chantal and I was puzzled that she had left a Montreal number for me to call her back at. It was too late when I got home, but I called first thing when I woke up this morning and sure enough she's back . . . to stay! She has known for, like, two months, but she wanted to surprise me.

Her dad's job was transferring him back here and at first she was going to move into a residence at Dalhousie. But then her boyfriend Jonas announced he was moving to Toronto and they decided to split up (they were together for three years!) and she figured she would rather come back to Montreal with her family – which includes me! She had switched programs from something science-oriented to an arts program, but even though she's artistic she found it too artsy fartsy for her liking, so she decided to take a break from school for a semester, which her parents aren't thrilled about, of course. So she'll be looking for a job. I always saw myself as the lost one who can't find my path in life, but I guess I'm not the only one.

I am floored. All these years of not having a best friend, and finally accepting I will never have a true best friend again, and now she's back! How did she keep it secret from me all summer??? I'm going to reread the letters she sent (not that many of them, in fact) and see if I missed any clues!

But first, a shower and off to class at Concordia University! Then Chantal is totally coming over for dinner!

• • •

Wednesday, Sept. 7, 1988
Dear Diary,
I can't say university classes feel much different from Cégep classes. Books to read, essays to write, what else is there to say?

Chantal did come over for dinner. Dave remembered her, but she didn't really remember him. He and Mom weren't officially dating yet when Chantal moved away so she had only met him one or two times. Mom kept going on about how Chantal has changed, how she looks older, and she's so mature now and all that. You know, the things parents say.

Though in fact it's true. I imagine I have changed in the last four years, too, but I feel like I'm the same party animal who doesn't like to study and can't stick with a guy for more than a few months; Chantal has had this three-year relationship, went to university for two years already, and has had all this life experience, living in a new city and everything else. Like she's been out to see the world and I've stayed in my same old messed up, shadow-infested life.

Yeah. The shadow-people are still there. I don't always bother writing about their visits, but I saw the dark, looming shape last night. There's not much else to tell. I know that what I have is called sleep paralysis, but I don't know much more than that. I should look it up at the bookstore! We have a whole section on dreams and dream interpretation. It's a good place to start, right?

• • •

Thursday, Sept. 8, 1988
Dear Diary,
Alex and Chantal both asked me to get together after work tomorrow night, so I've made a plan for the three of us to meet up at Carlos and Pepe's for tacos and frozen daiquiris. I wonder how they'll get along?

I have hardly any time to write these days, between work, school, Alex, and Chantal.

What can I say, I guess I'm finally popular!

• • •

Friday, Sept. 9, 1988
Dear Diary,
My old, perceptive friend still knows me too well.

Chantal and Alex got along great and we had a really good time. They're both nice and pretty sociable, and there was lots to talk about. I mean, even I don't know everything about her life from the last four years. Our letter-writing dwindled over time and we only saw each other once a year: the time I went to visit and the three times they came here.

Alex was being his usual sweet, doting self, sitting next to me, holding my hand, giving me the occasional compliment (but also the occasional disappointed look whenever I lit a cigarette). It's all a bit much for me sometimes; it's nice to be adored, but he does tend to make me want to unstick from him and reclaim some personal space. I must confess that I enjoyed the fact that Chantal got to see me in my near-perfect relationship after having been in one herself for so long. I was beginning to wonder if I would ever find a solid, long-term partner and then I met Alex, the ideal boyfriend. Why exactly had I been thinking of breaking up with him?

Once Alex left us (he was a bit pouty over the fact that I chose to leave with Chantal and spend the night alone) and Chantal and I hopped on the metro together, I asked what she had thought of him. "And be honest!" I insisted. "He's cute, though, isn't he? Aren't his eyes *amazing*? And he's so sweet," I continued.

"Yes, he is definitely good-looking and sweet. Great boyfriend material. So when are you planning to break up with him?"

"What is that supposed to mean?" I felt a bit hurt that she clearly didn't appreciate his long list of qualities. "You just said he's great boyfriend material; why would I break up with him?"

"Come on! All that hand-holding and adoration, the way he gazes lovingly at you every five minutes? It is indeed sweet, but it would be a lot even for *me*. For someone as independent-natured as you it must be all you can do to keep breathing when he's fawning all over you."

My initial reaction was to get defensive, but we both knew she was totally right. I hoped it hadn't showed too much in my demeanour during the evening and that her insight came from having insider knowledge about my character.

"Chantal, what is the matter with me? Why can't I fall head over heels for a guy like Alex? He's kind, responsible, and respectful. And he's good-looking and generous in bed to boot! He's everything I should want."

"Yes, but the answer is simple: *Il ne t'excite pas!*"

She was absolutely right: On paper he has all the right stuff, but my stomach hasn't flip-flopped when I see him for at least a couple of months.

"It's not my place to tell you what to do with your love life, but the longer you wait, the harder his heart's going to break when you finally do it."

She's right, I guess. And she still knows me. It's like she never left!

• • •

Sunday, Sept. 11, 1988
Dear Diary,
I'm spending tonight with Alex. He's been sad all weekend because I've spent it all working and hanging around with Chantal.

I know I've neglected him, but the pouting is really getting on my nerves.

I keep thinking about breaking up, but it just doesn't make sense to leave such a great guy. There is seriously not one good reason!

Maybe a night with just the two of us will make it better.

• • •

Monday, Sept. 12, 1988
Dear Diary,

Chantal found a job already! We were walking up St. Laurent and she stopped to check out the window of this really modern furniture store. Then she saw that there was a sign in the window that they had a sales position available. She went in to ask about it and came out with the job! She said she really clicked with the woman who owns the place, plus she studied design and has sales experience from Halifax summer jobs. She still has to give in her CV, but said it's just a formality. She's going in tomorrow!

Once again our lives are in sync: I want to be a writer and I work in a bookstore; she wants to be a designer and is going to work in a furniture store.

And now, about last night.

We ended up at Alex's place and I slept over. It was the usual routine: foreplay until I climaxed, then intercourse until he did. As usual he tried to cuddle with me to go to sleep afterward, but I needed room to breathe. I can't even sleep facing someone, let alone all snuggled up; I feel like I'm not getting enough oxygen. I explained it to him – again – and went to sleep feeling like the bad guy and annoyed because of it.

• • •

Wednesday, Sept. 14, 1988
Dear Diary,
Chantal and I met at Le Grand Café on St. Denis for a pitcher of sangria on the leafy back *terrasse* after work today because she wanted to talk to me about an idea she had, which is that we get an apartment together!

Seriously, I wasn't really even considering moving out. I have it good at home; Mom's not around that much and she pretty much treats me like an adult. I have my own phone line and I can go out as late as I want and even sleep at Alex's as long as I let her know.

But Chantal says since we both have paycheques, why not? She had been looking forward to being on her own when she was still planning to live in residence at school.

I felt bad, like I should have been more excited about it. I mean, the idea of our own place is pretty awesome, but I don't know. I need to think about it, and that's what I told her. I hope she's not hurt or angry.

● ● ●

Thursday, Sept. 15, 1988
Dear Diary,
OK, what is going on?

Alex met me at the store today for lunch . . . and asked if I wanted to move in together!

I was really caught off-guard and I somehow blurted out that Chantal and I had just agreed to move out and be roommates. I didn't realize I had made that decision, but I guess I have now. I better let Chantal know!

He's clearly hurt. But man, moving in? Why would he want to do that anyway? If I think I have it good at home, he has it great. He has the basement all to himself with a gigantic room and his own bathroom. He's living rent-free, which is perfect while he's in business school full time. Even if I were hopelessly in love with him (if only) I think it would be too soon for me. Maybe Chantal's right and I should just rip the Band-Aid off and break up now. When I imagine it I feel terrible because I picture him all heartbroken, but I also imagine myself all liberated.

Then I think of all the nice things he does for me, and how he kept me on the straight and narrow last semester so I could finally finish Cégep, and I think how good he is for me. The relationship deserves a shot, right? I'm not going to leave him yet.

• • •

3:15 a.m.

Dear Diary,

I just broke free from an episode of sleep paralysis. This was a new one.

After my initial panic subsided and I realized – as always – that I could still breathe, I grew somewhat calmer and I waited, as I've done countless times before. Then I felt a presence –right in front of my face. I couldn't see it; I don't even know if my eyes were open or closed, but I could sense it right there in front of my face, breathing, not inches from me. It breathed heavier and heavier, inhaling ever so deeply, sucking the air right out of my mouth and my lungs.

"If I don't scream now I won't have any breath left to do it later," I thought. As always it took time and effort, but I found my scream and I woke up. I think I didn't actually have enough lung capacity to outright scream, because I felt like I was gasping for air once I was fully awake.

Normally my one comfort through it all is that I can breathe, so I have that one thing to keep me calm and focused as I deal with the terror and the paralysis. Have they figured that out now? So they can rob me of my breath, the one thread I have to hold on to?

• • •

Saturday, Sept. 17, 1988

Dear Diary,

A bunch of us went out dancing last night. We went to Metropolis, which is right at the intersection between the Gay Village and the red-light district, so the entertainment starts before you even get inside the club, with the prostitutes in their shorts and fuck-me boots, the transvestites with bigger hair and better legs than me, the Harleys lined up along Ste. Catherine Street, and tons of tough and tattooed characters wandering past the lineups of us clubgoers waiting to dance the night away.

It was a girls' night out, which was just what I wanted. We were five: Belinda, Giselle, a friend of hers named Isabella, Chantal, and me. Chantal seemed a little shy at first, since she didn't know anyone else, but dark lights, loud music, a huge dance floor, and a drink took care of that before long. We each only had one rum and Coke, because they were expensive (eight dollars!) and weak, so between that and the cost of our entrance we were already broke.

Belinda was, in fact, almost too friendly with Chantal, if that makes sense. She acted super gushy when I introduced them, all "Poppy has told me so much about you!" and "You're so pretty!" and "We're going to be such good friends, the three of us!" It was kind of nice in a way, but it felt forced, like somehow she wanted to prove she's not jealous of our practically lifelong friendship.

I didn't notice Isabella being all that pretty when I first met her outside, but she's tall and confident and has really thick, long hair and everywhere she went guys' heads were turning her way. Belinda was her usual overt self, climbing up on the speakers in her skin-tight dress that put her best assets on full display and grinding her way through "Pour Some Sugar On Me," blond head thrown back and arms in the air. Chantal and Giselle are both more quiet in their good looks. Giselle is elegant, long-legged and chocolate-skinned, with short-cropped hair and the brightest, most stunning smile you have ever seen, while Chantal has grown into her classic good looks, with an elegance of her own as well as a subtle sexiness.

I can't say I had the best time; I'm PMSing, was feeling bloated, and my hair had gone frizzy so I felt a little homely and invisible compared to the rest of my gang, and I didn't manage to get lost in the music and dance the way I sometimes do. I think I was too caught up in comparing myself to everyone else, constantly noticing who has better dance moves, a nicer body, or more stylish outfit. And then I kicked myself for being so superficial and insecure.

After we left we went across the street to Burger King, where the after-hours parade of characters never disappoints. For example, there was a minor scuffle between two scantily-clad women whom I wouldn't want to mess with, and when I went to the ladies' room I found myself waiting in line behind an extremely tall blond, standing out in stilettos and a fur coat (in September!), who, when I got a better look, turned out to be no lady at all, if you get what I mean.

The five of us managed to find a cleanish table and absorbed ourselves in conversation so we wouldn't look too hard at any of the unsavoury and most likely none-too-sober characters. Chantal and I mentioned that we were starting our apartment hunting and right away Belinda jumped in with, "Can I come, too? It would be so fun to be roommates, the three of us!" She launched into plans for parties and wardrobe sharing, while Giselle and Isabella gave advice about neighbourhoods we should look at and things to ask our potential landlords.

Once we had left and Chantal and I were alone on the bus, she turned to me and said, "No offence, but no way am I moving in with that girl."

"Don't worry," I said, "I wasn't planning to. We're not even that close."

"I'm sorry, but I don't like her."

"She's a little – insincere and manipulative," I said, feeling slightly guilty for talking behind her back but also relieved because now I know it's not just my imagination.

"Mets-en!" Chantal asserted, which basically means, "You're telling me!"

Suffice it to say our roommate plans will be moving forward unchanged.

• • •

Monday, Sept. 19, 1988
Dear Diary,
We found an apartment!

It was the fourth place we called and the second we looked at.

No way did we expect to find something that fast. Especially since the official moving day in Montreal is July first, so there aren't as many places available at this time of year. But I guess luck is on our side, because it's a cute place on a nice street near a great park.

It's on Christophe-Colomb near Parc Lafontaine. It's the third floor of a triplex with an outdoor staircase. We're wondering how it will be in the winter with the snow and ice, but we'll know soon enough! It's going to be tricky to move in up and down all those stairs for sure, but I have always loved the look of those outdoor stairs: so typically Montreal (though a weird architectural choice for a city with winters like ours).

It's a four and a half, with room in the kitchen for a table, a decent living room, and two bedrooms, of course. I offered to take the smaller one; I'm pretty sure I can just fit my double bed with one bedside table. The closet is huge, the length of one whole wall with folding doors, so I will put my dresser inside the closet and still have room to hang clothes up next to it. I will have to measure, but I should be able to squeeze a dressing table into the room as well, on the wall at the foot of the bed, just next to the door.

I really want to put white sheer curtains on the window. I find that such a romantic look. And I was thinking of painting the walls pink. But then I would need new sheets, because my purple ones would clash.

We're going to have to buy a sofa and a TV and a table and chairs . . . it's going to cost us, but our parents will help and it's going to be so fun! Our very own place! Best friends together again!

We're supposed to move in on October first. It's so quick and we're not really ready, but we can't pass it up. It feels like a new beginning!

● ● ●

Thursday, Sept. 22, 1988
Dear Diary,
Moving plans are moving forward and meanwhile I've decided to cancel my annual mix-and-match birthday dinner.

Everything has happened so fast and there's so much to do, with lease signing and packing, shopping, reserving a truck and friends to help us move. Dave said he would drive the truck. Chantal has her licence – she got it in Nova Scotia – but she's never driven a van or truck and she said she's scared to drive in Montreal. The roads are much busier than in Halifax.

As for the party, we decided we'll wait and host one after we move in. It will be a joint birthday and housewarming party.

Speaking of everything moving fast, Mom's clearly annoyed with me about all of this. I think her feelings are hurt that I want to move out and she thinks it's all happening too quickly. So basically, she's taking it personally that I'm leaving home when I don't need to, and she thinks I'm being irresponsible by making all these decisions on the fly. She didn't actually say any of those things in so many words, we're too WASPy to be so direct, but she made herself understood in her passive-aggressive way.

Dave, always the peacemaker, said to give her time and she'll be just fine, which I know is absolutely true. I just have to remember not to take her reactions personally now.

● ● ●

Saturday, Sept. 24, 1988
Dear Diary,
Can't anyone just be happy for me?

Mom's still being curt with me and Alex is sulking. Why do they think it's all about *them?* This is about moving forward with *my* life, not about me wanting to abandon anyone else or choosing one person over another. Grrr.

● ● ●

Tuesday, Sept. 27, 1988
Dear Diary,
It's hard to find time to write these days with preparations for moving out added to work, school, and boyfriend. I'm trying not to show how overwhelmed I am, though, because Mom's still annoyed with me for being "rash and impulsive". She has a point, I admit, about timing this move right when I just started university classes, but I have never been one to think things through much, so why change now? Seize the day, I say!

Today as I was going through our bookshelves, deciding which of my books to take with me, to leave here, and to donate to the library, I decided to look up sleep paralysis in Dave's *Encyclopedia Britannica* collection. (Why did I never think of doing that before?) Well, it was there and it sure was interesting, so I thought I should write down some of what I found out.

First of all, sleep paralysis is something everyone has, in fact. It just means that when we're in the REM cycle we are paralyzed so that we don't physically act out our dreams and hurt ourselves. Some people occasionally (or often) wake up while they're in the paralyzed state, but not completely, so their mind is basically awake, but not their body.

I know all about that.

Then some people, not many, experience hallucinations where they see or sense some type of presence in the room watching them. In some cases the presence even touches them, often sitting or pushing on their chest making it difficult to breathe.

I know all about that, too.

I had chills reading about it. And I came to a realization: not only are the shadow-people sleep-paralysis-induced hallucinations, but so was the Curtain Lady! I can't believe I never made the connection before. It seems so obvious now. Suddenly all the connections are starting to link up in my brain, kind of like when you hear a new word for the first time and from that day on you start hearing it everywhere. (I remember that happened the first time I heard the word "innocuous.")

I feel like a light just came on that explains my whole life! I mean, there's a scientific name and explanation for all of it. I even read that some scientists believe all those stories of alien abductions are caused by episodes of sleep paralysis.

What a sense of relief! Ironically, it's as if a weight has been lifted off my chest, allowing me to feel so much less alone and so much less crazy!

● ● ●

Thursday, Sept. 29, 1988

Dear Diary,

Today is my twentieth birthday. I'm going to pack all day, have a quiet family dinner with Mom, Dave, and Alex then meet up with Chantal and Belinda for drinks and maybe dancing. I know Chantal doesn't love her, but she promises to be nice for my benefit, especially since it's my birthday. And Belinda's a little wild and always fun to party with. Alex won't be joining us because he has an important exam at eight thirty tomorrow. He's so responsible.

• • •

Friday, Sept. 30, 1988

Dear Diary,

While Alex may be the perfect boyfriend on paper, sometimes I think he really doesn't know me at all. Like he knows just what to do for a woman, but doesn't always take into account the personality of his *actual* woman, i.e. me. He gave me what was probably quite an expensive necklace, but it wasn't my style at all. First of all, it's gold and everyone knows I only wear silver, lots and lots of it. You really can't miss it. Second of all, the necklace is extremely classic and delicate, not my style at all. I like dangly earrings and chunky rings made in Mexico or Morocco and I've been building my collection of bangles since 1984. Third of all, the pendant is a teddy bear holding a heart. I am not the mushy, cutesy romance type, which I have outright told Alex many times. So is it that he doesn't actually get me at all or that he's just hoping (in vain) to change me?

I'm not actually the cold-hearted bitch I am making myself sound like, so of course I didn't say all those things to him. I kissed him, told him he was very sweet, removed the silver chains

I was already wearing, and let him put his token of romance and affection around my neck. This all happened over dessert and I could swear I caught Mom rolling her eyes for a second as I opened the box: I come by my lack of lovey-doveyness honestly.

In the end it was just Chantal and me for our night out. Belinda called at the last minute to cancel. She was chipper, but it was clearly feigned. Something was bothering her and I knew she wanted me to pry and coax it out of her, but I wasn't in the mood so I just said "OK, no problem," and promised to call her soon.

Chantal and I decided just to hit Crescent St. We started at the Thursday's dance club in the basement, but it lived up to its reputation of being a meat market full of older businessmen hoping to score with younger women looking for a good time and a thick wallet, and we got turned off pretty quick. Finally we ended up at Sir Winston's, where the vibe is similarly meat marketesque, but at least there's less of an age gap between the sexes. We ended up having a total blast dancing, flirting, and drinking just enough to let loose but not enough to get sick (I am finally learning).

We both had to work at ten this morning, so we left well before last call and took cabs to our separate homes for the last time.

● ● ●

Saturday, Oct. 1, 1988
Dear Diary,
It's moving day!

Dave has already left to pick up the truck and I have tons to do, but I had to tell you about the scare I got last night!

When I went to bed last night, I looked around my soon-to-be-former room, mentally saying goodbye, and my eyes came to rest on my window, where my old red curtains still hang. The curtains are staying – I've bought new sheer white ones for my new place – and I suddenly thought back to the Curtain Lady and got a little shiver. And then the curtains moved! I blinked, thinking my mind was playing tricks on me, but they kept moving and then they parted. I was frozen in place as I stared, fixated, waiting for the old silhouette to emerge – and out came a familiar shape, yes, but it was orange and fuzzy and jumped heavily down from the radiator.

"Pumpkin! You scared the shit out of me!" I gasped, going to pick him up for a final cuddle with my long-time roommate. "I'm going to miss you," I said, burying my face in his soft, plump body. But, as always, he only accepts affection on his own terms (I could learn a thing or two from him) so he squirmed, thumped to the floor again, and walked out on me.

A dark, looming shape came and visited my paralyzed self later in the night, so I'm not as well-rested as I had hoped to be. Why can't *he* walk out on me?

● ● ●

11:00 p.m.

Dear Diary,

We did it! We are moved in! There's so much to unpack, but at least our beds are set up and made and there are glasses in the kitchen cupboard and toilet paper in the bathroom so we can survive until morning when the work will begin again.

We had plenty of help with the move, but we're exhausted anyway. Our moms both helped us finish packing and load the truck and our dads helped get things moved into the new place. Phil helped, too, way more than I expected. He's thirteen and in high school now! I can't believe it. Obviously Alex was here with us all day (and is still here), being the faithful helper and even good old Stefano came to help, which was so sweet! Neither Chantal nor Alex had met him before and he made quite an impression with his hair, fast talking, and latest impressions, including all the main characters in *The Godfather*. Chantal was in stitches and almost spit out her beer – more than once – while we chilled out over pizza once everything was finally in the apartment.

• • •

Sunday, Oct. 2, 1988
Dear Diary,
Good morning!

After baptizing my new bedroom with Alex I had a long, peaceful sleep and I feel refreshed, optimistic, and excited about this new chapter in my life.

I hear voices and I smell coffee! Chantal is an absolute coffee addict, so there's going to be a lot of that delicious smell in our home. *Our home!*

I've got a long day of unpacking and organizing ahead of me, so off I go!

• • •

Monday, Oct. 3, 1988
Dear Diary,
Oh sweet, dreamless sleep!

I don't even care that it's pouring rain today. I feel awake and alive, even at nine in the morning.

Chantal had made coffee again by the time I woke up. She starts work at ten so she was already dressed and looking so professional! She got herself this really classy gray suit with a straight skirt and fitted blazer with stylish shoulder pads.

I'm not working today; I have classes. But I've been calculating expenses and I think I'm going to see if I can get my fifth day back at the store. My share of the rent is two hundred and fifty dollars, plus the phone and electricity bills. After paying for food I won't have any money left for fun working part-time at barely more than minimum wage.

Mom's coming over later, when she finishes work, to check out our place and lend a hand.

● ● ●

Tuesday, Oct. 4, 1988
Dear Diary,
Mom seems to have forgiven me and said lots of positive things about the apartment and the neighbourhood. She told me that the best poutine place in the city is just a couple of blocks away, so the three of us went. It's called La Banquise and it's very popular! And yeah, the poutine's good. It was cool to sit around with Mom and Chantal, smoking cigarettes and just talking like three friends. While we were there Mom told me two things: she and Dave are thinking about buying a place together, maybe a small condo, now that it's just the two of them. Also, Pumpkin is sick. She said he's lethargic and not eating much (very unlike him!) and she's going to take him to the vet later in the week if he doesn't seem better. She says he's probably just thrown off and a little sad because I'm not there and he needs time to adjust, but I've been away before, for way longer than four days, and he never acted like he missed me. Anyway, he's only fifteen and cats can live way longer than that, so whatever it is I'm sure it's not serious.

Everything's pretty much set up now. We're still waiting for our couch to come next week and we have some other finishing touches to do. I never did paint my bedroom walls. I'll get to it one of these days.

• • •

Wednesday, Oct. 5, 1988
Dear Diary,
So, last night Alex slept over and left his toothbrush behind. I called him later to tell him and he said he left it on purpose because then he wouldn't need to remember to bring one every time he sleeps over.

It makes sense, so why is it bugging me so much? I mean, it's just a toothbrush, but this is my and Chantal's apartment. Our *new* apartment. Is it normal for him just to assume he can keep his toothbrush here without checking with me or my roommate first? He left it in the bathroom and I took it out and put it in my room. It just doesn't seem right to me to see a third toothbrush on the sink when only two people live here. I didn't even mention it to Chantal.

So tonight we were talking about work and school and plans and everything and we came up with the perfect career: we should make our own magazine. Long ago we used to dream about it as we leafed through the pages of *Seventeen* – long before we ourselves were seventeen! But I want to write and she likes to design and we both love clothes and makeup, so doesn't it sound like a cool idea?

We can totally picture ourselves in a big, sunny office overlooking the city in our stylish clothes directing our staff and putting out our glossy pages. Still some details to work out, of course, but maybe Dave would know something about it. He works in book publishing, but he would have some information, no?

• • •

Thursday, Oct. 6, 1988
Dear Diary,
I can't believe how well I've been sleeping since moving in! I mean, I still have my same old bed and there's even more morning light that comes in with my new curtains, but I am sleeping like a baby.

• • •

Friday, Oct. 7, 1988
Dear Diary,
I can't believe it. Pumpkin is dead.

I love – loved – that cat and we've had him for what feels like my whole life. My whole life that I can remember, anyway. We've had him since before Dad died, when we still lived in our house in Montreal West.

Mom took him to the vet today. By that time he wasn't eating at all and could hardly walk. They basically said that they could run some very expensive tests, but that it was probably one of two things, both of which are terminal. So she decided to have him put down. She was going to call me, but I was at work and she didn't want to upset me, so she waited 'til the end of my shift and called to tell me after the fact. Her voice cracked and I could tell she was crying when she told me. She never cries; I don't remember ever seeing her cry except at Dad's funeral.

I went straight over and when I got there I hugged her and she burst into tears. I was crying, too, of course, but it was weird.

She felt small and somehow older, as if I had never noticed her aging or changing my whole life and all of a sudden it hit me that her hair is almost all gray and she has crow's feet and laugh lines that I never saw before, not even when we had poutine just this week.

It made me feel grownup to be a visitor in my mother's home and to have her cry on my shoulder instead of the other way around.

• • •

Sunday, Oct. 9, 1988
Dear Diary,
Yesterday was a day of blasts from the past, some better than others.

First, I wandered around yesterday on my lunch break. It was a gloriously warm and sunny day, and at this time of year I like to take advantage of those, because a long, cold, gray winter is just around the corner.

Speaking of just around the corner, I was walking along de Maisonneuve near Concordia and the name of a small place caught my eye: Pâtisserie Trinh. Of course, it's not an uncommon Vietnamese name, but I wandered in out of curiosity, and who should I find behind the counter but my old friend!

"Trinh!" I exclaimed.

"Poppy!" she said, flashing that familiar smile.

"Is this *your* place?" I asked. It was tiny, but clean and beautifully arranged, with row upon row of beautiful pastries, cute cookies, and impressive cakes.

"Yes," she beamed. "I just opened one month ago, after I finished school."

"I can't believe it! Congratulations!"

More customers wandered in and she had to attend to them so I bought a couple of mille feuilles – which I had to insist on paying for – and left. Oh, I'm so happy for her! And so impressed. But not that surprised, honestly. She's so smart and was always amazing at baking. And I remember that her parents were not too keen on her pastry chef idea so she probably has extra motivation to succeed.

After work Chantal and I agreed to meet at the Peel Pub Showbar for drinks. Halfway through our pitcher, a familiar voice said "Hey, ladies." I looked up, as recognition set in and Chantal leapt up and threw her arms around the speaker.

"Olive!"

He hugged her back, lifting her right off the floor.

"Poppy! It's Olive!" she said to me excitedly once her feet were back on the ground.

"Act normal, act normal," I said silently to myself as my stomach turned and my vision went this bizarre combination of blurry and super clear.

"Hi Olive," I said, forcing a smile to my lips and getting up to kiss him politely on both cheeks. Turns out he's an air-kisser, a trait I generally dislike but for which on this occasion I was grateful.

Olive introduced us to his friend, John, a co-worker, and Chantal immediately insisted they pull up chairs and join us. I lit a cigarette and ordered another pitcher.

If you weren't in my head, you would say the whole night went absolutely fine. We caught up with each other's lives, reminisced about old times, and drank vast quantities of watered-down draft beer. A part of me was really tempted to just forgive, forget, relax, and have fun with my old friend. After all, I have so many good memories of Olive, why should they all be outweighed by one bad night? But they are. My pride and my growing feminist sensibilities wouldn't let me let it go.

Then again, I thought, he never meant to hurt me, I'm sure of it. And he probably feels bad about it. I watched Olive all night for signs of discomfort or a guilty conscience, but couldn't discern any. Then again, even Chantal didn't detect the awkwardness I was feeling. Whether that was because of the beer or my acting skills, I don't know.

On the topic of the beer, I was definitely drunk, but clear-thinking enough to formulate a little plan. As the night wore on and I thought more and more about our eventual departure I became quite sure that Chantal and Olive would exchange phone numbers, and I definitely did not want that door opened. Phone calls, future encounters, what if she invited him over? One night of pretending all was well with the world was one thing, but I had no desire for a repeat performance. If he re-entered our lives I would be faced with the choice between brushing his violation and betrayal under the rug or eventually confronting him. Neither appealed to me.

Well, everyone knows I've been known to drink so much I get sick. So that's what I was going to do last night. Glass after glass was poured and downed, and when I felt I was just at the tipping point between tipsy and sick, I shot Chantal my most worried face, said, "I'm going to be sick!" and ran to the bathroom. Great friend that she is, she was close on my heels and waited outside the stall while I leaned over the bowl and made coughing, retching, and spitting noises for a good five minutes or so. I came out wiping my mouth, to the disgusted and sideways looks of many, rinsed my mouth out for show, and said, "Let's get out of here before I puke again."

"We should just go say goodbye to Olive before we go," she said.

"I can't wait," I said. "I'll get a cab." I staggered toward the stairs, gripping my stomach. She shot a guilty look toward our faraway table and reluctantly followed me out.

Our taxi driver was a little nervous about letting me into the cab, but we convinced him and I opened the window wide, being sure to say how much better it made me feel.

At home I headed straight for the bathroom. I actually only meant to go pee, but I realized I was actually pretty dizzy and would pay for it today, so I stuck my finger down my throat and emptied myself of what alcohol I had not yet digested. I was extra loud about it, as my closing act.

It was just about the most dishonest I had ever been with my best friend, and my lack of guilt over it surprised me as I lay in bed after apologizing sheepishly for having overdone it. I guess I was in self-preservation mode or something.

Well, karma comes back for you, doesn't it?

For the first time in over a week I woke up paralyzed, with the thin man watching over me. Though I should know by now I can't blink him away, I did try, but all my efforts did was make me see him (it) clearly enough to notice he was wagging his finger at me as if I had done something naughty. After a brief (but not brief enough) struggle, I broke free with a gasp . . . and made a run for the toilet to throw up, for real this time.

● ● ●

Tuesday, Oct. 11, 1988
Dear Diary,
We are planning our housewarming/birthday party for Saturday!

Chantal still feels bad about not exchanging numbers with Olive and wants to try to remember his old phone number in case he or Darius still lives in the same apartment. (I doubt it; it was a crappy apartment. I even saw a roach once!) I burned his number and erased it from my memory way back when, after, well, you know. Anyway I told her I didn't want to dredge up old ties to Ricky because of *those* bad memories. I also said I thought we should stick to a dinner party with a select few guests in order not to be too loud and make enemies of our new neighbours. She accepted my lame excuses, though I'm sure she's wondering by now if something fishy's up.

We're inviting: Alex, of course, Roseline (a co-worker of Chantal's), Trinh, Stefano, Giselle, and Belinda.

Also, they're baaack! Thin man made another one of his petrifying appearances last night. (He is *not* invited to the party.)

• • •

Thursday, Oct. 13, 1988
Dear Diary,
Party plans are advancing, but listen to this!

I called Belinda to invite her, of course. I've had mixed feelings about her over the years, as you know, and I've drifted away from her since we're not at school together anymore, but we hung out for, like, two years in Cégep and she's always wild and fun if overt and a little fake, and we're great spades partners. I figured she might be a little cold because I hadn't called her since she backed out last-minute on my birthday, but whoa!

At first she *was* cold, responding to me with a curt, "Oh, hi," when I said it was me.

"Is everything OK?" I asked.

"It was until now."

"I see . . . Are you mad at me?"

"Why would I be mad at you, Poppy? Huh? Because you fucking *abandoned* me as soon as your *best friend* showed up in town? Because you ignored me at Metropolis and never once came to dance on the speakers with me like we used to? Because you totally excluded me from your little apartment plan, like I'm not *good enough* to live with you but *she* is?" (What is with people accusing me of thinking I'm better than them?)

"Belinda, what the hell are you talking about?" I asked, trying to keep my tone light. "We danced on the speakers together like one time, and I'm sorry, but Chantal's been my best friend since Grade Four. She's like my sister."

Silence. Then, her voice softer and cracking, (for dramatic effect?) "I thought *we* were like sisters." (I could visualize a close-up of her face, a single tear rolling down her cheek. Also, I'm pretty sure neither of us have ever said that.)

"After everything we went through together and the way I have always held your hand and supported you. After the *secrets* I kept for you. Do you actually think," she continued, pausing again, "that I would come to your *housewarming* party when you cut me out of your *house*?"

"I'm sorry, Belinda. I didn't mean to hurt your feelings." No lie.

"Hurt?" Pause. "You *destroyed* my feelings you cold-hearted bitch!" And . . . click.

What the Hell?

I've always known she's a drama queen, but am I really a cold-hearted bitch? I don't know whether to laugh or feel terrible. Well, at least Chantal will be happy about that particular name being crossed off the guest list – and my friendship list, too, it seems.

Oh, the people who *don't* think I am the worst person to ever walk this planet and *will* be attending our dinner party are: everyone else on the list, plus Trinh's boyfriend.

● ● ●

Sunday, Oct. 16, 1988
Dear Diary,
Despite some initial guest-list related stress we had a fantastic dinner party!

Everyone showed up practically on time laden with gifts and food and drink. Girls being girls, they all brought something besides their assigned dish, so we are now one plant (Trinh) and two scented candles (Giselle and Roseline) richer.

Chantal is not much more of a cook than I am so we decided to make it a potluck and in the end, that luckily meant we hardly had to make anything. As an appetizer, Alex brought spicy Jamaican beef patties homemade by his mom. Roseline – whom I had only met once before and who overflows with so much personality and joy that I totally get why Chantal was drawn to her – brought a traditional Haitian pumpkin soup in honour of the season. Stefano brought a bottle of Italian wine and what turned out to be the best lasagna I have ever eaten. (Sorry, Mom.) Trinh, of course, brought dessert. Not mille feuilles or one of her expertly decorated cakes, but Vietnamese mooncakes: pretty, flaky little pastries filled with coconut, bean, and egg – which is so much more delicious than it sounds! Her boyfriend, Jean-François, brought another bottle of wine. Giselle, who was coming straight from work and doesn't cook, brought . . . wine. We made salad, bought baguettes, and served pre-dinner rum and Cokes. We also bought two bottles of wine. You know, in case there wasn't enough.

Once everyone had arrived, cocktails were served and we had crowded around our not-nearly-big-enough table, I looked around, quite satisfied with both the eclectic spread and mix of characters, and felt thoroughly warmed by the friendship around me – as well as the rum in my belly. As Alex opened and poured the first bottle of wine, someone yelled, "Toast!" and both Chantal and I stood and raised our glasses simultaneously. "You go," I laughed, and she said, "To friendships old and new," pretty much exactly what I would have said. Glasses were clinked to the tune of "Cheers!" and *"Santé!"* with reminders to look at the eyes of the person, not the glass, in order to fend off any danger of being cursed with seven years of bad sex.

Alex was his usual polite, helpful, and charming self and everyone kept remarking on what a "perfect" couple we are. With all the outside approval I must admit I'm feeling better again about my relationship.

We sat around the table for hours, until the last drops of wine and rum were drunk and the last crumbs of pastry devoured. Once everyone but Chantal and Alex had gone, we agreed to leave the dishes 'til morning (or afternoon) and went off to bed.

I wish this entry could have ended there. But I woke up paralyzed in the night *again*. I didn't see anyone (or anything) lurking about, but as I patiently focused on my breathing somebody had other ideas. I felt this sudden pressure on my chest, not like a slow push but an abrupt shove, like someone trying to resuscitate a dead person, except it kind of took my breath *away*. And again. And again. It didn't exactly hurt, but it was so . . . violent. I just lay there wondering, "Who?" and "Why?" until I finally came out of my paralysis with a terrified scream.

I must admit I was grateful to have Alex there next to me, to comfort me and make me feel safe so I could go back to sleep. Not sure how he felt about it, though. I think it's the first time he's witnessed one of my screaming episodes.

● ● ●

Tuesday, Oct. 18, 1988
Dear Diary,
I'm off to work soon. I've taken back my Tuesdays and dropped one of my university classes. Two per semester is enough to start. But I don't know what to do about Alex.

I mentioned that I was feeling better about the relationship and he must have sensed that, because now he's sleeping over every night, suffocating me in the process.

He just doesn't understand me or my point of view at all. Imagine if he actually knew everything about me? Just how many guys I've been with, the shady types I hung around with, and the things we used to get into in high school, not to mention my big secret from a year and a half ago. He's so conservative, kind of a goody-two-shoes, actually, that I'm sure he would never be able to see past such a thing and would totally judge me over it. Which is one of the main reasons I've never told him.

He left early this morning with a peck on my cheek and a presumptive "See you tonight." Then, just now when I went to the bathroom I saw his toothbrush had made its way back into the cup.

It's like every time I give him an inch he takes a mile – all of it inside my personal space.

$$\bullet \quad \bullet \quad \bullet$$

Wednesday, Oct. 19, 1988

Dear Diary,

Breaking someone's heart is awful. But it had to be done.

Alex came over last night. He went home after school to get a change of clothes first and in the meantime I noticed a T-shirt, socks, and underwear of his in my laundry hamper. We ate Chinese takeout in the kitchen with Chantal and I wasn't in the mood to be the bad guy yet again, so I kept my mouth shut about the toothbrush, clothes, and four-night sleepover.

I couldn't bear to have sex with him, so I told him I was on my period, which is a big deterrent for him. He doesn't like anything messy. "Already?" he asked. Evidently, he keeps track.

"You know how irregular I am," I said, shrugging my shoulders.

I lay awake for quite some time, annoyed with myself for remaining silent and vowing to broach the subject in the morning.

Once I finally did fall asleep I was subsequently quite rudely awakened. I was lying on my side turned away from Alex and could feel him pushing his erection right up against me from behind, which is so unlike him. First of all, there's the period thing, and second of all, he is all missionary position all the time.

Besides, he knows by now how much I can't bear to be touched while I sleep. I find it so disrespectful and hurtful that he would do such a thing. But I was so tired I couldn't rouse myself enough to stop him. It went on and on until I finally managed to drag myself out of sleep enough to push him away, but by then he had stopped and was back on his side of the bed, seemingly fast asleep.

I shook him till he responded and got really mad at him, and he flat out denied it, allowing only for the possibility that he could have done it in his sleep. But it was the last straw for me. I told him to take his clothes and his toothbrush and go, that he has suffocated me for too long and would be better off with someone who wants to be pampered and doted on. I wasn't very nice or gentle about it and he was obviously really hurt.

Do I feel bad about the way I did it? Yes. Do I regret the outcome? No.

But I do have this nagging doubt that maybe it wasn't him at all who tried to violate me in the night.

● ● ●

Thursday, Oct. 20, 1988
Dear Diary,
The thin man came to visit last night. I wanted so badly to ask what he wants from me, but by the time I was able to talk, he had vanished. As always.

• • •

Friday, Oct. 21, 1988

Dear Diary,

One of the reasons I like my job is all the access to books I have, not to mention my employee discount.

I also like it because while it is technically a retail job, I don't have to be much of a "sales" person, which I think I would be terrible at. I'm really just there to help people find what they're looking for, offer the odd suggestion and, of course, check customers out when they're done. The job also offers me a fair amount of down time, during which I can study, write in my diary, or peruse the merchandise.

Today I pulled out a bunch of books on sleep and dreams. I found lots of stuff that didn't say anything about sleep paralysis, one or two that mentioned it in passing, not offering anything much that I didn't already know, and one book that is, quite frankly, fascinating. It's called *The Terror That Comes in the Night*, by David J. Hufford. On the cover is a painting called *The Nightmare* by an artist named Henry Fuseli. It shows a sleeping woman stretched out on her bed with a demonic goblin sitting on her chest, presumably representing the suffocating presence I know so well – and he painted it in 1781! Between the title and the cover art I didn't even need to open the book to know I had found what I was looking for. (Also, I can't decide whether I never want to see that image again or whether I want to find a print of it to hang on my wall.)

I took the book to the front with me and sat down to browse. At first I was careful, as always, not to bend the spine too much as I read so I could slide it back on the shelves later good as new, but after reading a couple of pages I just went right ahead and bought it.

The book talks a lot about a folkloric legend from Newfoundland called Old Hag. Apparently, Old Hag was a curse and people could "hag" someone by sending them an evil spirit to terrify (or perhaps even kill) them in the night. They would experience pretty much exactly the same thing as me, although the "hag" didn't necessarily take on the same form as mine.

I have to say, I don't think anyone "hagged" me, considering this all started when I was less than five years old. (Maybe I should ask Mom if she had any superstitious enemies from Newfoundland while she was pregnant with me.)

The different thing about this book, from most of the other things I've read, is that this one treats the encounters as real experiences rather than assuming that they're all in the subjects' minds. I'm not sure if I'm comforted by that or not.

● ● ●

8:00 p.m.
Dear Diary,
I can't put this book down.

Its subtitle is *An experience-centered study of supernatural assault traditions,* which is important because, as the author explains in the introduction, he focuses on people's experiences rather than the question of whether or not they are "real." As he notes, the important thing is they are real to *them.* The book is chock full of interviews with people who have had first-hand encounters similar, or in some cases pretty much identical to, mine! It is fascinating to know that this has happened all over the world and for centuries! *En passant,* the author also says that these events could be the most frightening thing ever to be experienced by humans.

One thing I read that is so interesting is that it always happens to people when they are at home. I thought about it and it's true for me. Could that be why the Curtain Lady visits stopped after we moved out of our house in Montreal West? Because she simply couldn't find me? And why the shadow-people visits stopped again for a short time after Chantal and I moved into our apartment? Because they had to look for me again? I'm pretty sure that they have never visited me on vacation. I wonder what would happen if I went on vacation to Newfoundland?

So anyway, there I sat, engrossed in my book, reading interview after interview and getting goosebumps up my arms and chills down my spine as I read about footsteps on the stairs, white glowing figures appearing, dark creatures lurking and looming . . . all so familiar I wanted to cry with both fear and relief.

Then suddenly a figure materialized in front of me and said "Hello!"

As you can well imagine, I practically flew right out of my boots. After gasping and jumping a foot off my chair, I put a shaky hand on my thumping chest and said, "Hugo! You startled me half to death!"

He laughed somewhat apologetically and told me he'd been standing there for two minutes.

"You seemed so absorbed in what you were writing I didn't want to disturb you," he said. "But then I kind of felt like I was spying on you and – well, sorry I scared you."

Hugo's a regular customer – one of my favourites – and I can't even imagine how much he must read. He takes books from all the sections, from bestsellers to classic horror, fantasy, sci-fi, and plenty of non-fiction, too. He never walks out empty-handed and rarely with fewer than four books, often from our discount bins, and he's in here at least once a month. Of course, this isn't the only store he visits either.

He asked what I was reading and when I showed him the cover he assumed it was another horror story. In a way, I guess it is. It sure is scaring me as much as any Stephen King I ever read.

• • •

Saturday, Oct. 22, 1988
Dear Diary,
Allow me to document my case.

First, I want to state that it is so incredibly comforting to know I am not alone. Whenever someone says that about a bad experience I think, "How selfish!" as if we wish our misfortunes on others so they can share in our misery. But that's how it is. I am human and therefore unavoidably selfish, and I do feel better knowing others literally live the same nightmares as I do.

Well, not quite the same, I guess. I've read about dark shapes looming and watching and even shadowy beings that sound just like mine. But then there are people who can see the faces of the visitors and whose visitors even talk to them. The only time I can think of where those things happened was that evil elf with the axe who threatened to cut off my foot when I was a little kid. But that one could have been a dream, right? It was so long ago and I have so many dreams and nightmares besides the paralysis and the visitors it's hard to keep them all straight in my head sometimes. Which is why I'm going to try to write it out properly here and now.

So my first visitor was definitely the Curtain Lady. (I still can't believe it took me that long to figure out she was one of the shadow-people!) Then there was the evil elf with the axe who threatened to chop off my dangling foot. Then we moved and I don't remember any other visits until after I watched *The Exorcist* when I was eleven. That, I think, is when it all started again. Did I somehow let them in then the same way Regan let her demon in by playing with the Ouija board?

There were a few periods when the visits definitely stopped for a good amount of time. Definitely when I visited Chantal in Nova Scotia and when I went on the school trip to Greece last year. Also the summer after I graduated from high school was relatively peaceful. Even when I moved in with Chantal it took the shadow-people about a week to find me. There have been other breaks, too, I think, and it's not like they visit me every night or anything, but they don't usually stay away for very long.

Now for the visitors themselves. There's the black looming shape I can't picture clearly that just watches me and the thin man in a hat (who toys with me). There was also that demon-shaped creature that once crawled over the foot of my bed (a chill just went down my spine thinking about that one). Those are the ones I remember actually seeing.

Then there are the sensations, which I wouldn't necessarily have put together with the shadow-people on my own, but the literature about sleep paralysis and the Old Hag describes so many of the crazy night-time things that I have lived through. There were the crawling sensations and the pressure on my chest. And the levitation! Even that! I might have chalked that up to a dream, but as I've said before, it's different from, say, flying in dreams. I've been lifted and thrown around and pulled by a force. And I think I've also been . . . you know . . . fondled.

The thing is, the visits seem to be getting more frequent and more aggressive. What does that mean? Should I keep up with my research or push it from my mind? And now that I've done all this reading in some ways I feel more confused than ever: are they sleep-induced hallucinations created by my mind or are they beings from a parallel realm who have found just the right moment to show themselves to me? If that's the case, what do they want and what else might they do? In either case, is there a way to stop them?

• • •

Sunday, Oct. 23, 1988
Dear Diary,
Last night I had the strangest dream.

One of the things I read about during my research on nightmares and sleep paralysis is this thing you can do when you're dreaming called "reality testing." Basically, to figure out if you're dreaming or not, you can try a variety of techniques like jumping, trying to push your hand through a solid surface, or checking your reflection in a mirror to see if it behaves normally.

This is supposed to be a way to gain awareness of and control over your dreams, particularly lucid dreams, in which you are aware you are dreaming. Sounds cool and maybe useful for me as a way to eventually gain control over my night-time intrusions.

You're supposed to actually do your reality checks during your waking life first, so that they become a habit and you'll remember to do them when you're dreaming. I decided to start by checking my reflection in the mirror. Why not, since I spend a fair amount of time in front of the mirror already.

Before going to bed, I sat down at my dressing table and looked at my reflection in the mirror, asking myself if everything was as it should be, and the answer was yes. Everything, from my own image to the room itself, looked just as it should. However, my mirror faces my bedroom window, and as I looked at it behind me I had this certainty that the Curtain Lady was about to appear at any moment. As I stared intently at the darkness showing through the gap in the curtains I felt a growing pit of fear in my belly and I envisioned the ghostly silhouette of my childhood nightmares materializing. It was a truly terrifying thought that sent a chill right through me, but she did not, in fact, materialize.

I went to lie down in bed, but didn't fall asleep right away. Eventually I got up to go have a cigarette (I don't smoke in my bedroom) and decided to check the mirror once more. I looked at my face and it was all good, then I glanced past myself to the window, just to be sure, and there she was. *Inside my room.*

I was paralyzed with fear and wanted to scream, but when I opened my mouth no sound came out. She was back!

She began to approach me and I held out my hands to stop her, but toward her reflection in the mirror, and, incredibly, my hands went *into* the mirror. My God! I was dreaming! I stood up, turned to face her and said, "This is *my* dream!" Then, with all my might, I jumped and awoke with a start in my bed.

I hope I can read this entry in the future, because my hand is shaking pretty badly. But pretty cool, right?

Chilling though it was, I feel like it's a step (or a jump!) in the right direction.

Chapter 10
Winter 1990

Monday, Jan. 1, 1990

Dear Diary,

I wish I could say "Happy New Year," but it's hard for me to say happy anything these days. Even my most ecstatic moments are tainted by everything that haunts me.

We had another one of our weird, eclectic parties with guests from all our different walks of life: childhood friends, school friends, work friends. There were about twenty people, including Tony, whom we'll call a work friend. He's a regular customer at the bookstore and I've had my eye on him for a while. I can't remember whether I first noticed him because he's always in the horror section or because he's fucking gorgeous. He has slightly long black, wavy hair, a perpetual five o'clock shadow – actually, it's more of a two-day shadow – and an absolutely perfected style somewhere between stylish and I-couldn't-give-a-shit. Let's call it fashionable bohemian. I often amuse myself by watching the reactions of female customers, from teenagers to women Mom's age, try not to look too hard as he walks by, and I'm quite sure he's as amused as I am.

Anyway, one day he asked for my advice on what to read next and I suggested *Dracula*, thinking I was stating the pathetically obvious, but he had in fact never read it, so he bought it, loved it, and asked for more recommendations afterward. Little did he know (or perhaps he knew it perfectly well) my stomach churns and my heart rate accelerates every time he talks to me. Little did he also know that after I made that recommendation I spent the next ten minutes completely lost in a fantasy about him being a vampire and me a quite willing victim.

Then just my luck, when it was time to invite people to our New Year's party, he wandered into the store, I gathered my courage and asked him if he would come. Maybe I was emboldened by my new look, which I actually love. I had my hair bobbed, accentuated the red with a henna treatment (very messy but worth it) and was feeling pretty sexy in my own version of fashionable bohemian with my cropped T-shirt, broomstick skirt, and freshly applied red lipstick. To my surprise and delight, he accepted my invitation.

It really was a strange and fun mix of friends old and new at the party, like my eclectic dinners, but bigger. In the old friends department, Stefano, whom I hadn't seen in months, came and was truly the life of the party. I was really glad I had called him. He has actually calmed down some, but still talks a mile a minute and I even got him to do his old Barbarino routine, which was a hit. I ordered the cake for the party from Trinh's bakery. She delivered it in person, but didn't stay long. She never was much of a party animal. Giselle was there, and Roseline. Amy came, too. She's finishing her *first* university degree this semester and applying to law school for September. She brought her boyfriend, a super-nice guy who will probably be really successful, just like her. They've been together for, like, two years. He got annoyed with her when she got caught sneaking outside for a cigarette with me, but they seem pretty happy overall. I wonder if I'll ever have a real relationship like that. This past year has basically been a revolving door of flings and one-night stands.

Which brings us back to Tony. As soon as he walked into the party I knew he was there for one thing and one thing only. Which didn't bother me one bit. He drew plenty of attention and appreciative glances during the festivities, and at some point I even wondered if he would get whisked away by another enthralled guest. (Interestingly, Chantal doesn't find him that attractive. She's not a fan of the whole bohemian thing and tends to like her guys more clean-cut.)

After the countdown to midnight and the popping of several bottles of cheap bubbly, we all did the rounds of the room, giving the requisite two-cheek-kiss and wishing *Bonne Année* to each and every person. Tony and I saved each other for last and the two-cheek kiss was followed by a two-lip kiss.

The only thing missing at the party was there wasn't enough dancing. Chantal and I tried a couple of times to get people up. We put on an old Prince tape and blasted "1999" at one point, but instead of getting people dancing it got them all talking about how we can't believe it's already 1990 and how hard we're going to party when 1999 does come around. Of course, I'll be thirty-one by then, so I don't know if I'll still be doing much partying at that age – if I even live that long!

Not wanting to be the bad hostess who disappears halfway through the party, I continued to mingle and offer drinks until the crowd started to thin out and I felt I could sneak away and leave Chantal in charge. As you know, I'm not the most forward person, so it's not like I could just grab Tony by the hand and pull him into my bedroom, although I fantasized about doing just that several times through the night. No, I needed absolute confirmation that he wanted me as much as I wanted him, so I wandered nonchalantly into my room at one point to "look for something" and, as I hoped, I looked up and he was standing in front of me.

"Hey," he said.

"Hey," I replied, still telling myself the deal wasn't sealed.

Just in case I needed any extra convincing (which I didn't) he produced a baggie of white powder. I was at once taken aback and intrigued. I had told myself a million times I would never do real drugs, as in anything other than weed or alcohol, and I didn't love the fact that he was so openly plying me with illicit substances. But he was Tony, object of my vampire and other fantasies, and the idea of mental escape – with him no less –was beyond enticing.

"Got a twenty?" he asked.

Was he selling it to me!? Of course, I quickly realized he just wanted a bill to use for sniffing. Why a two-dollar bill or a five-dollar bill wouldn't work I don't know, but I did have a twenty, so I handed it to him and he rolled it up and showed me how to snort a line. I was a little scared and expecting something quick and intense with an immediate and obvious effect, but in fact I felt nothing, really. In retrospect I guess it sobered me up, kept me awake, and removed a few inhibitions. Needless to say the next hour or so was fabulous.

He dozed off after a while, but I did not, and as I looked at him, marvelling at his beauty and my recklessness, I thought, "Who is this dark stranger sleeping in my bed?"

One thought led to another and I wrote this poem:

Oh Dark Stranger
By Poppy Bell

Oh dark stranger who comes to me
Reminding me I will never be free
Oh friend – from where? – who haunts my nights
Taking my fear to unknown heights

No, not a stranger, much less a friend
Are you a sign I am nearing my end?
Who are you and why am I chosen
To lie in terror, my body frozen?

Why do you visit me, evil ghost?

Why have you picked me as your host?
Are you here to take me away?
Or just to torment me day after day?

Sometimes you watch me, silently
And I want to escape you, violently
Sometimes you touch me, cold and cruel
Engaging me in an unfair duel

And so I fight to wake again
To break your spell I scream and then
You disappear into the black
But this I know: You will be back

I'm no Poe, but while I was writing it I got really freaked out. At one point I glanced up at the window – the curtains were open – and was sure a shadow was going to appear at the glass any moment. I don't know if I'm a masochist or what, but the more I became afraid and even outright convinced that a face (or a familiar dark shape) was going to appear the more fixated I became on the window. I stared and stared, almost daring *it* to get things over with and show itself, but it never did and I finally looked away, back to my much more appealing dark stranger.

I guess I finally did doze off, because I woke up sometime later and felt like I was having a pretty messed up *déjà vu*. I was lying on my side and Tony was pushed right up behind me, trying to penetrate me from behind. Of course other people don't know how much I hate to be touched while I sleep for my many messed up reasons, but why do guys think it's OK to do it? Like you fall asleep next to someone and that gives them permission to do what they want to your body?

I was feeling incredibly heavy, which I attributed to the drugs and alcohol, not to mention lack of sleep. I had that stuck-in-quicksand feeling I couldn't pull myself out of so I lay helpless as it went on for quite some time before I eventually woke up enough to react. And when I did there was no one there. He wasn't next to me or behind me or in the room at all, and I still had my pyjama pants on. (I had put them on when I grabbed my diary to write my poem.)

Morning light was already shining through the window, so I got up and wandered out, feeling very disturbed as well as a little ashamed of myself for having been so shameless the night before.

"Happy New Year. Good night?" Chantal said from the sofa, coffee in hand.

"Very good." I said, with a knowing smile. Then I cleared my throat and said, "Did you see Tony? Is he still here or did he leave?"

"I haven't seen him, so I guess he left before I woke up," Chantal said.

"Huh. I could have sworn he was just in bed with me," I said, more nonchalantly than I felt. "Any more coffee?"

● ● ●

Tuesday, Jan. 2, 1990
Dear Diary,
I've decided to drop my courses this semester. I'm not quitting school or anything, just taking a break.

I'm not sure English Lit or even Creative Writing will get me any kind of a career, so I've been thinking about switching programs anyway. I mean, I'm an OK writer, but I'm not brilliant or anything, so what are the chances I could ever actually make it as a novelist? Mom has always encouraged me to pursue something more practical and realistic. Maybe I could eventually study translation and become a translator? I don't know. I have to think about it for a while.

But I'm too stressed and preoccupied and I need time to figure out what is wrong with me and how to fix it. I can't work full time, study *and* research my . . . condition . . . properly. Something has to give. Anyway, it's just one semester.

• • •

Wednesday, Jan. 3, 1990
Dear Diary,
I can't believe it. I was leafing through the newspaper at work and I spotted a photo of a face I recognized beneath the headline "Five arrested in sex-trafficking sting." There was a lineup of mugshots of the five, including one of my old nemesis, King. Actually, his real name is Tesler King, it turns out. There was also a photo of his younger brother, Samael. Basically, they were pimps and they were kidnapping underage girls, keeping them locked up in some basement, and prostituting them out. I can't say I'm that surprised, but I am definitely creeped out knowing that a criminal predator singled me out just a few short years ago. I feel like I was lucky to get off so easy.

Which made me think about predators. The flashers and the guys who grope you or follow you in the streets and the metros, not to mention the rapists . . . and the killers. I still can't believe that here, in our very own city, less than a month ago, some fucking woman-hating sicko just walked into a university and mowed down 14 women. Women my age. One of them went to FACE and was just one year behind me. I mean, I *remember* her. A beautiful girl and a beautiful singer – she played clarinet like me in band. And now she's just *gone.* All of them are just *gone.* Because they were *women.*

It's pretty fucking fucked.

• • •

Thursday, Jan. 4, 1990

Dear Diary,

I don't know if I'm crazy or haunted, but I need to get rid of these petrifying visions. I can't take it anymore. I'm not sleeping properly and half the time when I fall asleep I am convinced I will never wake up again.

When I have an episode of "sleep paralysis," especially when it includes a visit by the shadow-people, I am more and more afraid to go back to sleep, so some days I survive on two or three hours of sleep and a lot of coffee.

I need to get down to some serious research and find a way to stop this.

So far, these are the suggestions I've found:

1. Stick to a schedule.
2. Avoid caffeine and alcohol close to bedtime.
3. During an attack, try to relax and breathe normally to reduce its length and intensity.
4. Concentrate on moving one small muscle, such as a finger, to break the paralysis.

Some of them make sense, like sticking to a schedule and avoiding caffeine and alcohol (I have noticed that if I fall asleep drunk I am extra likely to have an "attack." Attack. I have actually never used that word before. But it's what it is, isn't it? The other word I found recently, to describe the shadow-people, is "intruders." That is such a perfect description I can't believe I didn't think of it on my own.) I like the suggestion about trying to move a finger to get out of the paralysis and make the intruders go away. Maybe it would be easier than trying to scream? I'm not at all convinced by the trying to relax idea. I have tried it, recently even, and it usually seems to make things worse. But that seems to be the prevailing advice, so I will keep it in mind.

• • •

Friday, Jan. 5, 1990
Dear Diary,
This is what the scientists say about sleep paralysis: Apparently the term was coined in 1928 by a guy named Kinnier Wilson. Basically, it is a state of "parasomnia," where your brain is awake but your body is still in dream mode (we're paralyzed during REM sleep so we don't hurt ourselves while acting out our dreams), and people like me often experience "hypnagogic" or "hypnopompic" hallucinations while in this borderland between sleep and wakefulness. In my case I guess the visions are "hypnopompic," because they happen as I am waking up rather than as I am falling asleep. Neither the paralysis nor the hallucinations are supposed to be dangerous, nor are they necessarily a sign of mental illness or anything like that.

Well, whether or not they *are* dangerous, they *feel* fucking dangerous.

But the phenomenon has been around for a lot longer than a few decades and there are tales and legends about it from all over the world. For example, have you ever heard the expression "the devil on your back"? Well, guess what it refers to? There are different names for it in Africa, Asia and South America, but the stories are all remarkably similar: you wake up, you can't move, and a presence appears to terrify and torment you.

So there are countless stories and explanations in science and folklore, but what no one seems to say is why. Why does it happen and why does it happen to *me?*

If you believe the legends from Newfoundland that call it the Old Hag, people can actually be "hagged" (basically cursed) by someone else. I wrote about it once before, when I read a book about it a couple of years ago, and I still doubt that I was "hagged" by anyone at the age of four or five or whenever it started.

Dave found a psychiatric article for me about the similarities between Old Hag and sleep-related hallucinations. (I told him it was research for school. I haven't told him or Mom that I'm dropping out.) I could have told you they're just two different explanations of the same nightmare. The word nightmare, by the way, comes from the Old Hag legend as well. Sometimes she, or it, was called the Night Hag or the Night Mare, which eventually became the word nightmare as we use it today. You learn something new every day, right?

If only I could learn how to get rid of *my* "Night Mare."

• • •

Monday, Jan. 8, 1990
Dear Diary,
Tony came into the store today.

I thought I had gotten him out of my system on New Year's Eve, but the flip-flop my stomach did when I saw him told me otherwise. I considered proposing a repeat encounter, but wasn't quite bold enough. Plus I'm slightly hurt that he snuck out, hasn't called, (does he even have my phone number?) and took more than a week to come see me at the store. Not that I asked or expected him to call . . . but I might have hoped a little.

"Hey," I said, casually, proud of my feigned nonchalance.

"Hey."

"Looking for anything in particular?" I asked.

"Just browsing. Wondering what's available."

He has a very mild accent that, of course, only adds to his charm. Did I mention it before? Spanish, I think, but ever so slight. He over-pronounces some of his vowels and all his s sounds come out as pure s, never z. So he said "browssing," not "browzing" and then lingered slightly on the "i" in available. Also, was that a suggestive comment? I cursed my insides for turning to liquid so easily.

I showed him the latest Stephen King, *The Dark Half,* and the latest Dean Koontz, *Midnight,* wishing I could think up something more original to suggest than bestsellers. I also told him I had both at home and could lend them to him if he wanted, choosing the opportunity to facilitate a future meeting over the opportunity to make a sale.

"Is that so?"

"If you're interested," I said, shrugging, and wondering if he would take my comment as suggestive.

"I might be," he said, then went off to browse the shelves some more.

So, did he come in for the books or for me?

I don't want to like this guy. He's too good-looking, too smooth, too mysterious, and did I tell you he's thirty? I really want to keep this one just for fun. I don't have time to get attached to someone, especially someone who won't get attached back. There's too much else on my mind right now.

● ● ●

Tuesday, Jan. 9, 1990
Dear Diary,
Stop me if I've told you this story before.

I woke up halfway through the night, at three-eighteen in the morning to be precise, and I couldn't move. I was terrified at first, feeling like I was drowning in mud, and then I calmed down a little as I realized I could breathe. I tried to move and I tried to speak, but I was paralyzed. So I focused on breathing.

Then I noticed a dark shape in the doorway. And I recognized it: the thin man in a hat, leaning casually against the doorframe, staring at me with his no-eyes. I knew he couldn't be real, that he had to be a figment of my middle-of-the-night imagination, so I tried to blink, but couldn't, so I concentrated on just refocusing my eyes, to see him, it, as a coat on a chair or some other thing that had a sane explanation, but he would not disappear. I could even feel him enjoying my fear, like that's what he was there for, to petrify me – quite literally.

The longer I stared and the longer he stayed, the more afraid I became, so I panicked, found my voice, and woke up. I didn't really scream, just kind of called out quickly, so I didn't wake Chantal or anything.

Tired of this same old story yet? I am.

● ● ●

Wednesday, Jan. 10, 1990

Dear Diary,

Chantal and I went to Stefano's restaurant for dinner. Well, not *his* restaurant, but the one where he works.

It's a small Italian (of course) restaurant on St. Laurent Blvd. He's a waiter, a really good one, super friendly and knowledgeable about the food. He dreams of being a chef and is thinking of applying to cooking school. Anyway, he told us it was better to go during the week so it would be less busy and he would have time to talk to us. The food was great, though he kept shaking his head at my conversion to vegetarianism, which limited my choices somewhat. I had pasta with spicy arrabiata sauce. Chantal went for his suggestion, osso buco, which is veal so I wouldn't have eaten it even if I weren't a vegetarian. She said it was delicious and I must admit, it smelled great. But caged baby cow? No thank you.

I always think of Stefano as *my* friend, but I guess by now he's *our* friend. He invited both of us to dinner, Chantal wasn't just tagging along, and they talk to each other like they've been buddies for years. Funny how things happen sometimes without you even noticing.

● ● ●

Friday, Jan. 12, 1990
Dear Diary,
Chantal and I decided to stay in tonight.

I'm not up to clubbing these days and I've been spending a lot more Friday and Saturday nights at home. Yeah, I worry about me, too.

We ordered a pizza and when the doorbell rang and I went to answer it, who should be standing there but Tony.

I told him it was presumptuous of him to just show up assuming I would be home.

"Yes, it is," he said. "May I come in, or are you busy?" It came out "bissy."

I pondered that one. I wasn't bissy, per se, but he would definitely be intruding on our girls' night and Chantal might not appreciate it.

"Come in," I said. "My roommate and I just ordered a pizza."

When we got upstairs and Chantal looked at me surprised, I said, "You remember Tony? He came by to borrow a couple of books."

"Did I?" he said. "Actually, I thought I was here for the pizza." Pee-tssah.

Right on cue, the bell rang again and I headed back down the stairs. When I came back up with dinner, Chantal and Tony were busy trying to pick which movie to watch, so it looked like he was staying. The choices were *Dirty Dancing*, *The Abyss* and *Working Girl*. I had been to the video store and had my couch-potato weekend all planned. We had all seen *Dirty Dancing* before, and *Working Girl* was deemed a chick-flick, so we settled on *The Abyss*. Sci-fi thriller fans unite! While we watched I kept glancing toward Chantal to see if she was annoyed at me after all and then back at Tony to see if he was disappointed in how his visit had turned out, but everyone seemed happy so I finally stopped fretting and settled in to enjoy the movie.

Against my better judgement, about halfway through I cozied up to Tony a little and he draped his arm around me. It felt very good and I cursed myself inwardly yet again for inviting emotions to interfere with my plan of unattached fun. Chantal acted like she didn't even notice, but once the movie was over it took her less than thirty seconds to say goodnight and head off to her room, giving us our privacy.

I went to the bathroom to freshen up and when I came back Tony produced another baggie of white powder. I raised my eyebrows.

"Do that a lot?" I asked, trying again to go for nonchalance while I mentally ran through all the reasons I should not partake.

"No, not a lot," he said, starting to clear a place on the coffee table. I wasn't sure I believed him.

I glanced uneasily toward Chantal's room and said, "Not here."

We headed to my bedroom and it didn't take much convincing on his part for me to give in again. But like the first time, I didn't feel much. Well, I didn't feel much from the drugs. I felt plenty from Tony. It's all a bit of a blur now, to be honest, but once again inhibitions went out the window and plenty of new and experimental fun was had. Which no doubt was his plan.

Why is it that it makes me feel cheap when I say that? I had plans of my own and was just as willing as he was. I was no naive or innocent victim and I had just as much fun as he did (twice as much, to be precise, but who's counting?), but inside I can't quite quiet the nagging, judging little voice that wants to call me that stupid word I swore I would never use to describe another woman. So I damn well shouldn't be using it on myself. Fucking double standards.

• • •

Saturday, Jan. 13, 1990
Dear Diary,
I was thinking about Tony and reading something in the store and the two things came together to give me this crazy idea.

About Tony: I was thinking how annoyed I am that I gave him my phone number but didn't get his, so I have essentially given him all the power in our non-relationship. He knows where I work and live and he can call me anytime he wants, so if I hope to see him again (I am trying not to hope) I basically have to wait around until he decides to make that call. Once I've gotten rid of these nightmares and have some time to think about other things I am going to learn to make my own choices. I'm going to choose my boyfriends instead of always letting them choose me. I mean, they've all chosen me, haven't they? Ricky, obviously, but even Mathieu and Alex. I guess it might have been me who chose Tony (yeah, I know, he's not exactly my boyfriend) by inviting him to our New Year's party, but I definitely let him take the reins pretty quick. Even my friends chose me. Sandrine and Chantal both came up to me. Don't get me wrong: I am grateful and in the case of Chantal, I could never have selected a better friend, but the point is, she made the selection.

About the thing I was reading, it was a not-very-good book about summoning spirits, but it got me thinking: What if I could summon the shadow-people on my terms? Make them appear when I want them to instead of waiting around for them to appear? How could I do that?

I guess I could try the Ouija board again. It's been years, but I still have it and I bet Chantal would be up for it.

I was also thinking I could take up meditation. It's supposed to be a spiritual experience, so it might get me in touch with my spirits, no? I don't really know how or where to begin, but I could start with some books on the subject. For sure we have some in the store.

Then I thought of Tony again and his baggies of white powder and I thought: magic mushrooms? They make you hallucinate, right? Could that work? Can you control hallucinations and if so, could I use them to contact the shadow-people?

So my plan is:

1. See if Chantal wants to do the Ouija board with me.

2. Read up on meditation.

3. Wait around for Tony to call (grrr) and ask if he can get some shrooms.

It's time to face my demons. Literally.

• • •

Tuesday, Jan. 16, 1990

Dear Diary,

I've started reading up on meditation. I actually didn't know a thing about it before. I always thought it was about emptying your mind, which sounds impossible to me as well as kind of pointless. But apparently that's not it at all. And there are all different kinds of meditation: mindfulness meditation, spiritual, mantra, and transcendental to name a few.

It sounds complicated, and how are you supposed to know which kind to start with?

One book I picked up said to just start by sitting in silence for five minutes a day. I could do that – I guess I will do that – but it sounds like a long process to get to a place of enlightenment or reach another plane or whatever in order to get in touch with my . . . spiritual side. Which is my goal, right?

Oh well, I guess I can try the sitting thing and see if it at least makes me feel less stressed, because that's about all I feel these days.

In the meantime I have to talk to Chantal and Tony. The question is, how much do I tell them?

• • •

Thursday, Jan. 18, 1990
Dear Diary,
I've been trying to meditate for three days now, but I don't know if I'm doing it right. I just sit there on the sofa with my legs crossed and try to focus on my breath, but I end up just thinking about random stuff and wondering constantly how long I've been sitting there until I finally give up after about ten minutes each time. With no timer or anything. It's always ten minutes.

I don't know what exactly you're supposed to feel when you meditate properly, but whatever it is I don't think I'm feeling it. We'll see how long I have the patience to continue.

• • •

Saturday, Jan. 20, 1990
Dear Diary,
My skin is still crawling.

I threw the Ouija board idea at Chantal out of the blue. We were eating take-out poutines from La Banquise and I just said, "Hey, you know what we haven't done in ages?"

She was already a little bummed out because again I didn't want to go out dancing. She wanted to go check out Thunderdome which is kind of alternative and has different floors and activities like body painting and Jell-O wrestling. The old, fun-chasing me would have loved it, but I'm just not up for dressing up, dancing, and socializing these days.

Anyway, she agreed to my stay-at-home plan less than enthusiastically and we dusted off the old board. We actually felt a bit silly and couldn't focus or get anything to happen, so we decided to set the scene a little better. We lit some candles, turned down the lights, and poured ourselves Diet Cokes with a big splash of leftover rum from New Year's.

Back to the board, we placed our hands on the pointer and said, "Is anyone there?" We couldn't help but giggle.

"Helloooo?" Chantal called out, suppressing another giggle.

"Helloooo?" I repeated.

"Hello," said the Ouija board. We both jumped a little and eyed the other suspiciously, but at least something was happening.

"Who is this?" I said, and Chantal giggled again.

"What?" I said. "Stop. Be serious." I suppressed a giggle of my own.

"Sorry. It just sounds like we're on a phone call with a bad connection."

We sat still for a moment, calming ourselves down.

"Is anyone there?" I said.

"Yes," the board said.

"Who are you?" I asked.

"U-S" the board spelled.

"Us?" Chantal said. "That's informative." Giggle.

"Who's us?" I said.

Nothing.

Weirdly, for no reason, I got a chill up my spine.

"Is it you?" I asked.

"Yes."

Chantal looked at me quizzically.

"Is it the shadow-people?"

"Yes."

"What are shadow-people?" Chantal asked.

"I dream about them," I said.

"No," the board said. We both stopped for a second and stared at it.

"I don't dream about you?" I said.

"No."

"You're not dreams?"

"No."

"Well, whatever you are, I am asking you, no, telling you to leave me alone."

"No."

"Yes."

"No."

"Well then, goodbye," I said.

"No."

"Goodbye," I said.

"Hello."

"Chantal, tell it goodbye."

"Goodbye," she said.

The pointer didn't move.

"Goodbye!" I said, much louder.

"Fuck it," Chantal said. "We said goodbye!" she shouted at the board, then she pushed the pointer to Goodbye and let go.

"I don't think you're supposed to do that," I said, not taking my own fingers off the pointer.

"Supposed to?" she said, visibly shaken. "It's a fucking game. Take your hands off that thing and let's go dancing."

There is still a rational mind inside me somewhere that is saying she was toying with me or maybe that I was even toying with myself, but meanwhile my hand is trembling as I write this.

Anyway, I have to go. I figured Thunderdome would be a good change of scenery after all and Chantal's waiting for me to get ready.

• • •

Sunday, Jan. 21, 1990
Dear Diary,
Last night was . . . interesting.

We downed another rum and Diet Coke and headed off to Thunderdome in our jeans and sexy tops. It was a beautiful night, just a couple of degrees below zero with the kind of light snowfall that storybooks are made of.

We hopped on the 24 bus along Sherbrooke then walked down Stanley, tipsy and arm-in-arm, fluffy snowflakes on our hair, best friends out for an enchanting night on the town.

When we got to the club, there was a crowd waiting outside and an arrogant bouncer picking and choosing from the bunch in a way that makes everyone feel insecure about their beauty and coolness quotient. At least it wasn't cold, and eventually, we found ourselves among the chosen ones invited inside. Once in, the lineup for coat check was long and pushy and once we finally got into the club itself we were in a less than magical mood. It's super-dark and a little grungy, I wasn't loving the music, and people weren't friendly or even flirtatious. Everyone was wearing black and was too cool to smile or even look you in the eye. We wandered around the different levels for a while and danced a little, in our own worlds like everyone else, when INXS came on.

Thunderdome is known for its wild themed activities, and last night was wet-T-shirt night (interesting how all the activities involve women in various stages of undress, but I digress).

Volunteers were solicited, space was made, and four braless girls in white T-shirts made their way to the performance space. The music blared, they started to dance and the water started to flow. And all of a sudden, as if choreographed, Chantal and I looked at each other, looked back at the contestants, then back at each other and said, "Is that who I think it is?" And oh yes, it was. My old friend Belinda from Dawson.

Suddenly we were more interested in the show.

Girl #1 got eliminated pretty quick. Her dancing was shy and her boobs, frankly, were too unimpressive for her to be a contender. Made me glad I wasn't up there. Applause determined the elimination of the second contestant, a very pretty and tough-looking raven-haired girl with a tattoo who looked pretty pissed to be out of the running. It was down to blonde, blue-eyed, big-breasted Belinda and a high-ponytail-wearing, long-legged knockout with a smaller bust size but better proportions. And it was on. Clearly, the contest was no longer really about what you could see revealing themselves beneath the drenched, clinging, transparent shirts, but about who could put on the raunchiest show.

At one point I wondered if we were still at Thunderdome or had been transported next door to the Chez Parée strip club. The girls were grinding and winding, checking each other out and one-upping one another every step of the way. And then ponytail lifted her T-shirt and unbuttoned her jeans, running her hands up and down her belly. So Belinda unbuttoned *and* unzipped her jeans and ran her hands everywhere. Ponytail turned around, bent over, and shook her behind, stripper style. So Belinda peeled her jeans down, down, down, turned around to reveal a g-string, and won the contest to an explosion of cheers and applause.

We considered going over to say hi and congratulate her, but she was surrounded by guys and enjoying every second of it. Besides, I had backed off that friendship because of her manipulative, attention-seeking ways and Chantal had never taken to her, so we decided to let her enjoy her win without us.

"I was rooting for the other girl," Chantal said as we wandered away.

"Yeah?" I said, laughing. "Why? I think Belinda was determined to win. She would have taken it all off if she had to."

"Oui, mais, elle est mal faite." Literally, she's "badly made." Mean.

"What are you talking about? She has those amazing boobs. I always wondered what it must be like to have real breasts," I said, looking down at my own practically non-existent ones.

"But they don't fit her body. Her legs are skinny and she has no butt. You're way sexier than she is."

While part of me relished the compliment and admittedly got some satisfaction from judging my very pretty ex-friend for turning out so trashy, I must admit there was a little part of me that was envious. Not just of her womanly shape but also her confidence in her own sexuality. She knew she was going to win that contest. It might not be the thing she'll brag to her grandchildren about, but I would never believe in any of my own assets enough to get up on a podium and flaunt them.

• • •

Monday, Jan. 22, 1990
Dear Diary,
I don't think meditation is for me and I definitely don't think it's going to get me anywhere in regards to communicating with the shadow-people.

I tried a kind of meditation called "body scan" today. I thought it might be just perfect for me because of some techniques I mastered a few years back with the help of certain substances. "Body scanning" involves paying attention to sensations in the body in a gradual sequence from your feet to your head. Basically the exact thing I used to do when I would smoke weed and go numb.

First of all, it is way harder to do without "assistance." But, I am proud to say, I actually did manage to concentrate well enough to create some tingling sensations in my feet and legs. I got pretty encouraged, actually, and thought maybe this was just the thing for me, but then the tingling changed to a kind of crawling feeling that reminded me of the times the shadow-people started creeping up my body. It's not that they were there today, but the feeling was too similar and kept making me think that maybe they would suddenly appear and take over or I don't know what.

I'm shelving meditation for a while and moving on to my next idea.

• • •

Tuesday, Jan. 23, 1990
Dear Diary,
I called Tony today. It is the first time I have used his phone number, which he gave me the last time I saw him, exactly nine days ago.

If I hadn't called him I wonder if he ever would have called me again or even come into the store. Believe me, I held back before picking up that receiver. For hours, maybe even days, I hesitated. But I have to try everything I can to face my fears and he's the only guy I can think of who might be able to get me what I need for my next experiment.

A woman answered the phone and I considered just hanging up. Was he married or something? But then I thought he wouldn't have given me his number if he were.

"May I speak to Tony, please?"

"One moment," she said. She didn't sound angry or anything.

I was afraid he would be unhappy to hear from me, like I should have gotten the message by now that he wasn't planning to see me again, but if he was annoyed it didn't show. We did the small-talk thing for a short time and then I decided it was time to broach the subject.

I know that people who deal in . . . substances . . . don't like to talk about it openly on the phone because apparently you never know who might be listening. Those fears usually sound like paranoia or a movie plot to me, and I don't think he actually *deals,* but I decided to try to kind of speak in code rather than talking about illegal things too overtly.

"I was wondering, you know the . . . samples . . . you brought when you came over?"

"Yes . . ." he said.

"Well, I was wondering if you had access to . . . experience with . . . any other types of . . . merchandise."

"That depends. What exactly did you have in mind?"

"Um, actually, I was thinking…" I couldn't come up with a good euphemism so I gave up on subtlety. "Mushrooms."

He laughed. "Mushrooms? Like you mean shiitake, portobello, or what?" I knew he was toying with me, as well as whetting my appetite with his most deliciously enunciated pronunciations.

"Actually, I was hoping for something a little more . . . magical."

"I see." Pause. "Let me see what I can do. I'll get back to you."

"OK." Pause. "Hey, Tony?"

"Yes?"

"Who was that who answered the phone?" It was really none of my business, I knew. I just hoped he wouldn't say that.

"My sister."

"Oh," I said, unable to tell whether he was making a joke or being honest. "I was just curious. I realized I don't really know anything about you, so . . ."

"Well, next time I see you, tell me what you want to know."

Next time? I mentally jumped for joy. Then mentally kicked myself for it.

"Sure. Get back to me about the . . . samples."

"I will," he said, then hung up without saying goodbye.

• • •

Thursday, Jan. 25, 1990
Dear Diary,
Well, that didn't take long.

Tony came into the store today, as welcome a sight as always.

Small talk didn't last long before he got to the question at hand.

"I have what you asked me for," he said.

"Yeah?" I said, looking around to make sure there weren't any customers nearby. "That was fast. Do you have it here? I guess I must owe you some money? Can you tell me how to . . . how I'm supposed to . . ." I searched for euphemisms and looked around nervously, thinking not for the first time that I wouldn't make a very good criminal.

"Listen," he said. "This is not the kind of thing you should do alone. Do you have a plan already? I mean, are you going to do it with a friend or something?"

"No . . . I don't have a plan. I was just going to do it by myself, I guess. I hadn't actually thought that far, to be honest."

"How do you feel about doing it together?"

How did I feel about it? My heart was singing and my loins were longing.

"Sure, OK. Why not?" Shrug. "When?"

"You tell me," he said, looking directly into my eyes with his dark chocolate ones. What were we talking about? Oh, right, the mushrooms.

"Saturday after work? I finish at five and Chantal is going to her parents' for dinner, so you could come over around six?"

"Sounds perfect."

Oh yes it does.

"I think we're going to have fun," he said with another direct chocolate stare.

Oh yes we are.

"See you Saturday," I said coolly.

I almost forgot the whole point of this was not to get it on with Tony on shrooms, but to confront the shadow-people. But I can do both, right?

• • •

Sunday, Jan. 28, 1990
Dear Diary,
Did I do the right thing? I cannot say. Did I do the thing? Yes, I did.

Tony showed up yesterday at six, as promised. I was tired and nervous. It had been a busy day at the store and I had slept badly because of the nightly intrusions. At least that meant I was feeling more determined than ever to confront the intruders and rid myself of them once and for all.

"You seem nervous," he said. "Everything OK?"

So he's perceptive.

I decided we had no time for niceties and we aren't very good at small talk anyway, so I just asked him if he had brought "them" and he answered in the affirmative. I asked him what I owed him and he told me not to worry about it.

"So?" I said. "What do they look like?"

He pulled out a baggie. It seemed like he was always pulling out baggies when we were together. In it were little things that looked like, well, pieces of dried mushroom.

"How do we do this?" I asked.

"Hang on," Tony said. "I was wondering if you would mind telling me why you want to try mushrooms."

I thought he might ask, so I had already decided to tell him just enough without revealing my *issues* in so much detail that he would end up running screaming from the room.

"I've been having a lot of strange dreams and sleep problems lately and I thought this might help me confront and deal with them."

He nodded. "So, they say you should always take magic mushrooms in familiar surroundings with someone you trust. Do you trust me?"

I thought about how I didn't know the first thing about him and how his "sister" had answered the phone when I called. But I had put my trust in him when I took other things with him, and had done very intimate, and even kinky, things I hadn't done with anyone else.

"Yes," I half-lied.

"I've never taken them before either," he said, surprising me. "I will take only a small amount, so I should be OK in case you have a bad trip or anything. Not that I think you will. Most of what I hear is pretty positive."

"OK."

"You don't have to go anywhere tonight? The effect lasts a few hours."

I was starting to feel like he was the pharmacist giving me advice when I filled a new prescription. Which I guess he kind of was.

"So, how do you take them?" I asked.

"You eat them."

I suddenly felt like I was *Alice in Wonderland* about to follow the rabbit down the hole and eat the cake.

"Just like that?"

"Well, I don't think they taste very good, so maybe we could mix them with food. What do you have?"

He followed me to the not-very-well-stocked kitchen. Chantal and I still don't do much cooking. I opened some cupboards and said, "We could sprinkle them on Kraft dinner."

He made a disgusted face and said, "I think I would rather eat them plain."

"Picky, picky," I said. "Hey! How about peanut butter and jam sandwiches?"

"Perfect."

I set about spreading the peanut butter on two pieces of bread and he sprinkled each slice with our magic ingredient, a little more for me than him. I topped them with raspberry jam and a second slice of bread, grabbed Diet Cokes from the fridge, and we sat at the table to dig in to our special feast.

"*Bon appétit!*" we said in unison and took our first bite. I couldn't taste them too much through the sweet and salty peanuttiness, and I think that was a good thing, because what little I could taste did not exactly add mouth-watering contrast.

After about five minutes I told Tony I wasn't feeling anything.

"Don't worry. I was told it can take at least half an hour to notice the effects."

I smoked a cigarette a little while after we had finished our sandwiches and then I figured I should do something about my tobacco-peanut breath so I went to brush my teeth. Wanting to shorten the time away from Tony I sat down to pee while I brushed. I was sitting there scrubbing back and forth and suddenly had the sensation that everything else disappeared and time slowed down. The only sound I could hear was the sh-sh-sh of the toothbrush, slow, clear, and rhythmic. It was a not unfamiliar sensation: I had felt a similar slowdown lying in bed in the morning a couple of times. Those times it had been accompanied by a sort of slow whooshing sound in my ears that reminded me of a train. This time it was the toothbrush. Sh. Sh. Sh.

I rinsed my mouth and washed and dried my hands and noticed that everything had slowed down, like my every action had a purpose and an importance to it. When I entered the kitchen, Tony was looking at me and I felt like even his gaze was slow, somehow.

"I think it's working," I said as I walked toward him at a snail's pace. "Everything has slowed down."

"I don't feel anything," he said, which inexplicably struck me as extremely funny and I started to laugh my head off. Rather than looking at me like I was nuts, he started to laugh, too, and I realized he was tripping also. He just didn't know it yet.

I stopped laughing when I suddenly felt nauseated. I got that cold, sweaty feeling you sometimes get before you throw up and I headed to the bathroom again. I sat on the floor, my hands and face clammy, waiting for the nausea to rise, and thought how ironic it was that I had been there so many times before after too much to drink . . . and then I couldn't remember the rest of the thought that was supposed to be ironic. I never did barf, though. The feeling subsided and I went happily back to Tony.

I can't remember the exact order of things through the night, and the trip went on for hours (but felt even longer) so I will just tell you the significant parts.

At some point I suddenly felt myself kind of . . . shrinking. It sounds like I was back to being *Alice in Wonderland* again, but

I didn't feel smaller physically as much as I had the liberating impression that I didn't matter anymore. Then I grew again, like a flower blooming, or as if I were waking up for the first time and I felt like I was made of light, beauty, and colour, in harmony with everything around me.

I looked at Tony and felt this intense closeness to him, like he and I were one person.

"We're so beautiful!" I said at some point (the words feel gigantic in my memory, as if saying them took hours and repeated itself over and over).

I think he touched my face when I said that and I remember this sense of intense joy. There was no more *me,* just *us.*

Sometime later, it feels both like it happened right then and hours later, my gauzy curtains started to move in slow waves and to change colour, with one colour just blending into the next like a lava lamp. They went from white to yellow to orange to blue, billowing and bubbling. Then they parted, giving way to bright light (I remind you it was nighttime outside), which took shape and suddenly before me stood, or more precisely, floated, the Curtain Lady. She was so beautiful, gray, and pale, her svelte shape kind of radiating soft light.

I was not afraid. She was like an old friend who had come to take me somewhere safe. I had complete trust in her, and felt as if she was a part of me and I of her. I remembered Tony asking me if I trusted him and I realized it was *her* I needed to trust, her I *did* trust. I couldn't get over how radiant she was and all I wanted to do was touch her, hold her hand, let her take me away with her. Even now, I feel this faint but slightly aching desire to see her again and disappear with her. And it felt so good, so liberating not to be afraid of her. I remember thinking that it wasn't even because she was no longer sinister, she still was, but it didn't matter. If anything, that made me want to be with her more.

"What are you staring at?" Tony asked.

"Don't you see her? She's so beautiful," I said, and then she started to move in a wiggly, wavy pattern, bending and stretching like an image on a TV with bad reception or a strange belly dance.

It struck me as hilarious and I laughed and laughed, and it felt so good to laugh like that, as if I didn't have a worry in the world. Tony laughed too, a laugh of pure, uninhibited joy, like a child who hasn't yet learned to be self-conscious. We kept laughing for what felt like forever and at some point I thought, *this* is euphoria. And I kept laughing.

Later (minutes? hours?) we went for a walk and I smoked a cigarette. Under the streetlights we watched the smoke rising and swirling and it suddenly twirled itself into little ghost-shaped forms. As I watched them float up, up, up, I realized they were actually tiny dancing Curtain Ladies and they were beckoning to me. I tried to touch one and it turned back into a wisp of smoke, which made me sad for a moment, then I started breathing the smoky air back in, inhaling the little dancers back into my body.

Tony watched me in fascination, probably seeing something else entirely.

In case you're wondering, we did not have sex. When we made our plan and when he arrived I was quite sure we would, but then the trip took over and I don't think we even thought about it because we were too busy experiencing everything else.

I realize that the one thing I forgot to do was to try to get the shadow-people to leave me alone, which was my whole goal in the first place. I mean, I didn't actually see any of them besides the Curtain Lady, but I was supposed to ask her what she wanted and find a way to send her away for good. But last night that was the furthest thing from my mind. Last night she was lovely and enchanting. Even now I feel like all my fear has dissipated like a fragile little wisp of smoke.

● ● ●

Monday, Jan. 29, 1990
Dear Diary,
I'm back to myself again. I had this dreamy, happy, calm feeling all day yesterday and wondered 1. if maybe my new Zen attitude would last and 2. if I was still tripping.

I don't know the answer to Number Two. As for a new attitude, maybe.

The dark, looming shape visited me in the night. So the Curtain Lady didn't tell him/it to stay away (but I also didn't ask her to) and my problem is not solved. But I wasn't afraid. I mean, I dug for a scream to wake myself up as usual, but it was almost like I was doing it out of habit or ritual rather than actual fear. I'm sure that doesn't make any sense, but it did in my own head as I was writing it.

I haven't heard from Tony since we took our little magic carpet ride together. It hasn't been very long, so I'm not surprised. He slept with me for a little while on Saturday night (or Sunday morning), but left pretty early. He's clearly not the sleep-in-and-have-breakfast-together type. I don't know what to think about him and I can't figure out if I feel anything at all. It's like how I felt about the dark shape last night: I think I *should* feel insecure or jilted or something, but I'm not sure I actually do.

Still, I can't help but ask myself why I can't be attracted to someone more normal. Why do I keep picking the mysterious, non-committal types to become infatuated with? Whatever. I have more pressing matters on my mind these days.

• • •

Tuesday, Jan. 30, 1990
Dear Diary,
Last night I levitated.

It wasn't the first time, but I experienced it differently.

The other times I had similar experiences, they were a mixture of wonderful and terrible. This time, it was just wonderful, almost like flying. I was paralyzed, but I wasn't bothered by it. I was lifted off the bed and I lay there floating on air as if it were water.

I didn't even want to fight, but at the last moment I did. It was like a reflex, one I even tried to resist, but then I jolted awake with a gasp, lying quite heavily on my bed.

Then I curled up and cried myself back to sleep.

• • •

Wednesday, Jan. 31, 1990
Dear Diary,
The thin man came to me last night. He's the scariest one. I knew that, I remembered it, but I didn't feel it.

I stared at him as his eyeless face stared back, waiting for the time to scream myself awake. Then I suddenly remembered this technique I had read about concentrating on moving one finger to break the paralysis, so I thought, quite calmly, I would try that.

I could swear that as soon as my attention shifted to my finger, the index of my right hand, to be precise, the thin man shook his head at me. But then it worked. I was suddenly back in this waking world with no jolt, no gasp, no scream.

And then I became frightened. I lay there in the dark and thought, where has my fight gone?

• • •

Thursday, Feb. 1, 1990
Dear Diary,

It's like they've seen my weakness and they're coming on with a vengeance, wearing me down so I don't even know what to feel anymore.

It's three fifteen in the morning and I just woke up from what should have been a terrifying encounter. First, I went to sleep on my stomach, like all the literature says. Everyone says that either it only happens when you're sleeping on your back or at least it's more likely to happen when you're sleeping on your back. But I know things have happened to me when I'm lying on my side. And I also remember that when I was little I hardly ever slept on my back, because of the Curtain Lady, but I must have turned over in my sleep because I'm pretty sure I was always on my back by the time she appeared.

However, the finger-moving technique has worked and the books say to sleep on my stomach, so that's what I did.

Sure enough, a few hours later I woke up. Well, you know how it goes. My mind woke up, but my body did not. I had the initial moment of panic when I realized, once again, that I couldn't move or make a sound. I also realized I was still lying on my front, so, I thought, maybe I was safe from the intruders at least.

Then something touched my back. Fingers. Fingers touched me and slowly started to scratch, working their way up and down my spine, up and down. And I lay there, breathing, feeling, enduring. But where was the fear? Something in me has changed. My brain told me to stop it, to wake up, but the feeling of terror just wasn't there. In fact, the presence was almost . . . comforting. I thought maybe I would just stay and see what happened. Would it continue? Would it stop? And then what? But I wasn't ready.

So I fought. I forgot all about the wiggle-one-finger technique and I dug deep, deep, deep for a scream. And I screamed *loud*. Like I used to when I would wake up the neighbours. I stopped pretty quick once I woke up properly, but

Chantal came running anyway, all puffy-eyed and dishevelled and worried.

"Sorry," I said, embarrassed. "I just had a nightmare."

"Oh! Thank God. I thought, I don't know, someone broke in or something. Must have been some dream. What was it about?" she said, rubbing her eyes.

"Something came up behind me," I said, wanting to keep her there for the comfort and company, but knowing she would be out in seconds if I let her return to bed. "But I don't remember anything else. Never mind, I'm fine, go back to sleep."

I didn't need to say it twice. She was clearly grateful to go back to her room. I, however, don't want to sleep, but my eyelids are very, very heavy, so I think I have no choice. Maybe I'm exhausted enough that the shadow-people will leave me alone and let me get through the rest of the night in peace.

● ● ●

4:30 a.m.
Dear Diary,
No such luck. As if luck had anything to do with it. They're on a mission. I don't know exactly what they want, to kill me or take me away or something else, but I know they want *me*. And none of us are resting until they've got me.

Fuck, fuck, fuck, I'm so tired I'm about to nod off again already, but I have to tell you what happened, in case I don't come back next time. (There I go sounding crazy again.)

I remembered to sleep on my stomach again, for all the good it did last time, exposing my back to those scratching fingers.

Well this time, as I floated in that in-between place, face down, my back exposed and waiting, it came up behind me again, but although I could sense its presence it didn't touch me right away. I couldn't see it, of course, so I don't know which one it was, thin man, dark shape, Curtain Lady or someone new, but after what felt like an eternity of anticipation it finally touched me. To be specific, it pushed the back of my head. Not with its hands, though. It used something, another pillow, perhaps? Somehow I could still manage to breathe – maybe my head was turned to the side? – even though it was pushing me deeper and deeper into my pillow – and then I realized that again I wasn't actually scared. I was calm. I enjoyed the calm for a while, as my head continued to be shoved into the pillow. "Why am I so calm?" I wondered, and the answer came to me: "They're not real," I thought. But I thought it out loud somehow, even though I couldn't actually speak. "You are not real!" I screamed inside my head. I guess it heard me, because in response it pushed *harder*. "You are not real! You are not real! You are not real!" I inwardly screamed, like a mantra. And it pushed deeper, deeper, deeper.

So I kept screaming it over and over until I woke up screaming for real with Chantal already beside my bed, her hand on my shoulder, saying "Poppy, Poppy, wake up. It's just a dream."

I might not have been scared then, but I'm pretty freaked out now.

This time I couldn't resist. I asked Chantal to stay with me, told her I know how weird that is, but that my nightmares are out of control and I just don't want to be alone. She said of course she'll stay. She'll come back and sleep in my bed with me. She just went to the bathroom and to get a glass of water.

Maybe they won't come back if I'm not alone. But if they do, that's it. No more screaming. I am going to try the one thing I have never tried: giving in. No matter how long it lasts or what they do, no matter how enticing or terrifying they are, I will not fight. For my whole life I have said I would try giving in and every time I end up panicking and resisting. Every single time. This time I am determined. I will not struggle to break free. I will lie still and calm no matter what. The night is almost over anyway. What's the worst that could happen? Soon morning will come, Chantal will be here and I will wake up.

Epilogue

Sept. 29, 1990

Chère Poppy,

You are twenty-two today and I really miss you.

You have been in this coma, or whatever it is, for eight months now. It's not actually a coma, technically, because there is no brain injury or damage, at least none that they can find. You're basically asleep and paralyzed, but able to breathe on your own, and your brain seems fine, as if you could just wake up at any moment. I wish – we all wish – you would!

If only you knew what a miracle of science you are! All the doctors say they've never seen anything like it.

I don't know if it would be better for you if you knew what was going on around you and how many people have been spending time with you trying to bring you back and just keep you company, or if it would be better for you to be totally unconscious. I hate to think of you trapped and awake for all these months, living in a never-ending nightmare. In case you don't know it, well, besides your mom and Dave (I'm so happy they found each other), who are here every day, there is me. I'm not here every day, but almost. Wonderful Stefano (more about him later!) visits two or three times a week. Trinh came by a few times and Sandrine stopped in while she was in town to see her sister and brother. I can't believe she already has two kids! Oh, and Amy, too. No, she doesn't have kids! She was back in town for the summer and came to visit a bunch of times. My mom has come more than once and even Phil came once. He was really uncomfortable! But you remember being fifteen. Your aunt and cousin Cathy visited from Ontario and a few work colleagues stopped by, too. And one customer. That's right: Tony. I must admit I was a little surprised, even if it was only the one time. I always saw him as just using you for sex, but maybe I didn't give him enough credit. Then again . . . we'll get back to him later.

I put out a guest book for people to sign and write you messages, so when you wake up you will know everyone who came to see you. You'll have a lot of thank-you cards to write!

I am feeling guilty about some things and I have two confessions to make to you.

The first is that I didn't climb into bed with you the night you never woke up and I will always wonder what would have happened if I did. I came back with two glasses of water and you were already fast asleep, so I put your glass on the bedside table and went back to my room, almost tripping over the corner of the bed in that tiny room of yours along the way.

The second is – and I hope you won't be too mad at me for this one – I read your diaries. All of them. I know that they are secret and sacred and you said you would never forgive someone for reading them. So if – when – you wake up, I hope you will forgive me.

I must say, I know you more now than ever. I think you never really know people, even your family or your best friend. But if you can read their diary, the one they never meant for anyone to read, well, that's a different story. There were some parts I was embarrassed to read, about the kind of stuff we do in private that we don't tell people; there were parts that hurt me, like the stuff about Olive! I was hurt *for* you, because of what he did to you (and yes, it was rape, whether he meant it to be or not), and I was hurt *by* you, because you didn't confide in me. I'm not angry, though. There's stuff you don't know about me, too. Things I wish I had told you, and still will if – when – you come back!

There were some great memories in there, stuff I hadn't thought of for years, like the birthday bumps, the Paladium, and what about Mr. K.'s Grade Six English class! How could we have lived it so differently? I hated him so much, meanwhile he was your inspiration to start writing! And, of course, there was the scary stuff. I had no idea the nightmares you've been living with. I mean, we all have bad dreams, but those shadow-people. I don't know how you kept your sanity. (Also, why do you like horror so much? Didn't you have enough of it in your own life to not need to seek it out in all those books and movies?) Weirdly, the Curtain Lady is the one who scares me the most. Who terrorizes a little kid like that? I know you had told me about her, but I always kind of thought you just made her up, or at least imagined her. Well, I don't think that anymore.

Please wake up, Poppy, so we can make more memories.

I also want you to know I didn't show your mom your old diaries. I don't think that would have been good for anyone. She read your very last one, which only covers a few months and is mostly about sleep paralysis and shadow-people and you're right that some of it makes you sound a little crazy. But it gives the doctors a place to start without traumatizing your family with too many stories of our wild teenage years. There is the stuff about Tony, but that's it. At least he came to visit *before* we read about him, otherwise he probably would have received a quite different welcome. (I know now is not the time, but coke? Mushrooms? *Sérieusement*?)

So the question is, is your coma a brain glitch that is some kind of prolonged version of sleep paralysis, or are the shadow-people real and they have you trapped somewhere, like in that place you call the in-between? I would never say that second part to your mom or the doctors; then they would probably trap *me* somewhere! But if medicine can't explain this and can't help you, maybe it's time to look in another direction. And what I really think is this: The shadow-people *are* real, because they're real to you. Even if no one else ever sees them, they exist to you, which means they exist, don't they?

It's decided. I'm going to do that. While the rest of them keep looking for psychological explanations and medical miracles, I am going to look into dreams, legends, and ghost stories and see if I can find a way to get to you and bring you back. (No exorcists, though, I swear!)

Oh, and one more thing. You are not going to believe it! Stefano and I are dating. Now if that doesn't shock you out of your dream world, I don't know what will!

Bisous!

Your best friend always,

Chantal

Acknowledgements

I am lucky to be surrounded by a large number of people who have helped me in so many different ways.

A big thank you to Michael Occhionero, Luis Carlo Parga and the rest of the team at AOS Publishing for your hard work and for taking a chance on me and my novel.

Thanks to the organizers of the NaNoWriMo writing challenge, which got me to sit down and churn out thousands of words every day for a month (and beyond), until I had my first draft.

Thanks to my first readers for taking the time to read that first draft and give me your opinions and advice: my daughter, Mia Mercado-Shepherd; my life partner, Wolf Mercado; my childhood friend Dawn Lemieux; and my friend Anca Negut.

Thank you to excellent editor Laura Major for your thorough beta read and pages of invaluable comments, questions and suggestions. It was your encouraging feedback that made me believe my story was worth publishing.

I am immensely grateful to my family members, who have always believed in me, supported me and been proud of me in my writing and other creative endeavours: my parents, Harvey and Jean Shepherd; my children, Mia Mercado-Shepherd and Shane Shepherd; my brother and sister-in-law, Hugh Shepherd and Sandra Cohen; and my life, love, parenting, dance and business partner, Wolf Mercado.

They are too many to name, but I am thankful to all those who shaped me and the people and situations in my story. A big thanks as well to all the people who through the years have said to me, "You should write a book!"

Thanks to the real-life "Mr. K.," whose classroom diary project got me to start writing every day. I did not stop for decades.

Finally, I must acknowledge the "real-life" Curtain Lady of my early childhood, who terrified me, but also inspired this story.

Andrea Shepherd
By Isabelle-Blanche Pinpin

About the author

Born in Toronto and raised in Montreal, Andrea Shepherd has written and danced all her life.

In school, English was always Andrea's best and favourite subject. She started keeping a diary at age 10 and wrote just about every day for 20 years. In 1989, she got a clerical job at the *Montreal Gazette,* where she gradually worked her way up to a copy-editing position and did some occasional feature writing.

Outside school and work, Andrea studied classical ballet for years, then fell in love with Latin dance, especially Argentine tango.

In 2008, Andrea left her newspaper career to pursue dance full time. She and her partner opened a tango school, which has since become one of the top Argentine tango studios in Montreal.

During the COVID-19 pandemic, Andrea published her first book, a collection of essays titled *25 Tango Lessons.*

The Curtain Lady is her first novel.

Andrea lives in Montreal with her family.

Find out more at andreashepherd.ca.

www.ingramcontent.com/pod-product-compliance
Lightning Source LLC
Chambersburg PA
CBHW061147210726
48294CB00006B/1606